HARLEQUIN'S SUP

Harlequin began spons
Big Sisters of America
Sisters of Canada in April 1988. Since then,
we have become the largest single sponsor of
Big Sisters Programs and related services in
North America.

This fitting association between the world's
largest publisher of romance fiction and a
volunteer organization that assists children and
youth in achieving their highest potential is a
wonderfully different kind of love story for
Harlequin. We are committed to assisting our
young people to grow to become responsible
men and women.

Brian Hickey
President and CEO

For more information, contact your local
Big Brothers/Big Sisters agency.

Dear Reader,

Writing *Star Song* presented me with two
challenges. First, I would be writing about Big
Brothers/Big Sisters of America, an organization
about which I knew very little. Second, I wanted to
write about two deaf characters—and what I knew
about deafness was even less than what I knew
about the Big Sister-Little Sister program. So I did
what any conscientious writer would do—I
researched.

What I discovered was that the Big Brothers/Big
Sisters agency is a fine service organization that
has enriched the lives of countless young people. I
learned, too, of the difficulties with which the
hearing impaired must cope daily—and of their
determination. I also discovered the eloquence of
sign language. All in all, writing the book enriched
my life—it taught me of the common goodness of
people and of their uncommon courage.

Writing the book also allowed me to indulge a
couple of fantasies—what it would be like to have a
sister (in this case, I got two!) and what it would be
like to have a drop-dead handsome movie star in
love with me (of course, I put myself in the role of
the heroine). I hope that *Star Song* leaves you
believing in the magic of love.

Sandra Canfield

STAR SONG

Sandra Canfield

Harlequin Books

TORONTO • NEW YORK • LONDON
AMSTERDAM • PARIS • SYDNEY • HAMBURG
STOCKHOLM • ATHENS • TOKYO • MILAN
MADRID • WARSAW • BUDAPEST • AUCKLAND

To my parents-in-law,
Vivian and Charles Canfield,
for taking me so lovingly into their hearts

Published October 1992

ISBN 0-373-70519-0

STAR SONG

"Is it so bad being Nash Prather?"

Claire asked.

"You don't get it, do you?" Nash said softly. "It's not a question of good or bad. It's a question of existing at all. Nash Prather isn't real. He never has been, he never will be."

Claire pondered Nash's remark. Whether Nash Prather was real or not, the man who'd stood framed in her doorway had been as real as any man she'd ever seen. And she'd felt the realness of his pain.

More importantly, she'd felt the real warmth of his skin beneath her hand. It was a warmth that had burned to the very core of her being....

CHAPTER ONE

IT WAS JUST POSSIBLE that for once she, the woman who daily battled the world and won, had bitten off more than she could chew, Claire Rushing thought as she glanced at the taciturn sixteen-year-old sitting across from her. Without question she hadn't expected this degree of bitterness. Some bitterness, yes— you couldn't suffer the loss this young woman had and not feel that life had dumped on you in a major way— but not so much bitterness that it swelled into a full-hearted hostility that allowed no room for any other emotion. Or for that matter, any room for life and the abundance it had to offer.

"You don't like the ice-cream sundae?" Claire signed with her hands at the same time her lips formed the question.

AmyAnn Williams, tall, slim and with short curls as golden as the San Francisco sun burning through the ice-cream parlor window, glanced quickly around the room to see if any of the other customers had observed the sign language. Satisfied none had, she shrugged. "It's okay," she answered, speaking the words instead of signing them.

Because Claire herself was deaf and had been from birth, she was equally fluent in both lipreading and signing. She was also astute enough to know the game, the destructive game, that the young woman was playing. Lipreading didn't betray one's deafness, while signing, on the other hand, silently advertised it to the world. After only a few minutes with AmyAnn, Claire had noticed this classic denial behavior, which translated to, "I'm not going to let anyone see I'm different."

Even had Claire not recognized AmyAnn's denial, she had been warned about her attitude by Peggy Pannell, director of the Hearing-Impaired Program— HIP—of the San Francisco Big Brothers/Big Sisters agency. The vivacious, enthusiastic Peggy—the one who could sell the Golden Gate Bridge to a miser, the one who'd talked Claire into involving herself in the volunteer program even though she wasn't certain she had the time to spare—had warned Claire of Amy-Ann's resistance to learning sign. The resistance would eventually pass, Claire knew. That is, if the bitterness didn't obstruct its departure.

"If you'd rather go somewhere else—" Claire began to sign, but was cut off sharply.

"I can lip-read," AmyAnn said, amending it to, "At least I'm trying to learn."

With casualness that said the issue was no big deal, Claire took another bite from the sinfully sweet scoop of caramel nugget ice cream before placing the dish on the floor for the black fluffy-haired dog. The canine, trained as a hearing-impaired person's companion, gave a whine of appreciation that said she at least was glad they'd chosen this particular outing for a January Saturday afternoon.

"Lipreading is important," Claire signed, deliberately ignoring AmyAnn's objection, "but so is signing."

At Claire's stubborn insistence, AmyAnn's soft, doe-brown eyes hardened. She shoved the half-eaten ice cream from her. The glass scraped across the table, though neither woman heard the sound.

"Signing is too hard," AmyAnn said, establishing the fact that she, too, had a stubborn streak—and that it was the same mile long, the same mile wide. "I've tried, but I can't learn it."

Claire recognized the statement for the lie it was. She knew that AmyAnn's academic record was exceptional. In fact, that was part of the problem. AmyAnn was so intellectually gifted that her career choices were virtually limitless. Now, however, some doors had been closed—slammed in her face—by the deafness, making the disability an extraordinarily bitter pill to swallow.

"You can't expect to learn sign in three months," Claire pointed out, again with the use of sign.

AmyAnn's hard stare turned cold. "I don't understand what you're saying."

"You...can't...expect—"

"I told you I don't understand sign."

At that moment Claire would have loved to tell Peg Pannell to find someone else to deal with this kid, that she had neither the time nor the inclination for it. She'd also love to tell the kid that self-pity fed on itself until, nourished to the fullest, it took over your life, ruling like some sultan perched on a satin pillow. Claire took a deep breath, reminding herself how recent Amy-Ann's loss was. "You can't learn sign in three months," Claire said, leaving aside the hand gestures.

"I can't learn it at all."

"Of course you can—"

"I can't."

The two women, Claire with eyes almost as dark a
her ebony hair, which at present was swept back into
ponytail that made her, despite her thirty-one years
appear almost as young as AmyAnn, stared at eac
other with a look that said neither intended to give a
inch. The dog, a red bandanna tied around her neck
glanced from one gladiator to the other. Finally, Clair
nodded toward the abandoned tulip-shaped glass sit
ting in the middle of the table. The unspoken question
was, Are you finished?

Wordlessly, AmyAnn pushed back her chair and
stood. Just as wordlessly, Claire signed to the dog, who
immediately rose from her haunches and started for th
door. Claire's triumphant look in AmyAnn's direction
said, See. Even a dog can learn sign.

The same sullenness, the same hostility, character
ized the drive back to AmyAnn's house. Claire asked
the questions; AmyAnn answered them as briefly a
courtesy allowed, sometimes stretching civility to it
breaking point. It was obvious that AmyAnn would
rather have been anywhere else on earth . . . preferably
with someone who wasn't a constant reminder of he
own inability to hear.

"You haven't enjoyed our outing," Claire signed
when she stopped the van in the driveway and turned
to face AmyAnn. The dog, Smudge, sat in the back
seat with her huge head hung over into the front. As
always, the animal was relieved to be out of busy traf
fic, which she hated with a passion, so much so that the
only way she would travel in a car was if a seat belt was
securely fastened around her.

AmyAnn shrugged at Claire's accusation from the
far side of the passenger seat. Her hands were buried
deep in her hot-pink windbreaker. Because sign lan

guage made one particularly sensitive to body language, Claire recognized the gestures—the disinterested shrug, the distancing, the shoving of AmyAnn's hands into her pockets—for what they were, all signs of rebellion.

"It was all right," AmyAnn answered, proving that she could indeed understand some sign, perhaps even more than she realized.

"Joining the Big Sister-Little Sister program wasn't your idea, was it?" Claire signed, but this time it was clear that AmyAnn hadn't followed the discourse, either manually or orally.

It took a couple of frustrating attempts before AmyAnn pieced the message together. When she had, she answered, "No, my mother wanted me to."

"Joining the program wasn't my idea, either. In fact, I'm not any crazier about the notion than you are."

Claire's candor surprised the young girl. Her expression plainly asked, Why are you here, then?

"I know the director of the Hearing-Impaired Program. She asked me to be a part of it."

AmyAnn gave a simple "Oh."

"So," Claire said, "you don't want to do this. I don't want to do this. What do we do now? Call it quits?"

The young woman stared straight ahead, while a hand slipped from her pocket and slid the length of her jean-clad thigh. Claire wore jeans, too, and a denim jacket on which she'd painted a scene of sea and sky and the caption Old Artists Never Die, They Just Shade Away. The jacket, a pale blue that matched the dab of paint on her chin—more often then not, she accidentally accessorized with paint—was the perfect foil for the kitten-playful winds that blew off the bay but did little to counteract the chill that emanated from the girl beside her.

"I promised my mom I'd give it a try," AmyAnn said just when Claire thought she'd forgotten the question.

Claire tapped the young woman's shoulder, bringing her eyes to hers. "You'll have to look at me when you talk. Otherwise I can't read your lips."

"I said, I promised my mom I'd give it a try."

Claire nodded, as though she understood the honoring of such a commitment. "And I promised my friend I'd give it a try." A few seconds of silence passed. "So, you want to try again next week?"

AmyAnn nodded.

"Saturday afternoon?"

AmyAnn repeated the nod, though it was far from enthusiastic. Claire wondered if that was her response to all of life now or just to the Big Sister-Little Sister program.

"Where do you want to go?" Claire asked.

"It doesn't matter."

"Shopping?"

"It doesn't matter."

"A picnic?"

"It doesn't matter."

"Fisherman's Wharf? We could eat there."

"It doesn't—"

"I know, it doesn't matter," Claire said, frustration nibbling at her patience. Signing slowly, speaking slowly, she added, "Look, you're going only because your mother wants you to, and you're willing to go wherever I want to go. That's nice and accommodating, but you're part of this, too. What do you want?"

AmyAnn, who'd struggled to understand what Claire was saying, didn't in the least struggle for an answer. "To hear again," she said simply and without hesitation.

TO HEAR AGAIN.

On the drive home, the words played over and over in Claire's mind. Each time she heard them, she also heard the anguish with which they'd been spoken—the out-and-out, from-the-soul anguish. It was the kind of anguish that no sixteen-year-old should know. It was the kind of anguish that, in all fairness, no one at any age should know. But then, life wasn't fair. If it had been, she herself would never have been born deaf. On the other hand, being born prelingually deaf was a burden that no postlingually deaf person could ever fully understand. On the other hand, never having heard alleviated the bitterness that almost always came as the result of losing one's hearing. But—and this was the crux of the matter—people of substance, no matter how badly their lives had been shattered or at what point they'd been shattered, always managed to piece those shattered lives together and forge ahead.

And so would AmyAnn Williams...if she had grit. And grit was something you either had or you didn't have. No one could give it to you or instill it in you, which was just another excuse, Claire realized, to bow out of this commitment.

Drat it to high heaven, she didn't need this kind of complication in her life right now! She was up to her ears in art projects, which was the delightful predicament she'd worked long and hard to be in. Finally, her artistic endeavors were beginning to be taken seriously by the art community in general and by art patrons in particular. People were paying large sums of money for her bold, colorful paintings. Her agent was even talking about a one-woman art show.

And, as if these projects didn't occupy twenty-five out of every twenty-four hours in the day, she also taught art at a local university. Add to that the community theater commitment. She and her students were responsible for the scenery for two plays each year. It was a wonderful experience for the students and something she herself enjoyed. She certainly didn't need another responsibility—not one that would require four to six hours every week for the next year— the standard commitment a volunteer made to the Big Sister-Little Sister program. More to the point, she didn't need a responsibility the magnitude of AmyAnn Williams.

"Right?" she spoke out loud for the dog's benefit. Smudge, who now sat in the front seat beside her, the seat belt strapped safely around her, woofed.

Right, Claire confirmed. So, she'd just tell Peg Pannell that AmyAnn Williams was more than she'd bargained for, that she was uncooperative, uncommitted and that she really didn't want this arrangement, either. She'd just tell the program director that AmyAnn wanted...

To hear again.

The words once more broke through Claire's thoughts, bringing with them the image of the sixteen-year-old. Claire could see the pain in her brown eyes, the bewilderment, the "I don't see how this could have happened to me." She could also see beyond the hostility to the silent entreaty for someone, anyone, to explain to her why her world had suddenly fallen apart. She saw, too, AmyAnn's plea for help: *Help me make it through the day, the night, the rest of my shattered life.*

Claire sighed, admitting what she'd known all along—that there was no way she could turn her back on AmyAnn. There was no way she could close her eyes to the young woman's emotional suffering. And she couldn't do it for two basic reasons, both of which Peg had counted on from the beginning. One, she wasn't the kind to hang around on the fringes of life— she always stepped right into its middle, and two, she hadn't even the vaguest concept of what quitting meant. An overachiever, an individual who had never tolerated failure, she knew only how to do one thing: win. She'd made up her mind a long time ago that she wouldn't settle for less simply because she was deaf. And she hadn't. Nor would she let AmyAnn Williams.

She, with the help of professionally trained Peg, would find a way to reach the tortured young woman, even if it killed all three of them!

AMYANN CLOSED THE DOOR to the gray-shuttered, blue frame house. Even if she'd been able to hear, she knew she would have heard the sound of silence. The late afternoon sun, peering through faded, crisply starched and immaculately ironed curtains, provided the only light, giving a deserted, lonely look to the small living room. Shadows had already begun to pool in the corners and beneath the worn, carefully polished furniture and beside the potted palm that had thrived despite being haphazardly watered while AmyAnn had been in the hospital. AmyAnn fancifully, painfully imagined that the shadows whispered secrets, secrets about her.

She's deaf.
She's been ill...spinal meningitis...she almost died.
She's deaf.
Poor thing...she'll never hear again.
She's deaf...deaf...deaf...

With a vengeance that broke a fingernail, AmyAnn switched on the light, fracturing the shadows and silencing the heart-sickening secrets. As she crossed the room, she simultaneously nursed her nail and shucked her windbreaker. She threw the nylon jacket onto the sofa as she headed for the kitchen. There, the wall clock in the shape of a kettle said five minutes to five. Her mother would be home shortly, exhausted after working two jobs all week. By day, she worked as a seamstress at a department store; three nights a week and on Saturdays, she supplemented the meager income by sewing draperies for a well-known interior decorating firm. AmyAnn wished that her mother didn't have to work so hard. She wished that her illness hadn't piled up a mountain of unpaid medical bills. She wished that her father hadn't died five years before. She wished she could hear!

Anger, like caustic acid, bubbled through her, leaving a corrosive froth that ate away at her tender senses. She felt empty, removed, as though she were standing on the outside of the window of life looking in. She cherished this anger, however, for she intuitively knew that it was the only thing holding her together. Holding on to the anger sometimes caused her to lash out at others. It was anger that had made her act the way she had with Ms. Rushing, who, if truth be told, had really been kind of nice. She wasn't proud of her behavior, but it was the best she could do. She just wanted people to leave her alone, to quit telling her that everything was going to be all right when it wasn't—people like her mother, her friends, Ms. Rushing, sometimes even her boyfriend, Curt.

Curt. He was the only sanity left in her insane life. AmyAnn frowned as she placed two frozen dinners in the oven. It wasn't like him to cancel their Saturday night date, though she supposed he couldn't help it if his parents insisted he go with them to his grandmother's house for dinner. Actually, she needed the time to study. The illness had put her behind. Her mother, even a couple of her teachers, said that she shouldn't work so hard to catch up, that she didn't have to make an A in everything, but they didn't understand. She'd made A's when she could hear. She had to make them now to prove that she was no less a person than she had been before the illness.

Leaving the kitchen, she headed for her bedroom. In the hallway, she noticed that the hands of the grandfather clock read precisely five o'clock. The chimes would be ringing. In her mind she heard them—sharply, clearly, bitterly. The acid-anger began to bubble again. She tried to ignore it, but everything in her bedroom only added insult to injury: the telephone, the radio, the clock that used to alarm every morning at six-thirty, the stereo that had been silent for three months, the bare spots on the wall where movie star posters had hung once...before she'd ripped them down in the throes of hysteria when she'd realized her dreams of a career in drama would never be realized.

On the dressing table, as still as nesting cardinals, lay a pair of red pom-poms. As always AmyAnn's gaze came to rest here. She remembered vividly the day she'd been told that she would have to give up her position as cheerleader. How could she cheer when she couldn't hear the synchronized calls? It was the same day the drama coach had told her that he thought it best if her understudy took over the lead in the junior class presentation of *Bye Bye Birdie*. AmyAnn had cried for hours, until her eyes had burned and her throat had ached. She'd promised herself then and there that she'd never shed another tear because she was deaf. And she hadn't. She'd simply let the tears build into a hot, fierce anger.

AmyAnn turned on the bedside lamp, reached for her chemistry book and took out the notes that her "buddy" had taken for her. To help her at school, she had been assigned a peer in each class who made a copy of the notes for her. Three days a week, she saw a special instructor whose job it was to teach her sign language. AmyAnn knew that her teachers, her mother, everyone wanted her to consent to having a signing interpreter beside her during each class to help her to better understand what was going on, but she'd adamantly refused. It would only further emphasize that she was different. It would only give her classmates another reason to look at her out of the corner of their eyes when they thought she wasn't watching. She longed to tell them that she was deaf, not blind.

Spreading the sheets of paper across the bed, AmyAnn studied the notations. She was painfully aware of how she had to work twice as hard to get half as much done, of how difficult it was to assimilate facts received secondhand. Her thoughts rushed to the woman assigned as her Big Sister. Had she attended a normal school? Did she have to work twice as hard as everyone else? Did she sometimes feel so overwhelmed that she broke out in a sweat? Did she sometimes feel afraid?

Afraid.

Fear had become her constant companion, AmyAnn thought, but, like her being less complete than she used to be, it was something she knew but couldn't acknowledge. Refusing to admit it, however, didn't keep her from feeling the fear. Right down to the marrow of her bones. On a sigh, AmyAnn gathered up the notes and slid them into the chemistry book. She closed it. As she did so, her gaze returned to the pom-poms. Slowly, she eased from the bed, crossed the room and picked one up. It felt familiar yet foreign, as though it belonged to her, but in another lifetime. She shook it, letting the feathery streamers flutter. She imagined the rustling sound they made and the roar of the crowd when someone, more often than not Curt, made a touchdown. She imagined, too, the echo of a deserted theater as she stood on stage staring out at the empty seats. And at other times the applause that thundered about her when she took a final bow at play's end.

Lost.

All those sounds were lost to her.

For forever.

The pom-pom still in hand, AmyAnn climbed back onto the bed. She stretched, turned off the lamp and settled against the headboard. Immediately, shadows began to scurry across the room. The pom-pom, a symbol of all that was now denied her, clutched to her heart, she listened as the shadows began whispering their secrets.

She's deaf.

She's been ill...spinal meningitis...she almost died.

She's deaf.

Poor thing...she'll never hear again.

She's deaf...deaf...deaf...

IF CLAIRE HAD THOUGHT that the next meeting with
AmyAnn was going to be a significant improvement
over the first, she was sorely mistaken . . . and sorely
disappointed. AmyAnn seemed unusually moody, a
condition that quite possibly could be blamed on the
fact that she'd just received the first B of her life. Never
before, Peg Pannell had informed Claire earlier that
afternoon, had the young woman made less than a
perfect score on her report card. Claire also had to
contend with the fact that AmyAnn still refused to sign
and that she was openly hostile whenever Claire did,
which was often, because Claire refused to knuckle
under to her young friend's unhealthy attitude. The
only bit of encouragement came as they were finishing
their meal at one of the restaurants on Fisherman's
Wharf.

"Did you go to regular school?"

The question startled Claire. Not its content, but
rather that AmyAnn had initiated the dialogue. It was
the first time she had done so since Claire had picked
her up an hour and a half ago.

With her other fingers curled, Claire brought her
index and middle finger down to meet her thumb in one
motion. At the same time, she mounted, "No."

As before, it was obvious that AmyAnn would have
preferred the verbal response alone, though for once
the young woman seemed more interested in the subject than in glancing around to see if anyone was
watching them.

"You went to a deaf school?"

Claire folded her right hand into a fist and shook it
up and down, as though the fist were a head engaged
in a simple nod. She was gratified to see that AmyAnn
recognized the sign as yes. Claire then added manually

and with lip movement, "I went to the California School for the Deaf, in Fremont, then to Gallaudet University in Washington, D.C. Gallaudet is the only liberal arts college for the deaf in the United States."

"Why weren't you mainstreamed?"

"Mainstreaming wasn't that common twenty-five years ago. Even it if had been, I would have still gone to schools for the deaf. I had little choice. I was born deaf. I needed to be specially tutored from an early age."

Claire wasn't sure just how much of the conversation AmyAnn was picking up, nor was she sure how to tell AmyAnn what she'd wanted to from the beginning of their tenuous relationship. She decided that straight out was probably the best route to follow.

"You may not believe this, but you're lucky." Claire signed this last word again—touching her chin with her middle finger, then turning her hand quickly with the palm facing out—to make certain that AmyAnn understood.

AmyAnn did, if the sneer that crossed her face was any indication. "Yeah, sure, I'm real lucky."

"You are. You didn't lose your hearing until your language skills were in place." The young woman said nothing, though a spark of interest lighted her eyes. "Everything you learn—your culture, your humanity—is transmitted through language. If it can't be oral, then it has to be some other expression of communication. Sign language is very expressive, but it has to be introduced early in a child's life or else those first years are spent in a kind of soundless prison. Also, most hearing people can't converse in sign language."

At the blank look on AmyAnn's face, Claire knew she'd lost her, so she repeated what she'd said, even scribbling down a couple of the hardest words. Finally, she added, "So deaf people have to learn to speak to compete in the real world, but it's hard to speak when you've never heard words. It would have been easier if I'd had the memory of words to call on. I have no idea what a word really sounds like. I know only what I've been taught it sounds like, and I've had to work very hard to develop verbal skills. Very hard."

"Do you sound funny?"

Claire grinned elfishly. "I don't know. I can't hear."

AmyAnn failed to see the humor. "The sign instructor said I wouldn't sound normal after a few years," she said, shoving around the food on her plate.

Claire heard the young woman's concern and sobered accordingly. "After two or three years, your voice will become a little distorted. And no, I don't sound normal. But so what?" she added on a shrug. "What you say is more important than how you say it."

AmyAnn was not prepared to be so blasé. She pushed her food around a little more before asking, "Did you make good grades?"

Claire grinned again. "Yeah. I was an over-achiever...like you." When AmyAnn offered no comment but seemed to retreat into herself, Claire continued—nonchalantly, "How's school going?"

"Okay. I guess."

"Do you have a classroom interpreter?" Claire knew the answer, but she wanted to see AmyAnn's reply.

AmyAnn shook her head. "I don't need one."

"I see. You understand everything that's going on? You understand the questions that your classmates ask? The answers that your teachers give?"

"I don't need an interpreter," AmyAnn said with the same implacability with which she'd insisted she couldn't learn sign language.

Claire didn't point out that the young woman had just received her first B, which meant she obviously hadn't understood something.

Quietly—the tone was imparted by slow, serene movements of her hands accompanied by soft facial gestures—Claire said, "There's no shame in asking for help. There's no shame in being deaf."

AmyAnn said nothing. Her silence continued for the remainder of the outing.

"CAN WE GO SHOPPING?"

Claire almost passed out cold at AmyAnn's animation the following Tuesday afternoon, when she picked her up after school.

"Sure," Claire answered, wondering what had caused the sudden change. She didn't have long to wonder.

"I need shoes for my dress."

"You have a new dress?"

"Yeah. Or I will when Mother finishes it."

"What's the occasion?"

"A party Saturday night."

"You didn't tell me you were going to a party," Claire said, then thought to herself, *Nor much of anything else, for that matter.*

"I didn't know until yesterday. Some of the parents are having a party for the football players and their dates."

"Sounds like fun," Claire said, maneuvering the van out of the residential section and onto the crowded street. Smudge whined and flapped an ear over an eye, as though hiding from the darting cars. "So you date a football player?"

Claire was pleasantly surprised that AmyAnn was dating. She'd been told that the young woman had withdrawn from her friends. Obviously she hadn't withdrawn from one. Which was good. Real good.

"Yeah," AmyAnn answered. "The quarterback."

Claire arched a brow as dark as her raven-black hair, which was piled atop her head except for a few wayward wisps that appeared to have made a daring dash for freedom just in the nick of time. She wore a red leather jumper that came to midcalf, a black cowlnecked sweater and enormous gold loop earrings. A dab of paint on her cheek, aubergine in color, bore testimony to the fact that she'd just come from her studio.

"Quarterback?" Claire said. "I'm impressed."

AmyAnn grinned. With her shock of blond Little Orphan Annie curls, Claire was suddenly reminded of just how young sixteen really was. It was an age that thought it knew it all, but mostly it was an age of bravado. It was an age when self-image was all-important and peer pressure was at its greatest. It was a lousy age to have your life turned topsy-turvy.

"Do you have a boyfriend?"

"What?" Claire asked, making out only a part of what her friend had said.

"Do you have a boyfriend?"

A hollowness dented—not carved, just *dented*—Claire's stomach. "No," she signed, thinking of Bill Gaensehal.

He constituted the only significant relationship she'd ever had. It was a two-year relationship that had ended almost nine months ago. Although he, a teacher at the

California School for the Deaf, was also deaf, they
hadn't found enough common ground to keep them
together. The relationship, which had slowly fizzled
into a friendship, had been terminated by mutual consent. She still missed him, or rather missed having
someone in her life. Despite her busy schedule, she was
sometimes lonely. Maybe that was one reason she'd let
Peg talk her into getting involved in the Big Sister-Little
Sister program.

"I did have a boyfriend," Claire added, "but we
broke up."

"Was he deaf?"

"Yes." Then, grateful for the opportunity to change
the subject, although she had no idea why she felt the
need to do so, Claire parked the van and opened the
door.

"Let's go shop for those shoes," she said, slinging
an enormous tote bag over her shoulder.

Smudge, obviously happy to have survived the traf-
fic, jumped onto terra firma, or in this case concrete
firma, and wagged her tail in solemn thanks to the gods
who watched over canines in cars. She then dutifully
took her place at Claire's side. The dog's red leather
kerchief matched her mistress's jumper.

Within the hour, it seemed as though AmyAnn had
tried on every pair of shoes in the mall. None fit the
bill. Down to what had to be the very last pair, both
Claire and Smudge eagerly awaited a verdict.

AmyAnn stood, walked the length of the chairs, then
returned to stand before the mirror.

"What do you think?" Claire asked.

AmyAnn smiled. "They're pretty."

Claire and Smudge sighed in relief, with Claire adding, "They look pretty."

"They're more than pretty, they're perfect," AmyAnn said, turning once more to observe the gold-and-bronze shoes in the mirror.

A warm feeling washed through Claire. AmyAnn had signed the word *pretty*. Not that she was aware she had, but, like it or not, fight it or not, AmyAnn was beginning to think in sign. Claire smiled, then repeated the sign, "Pretty."

If the shoes were perfect, the outing proved no less, except for one minor complication. As they were leaving the mall, they ran into two of AmyAnn's schoolmates—Candace Jordan and Leah McCleary. At the sight of the girls, who were AmyAnn's best friends, Claire sensed AmyAnn's immediate tensing. It was a subtle kind of thing, which only body language revealed. AmyAnn clutched the package to her chest, as though shielding herself from two enemies who'd suddenly sprung upon her. The three exchanged polite words, though AmyAnn said very little. The other two also seemed ill at ease. As was often the case when hearing people spoke to deaf people, they exaggerated their lip movements, making it more difficult to lip-read.

"They think I'm a freak," AmyAnn said seconds later as she, Claire and Smudge made their way to the parking lot.

"No, they don't. The truth is, they don't really know what to think. They're waiting for you to cue them. If they sense you feel at ease with your deafness, then they'll feel at ease, too."

"How can I feel at ease when I hate what's happened to me?"

Claire saw the girl's anguish and wished that she could miraculously make it disappear. But she couldn't. Any more than she could change the fact that, in a very real sense, AmyAnn *was* different now. Certainly not a freak, but nonetheless an oddity. It was a change that could lead to isolation if one didn't constantly fight against it. It was all in one's attitude. She herself had had an advantage. She'd had a family with a positive attitude, a family that had allowed her to have no less. A long time ago she'd chosen to project the image of an artist who just happened to be deaf not the image of a deaf person who just happened to be an artist. A long time ago she'd rejected the road of isolation and had chosen the road of inclusion. AmyAnn would have to find her own road to travel.

"Give yourself some time," Claire advised, adding, "Focus on what you have, not on what you don't have." At AmyAnn's skeptical look, Claire said, "You have a boyfriend, a new dress and a pretty pair of shoes."

Despite her sullen mood, AmyAnn smiled.

Claire smiled, too, and thought for the first time that maybe, just maybe, this relationship was going to work, after all. Maybe, just maybe, AmyAnn was taking her first tentative steps toward healing.

CHAPTER TWO

THE HIGH SCHOOL HALLWAY rang with noise. Lockers banged, feet pattered, voices sang in choruses of chatter that were punctuated by raucous shouts and shrill laughter. AmyAnn heard nothing, or more precisely heard only gurgling sounds, weird babbling that occasionally rumbled through her silent world. All the noises, she knew, were coming from within her own head. Just as she knew deep down that believing everyone was looking at her and talking about her was only part of a vivid imagination.

Even as she thought this, a couple of girls a few lockers away stopped talking the second they spotted her. They smiled—awkwardly, AmyAnn thought—waved, then quickly turned away. One of the girls looked back, but, embarrassed at being caught doing so, she jerked her gaze away. The episode, in one form or another, had been repeated all morning, or at least it seemed so to AmyAnn. She'd felt herself the object of everyone's stare ever since she'd returned to school following her illness, but never had she felt so blatantly scrutinized, or rather, so covertly scrutinized. Hadn't every eye turned her way when she'd walked into chemistry class, and hadn't the same gazes staggered over themselves trying to find something else to look at? Hadn't more than one person scurried away rather than face her? Hadn't Candace and Leah acted downright odd?

Reining in her paranoia, AmyAnn told herself she was just imagining things. She had to be. Though *her* every thought was centered around her deafness, logic told her that other people didn't concentrate on it every minute of every day. They had their own problems to contend with.

Besides, things were looking up. For the first time in a long while, she was excited about something. The upcoming party was more than a party. It was her chance to do something "normal." It was her chance to *be* normal, if only for an evening—even if she had to pretend. But she didn't have to pretend that her dress, which her mother had worked long into the night to finish, was pretty. Just as there was no need to pretend that her shoes were pretty. Pretty and perfect. Curt would love both the dress and the shoes.

An uneasy feeling pricked AmyAnn as she dialed the combination lock on her locker. She hadn't seen Curt all morning, which was strange. He usually showed up to walk her to the next class and to steal a quick kiss or two. As though seeking protection, she burrowed deeper into his letter sweater. He'd given her the sweater when they'd started going steady at the beginning of the fall. Out of the clear blue, he'd just asked her if she wanted to be his girl—plain, simple, no gushy sentiment. When she'd answered that she did, he'd taken off the sweater and handed it to her. The three months she'd been ill, the longest months of her life, she'd often worn the sweater over her nightgown. It had made her feel that Curt was near even when he wasn't. And he had come to see her every week. Well, every week that he could. Football practice and foot-

ball games often got in the way. Everyone knew that
every college coach in the area was scouting him now
that he was a senior and would be graduating in the
spring, though he never talked much about the way he
was being courted and wooed.

No, she thought, opening her locker, depositing
some books and retrieving those for the next class, Curt
wasn't much on words. Which was probably why he
hadn't said anything about the party Saturday night.
Even considering his typical reticence, however, it
nagged a little that he hadn't mentioned anything about
the two of them going. As part of the team, he would
have to be there, and since she knew for a fact that the
guys were bringing dates—both Candace and Leah
were going—she was certain she was going, too. After
all, she *was* Curt Knight's girl.

At the tap on her shoulder, AmyAnn turned, more
than half expecting to see Curt. Instead, Candace and
Leah stood beside her. According to AmyAnn, who
compared all people to movie stars, Candace looked
like Meg Tilly, while Leah was a dead ringer for Molly
Ringwald. Right now, they both looked even more ill
at ease than usual.

"Hi," Leah said.

"Hi," Candace chimed.

AmyAnn read both pairs of lips and responded with
the same, "Hi." She spoke softly, in barely more than
a whisper, because she was afraid that without the
ability to monitor her pitch, she would end up shouting. That thought mortified her.

As always, the same awkward "What do I say
now?" jumped among the three friends. AmyAnn
hated the awkwardness but didn't know what to do
about it. Since the illness, since the loss of her hear-

ing, she no longer belonged. Overnight she'd felt as if she'd grown two heads, while her friends continued to have only one each. She sensed her friends wanted to apologize for having only the single head, while AmyAnn, try as hard as she would, couldn't help but resent that she now had two. A part of her, a shameful part of her, even wanted to blame them for remaining normal.

Leah looked at Candace, Candace looked at Leah, as if each were prodding the other to say something.

"How did you do on the algebra test?" Candace blurted out.

Leah looked at her friend, her expression saying that that question was not what they'd planned to ask. AmyAnn sensed this. Both curiosity and something that could only be called trepidation washed through her.

"I, uh, I made a ninety-eight," AmyAnn answered absently, studying her friends, who now seemed to be sweating blood.

There was another brief silence during which Leah jabbed Candace with her elbow.

"I made a ninety," Candace spat out. "Leah made a—"

"What's wrong?" AmyAnn asked at the exact moment that Leah elbowed her friend again.

After a yelp of pain, Candace rounded on Leah. "You ask her, then!"

"Ask me what?" AmyAnn said, a cold feeling crawling over her.

Both Candace and Leah turned back to AmyAnn. Each looked troubled.

"Will you tell me what's wrong?" AmyAnn repeated, now not caring about the pitch of her voice.

Like water pouring over the side of a cliff, Leah plunged ahead. "Was Curt with you Saturday night?"

The question so startled AmyAnn that all she could say was, "What?"

"Was ... Curt ... with ... you ... Sa ... tur ... day—" Leah started to repeat, again exaggerating her lip movement.

"I understand the question," AmyAnn interrupted, her voice overly loud. Several nearby students glanced toward her. "I just don't understand why you're asking the question."

"Was Curt with you?" Leah persisted. Compassion in her Molly Ringwald eyes pleaded for AmyAnn to tell her that he was.

AmyAnn felt the earth shift beneath her. She'd had the world-spinning feeling only once before—when the doctors had told her that she'd never hear again.

"Was he?" Candace asked determinedly.

"He was at his grandmother's," AmyAnn answered. "His parents made him to go dinner..." The words trailed off, suddenly sounding as hollow as tin bells.

"He was out with Heather Blakely," Leah said.

Heather Blakely. *Madonna. Of the white-blond hair and drop-dead sexy body.*

The earth split wide open beneath AmyAnn. She fell into the yawning chasm. When she could find her voice, she asked, "Why—why are you lying to me?" She knew, though, that her friends weren't lying. Something deep in her feminine heart knew they were telling the truth.

"I'm not lying," Leah said, her own voice strained. "It's all over school."

As though on cue, two boys, both football team-mates of Curt's, passed by. They glanced in Amy-Ann's direction but couldn't look away fast enough.

"I'm sorry," Leah said. "I wanted you to hear it from us."

"Yeah," Candace said, "I'm sorry."

"...sorry...hear...from us..." AmyAnn caught only bits and pieces of what her friends were saying, though she didn't miss a single nuance of the pity she saw on their faces. Pity. She was sick to death of seeing pity on everyone's face! First there'd been pity because of her handicap, now there was pity because her boyfriend had thrown her over for Madonna. No wonder he hadn't mentioned the upcoming party!

Slamming her locker shut with such force that it rattled, AmyAnn whirled and plowed her way through the sea of students, all of whom she felt staring at her. Her own eyes stung with tears that begged to be shed, but her pride made her shut them tightly away. Instead, she'd find another outlet for her hurt—anger.

"AmyAnn!" Leah called.

"Wait!" Candace cried.

AmyAnn, taking the stairs two at a time, disappeared without a backward glance. She found Curt just as he was entering his physics class. His expression said that he wasn't expecting to see her.

"Hi," the tall, sandy-haired Kiefer Sutherland look-alike said, as quick on the uptake as he was at snapping the football. "Where ya been? I've been looking for you all morning."

AmyAnn knew he was lying. In fact, she now realized the truth was that he'd been avoiding her. "Have you?" she said, throwing him the rope necessary to hang himself.

"Yeah. Where ya been?" he repeated.

"The usual places," she answered, tossing him a fe'
more inches of the rope.

"Look," he said, shuffling his foot, glancing dow'
at the gleaming Gucci loafers he took such pride i'
then back up, "I need to talk to you. What about ha'
ing lunch—" When he saw that she wasn't followin'
what he was saying, he opened his notebook an'
scribbled out the message.

Her response was "Why wait till lunch? How abou'
talking now?"

"I have class."

"Now."

AmyAnn's unusual insistence caught him off guard'
like a football tackle coming from out of nowhere. H'
looked at AmyAnn as though seeing her for the firs'
time.

"Hey, Knight, you coming to class?" one of hi'
buddies called out as he passed by and stepped into th'
classroom.

Curt's eyes never left AmyAnn. "Yeah. In a min'
ute. Look," he began, "about the party Saturda'
night..."

When AmyAnn said nothing, Curt started to writ'
down what he'd said.

"I understood you," she informed him. "Wha'
about the party Saturday night?"

The young man at least had the decency to look un'
comfortable. "Well, I was thinking... I mean, abou'
the party... I thought you probably wouldn't want t'
go...with the dancing and all... I mean, you wouldn'
be able to hear...you know, the music and...and all."

Curt's awkwardness, his "Gucci loafers carry m'
away" look, said that he knew he was acting like '

irst-class jerk. AmyAnn had never noticed before how
perfectly the role fit him.

"Gee, Curt, what a sensitive guy you are."

Curt hadn't the foggiest idea whether AmyAnn was
being sincere or sarcastic. The tone of her voice could
have gone either way. He chose to belive she was being
sincere.

"Yeah, well, there's no need you going if you don't
want to." He looked down at his loafers again, then
forced his gaze to meet AmyAnn's. "I thought…well,
since you weren't going…I didn't think you'd mind…
I thought I might take someone—not a date," he
amended quickly, adding, "You know, just someone
to dance with."

Miraculously, AmyAnn had followed what he'd
said…or at least enough of it to feel the dagger plunge
deep into her heart. "Someone like Heather Blakely?"

At the mention of the name, Curt, noted for his on-
field bravery, paled.

"Did you take her out Saturday night?" AmyAnn
asked point-blank.

Curt went from pale to ashen. "Where did you hear
that?" he asked, his voice shredding into sliver-thin
threads that AmyAnn would have appreciated if only
she could have heard them.

"Apparently everyone knew it," she answered.
"Well, not everyone. I just found out about it."

"Look, it wasn't a date. I just ran into her." At her
confused look, he again wrote down what he'd said.

AmyAnn read the words, then looked up defiantly.
"You ran into her at your grandmother's?"

"No, at Dennison's!" It was the place where all the
high school kids hung out.

"I thought you were having dinner at your grand mother's house."

"I was, but..." Panic skittered across Curt's hand some face. AmyAnn could see he was searching fo some logical excuse as to why his plans had changed He seized the first thing that occurred to him. "She go sick! The flu!" This last he scrawled so hard he brok the lead on his pencil.

"So you went cruising?"

"I did not! I just went by Dennison's. Heather an I got to talking and... Look, it wasn't a date. You jus misunderstood what someone told you. For heaven' sake, you can't hear. You just got it wrong!"

Something snapped in AmyAnn. "I'm deaf, Cur Knight, not dumb!"

Though the hallway had cleared except for a few stragglers, these few looked over in the direction of th feuding couple.

"Sh!" Curt whispered, placing his hand on he shoulder to calm her. "Will you be quiet? Everyone' gonna hear you!"

She jerked her shoulder away. "You lied to me. You never were going to your grandmother's for dinner," she accused, juggling her books from one hand to the other and wrestling out of his sweater. She threw it a his feet and stalked away. After only a few steps, she turned back. "For your information, I wasn't plan- ning on going to the party. I've got better things to do with my time than date a lying, two-timing jerk."

As she bolted through the hall door, she wondered if God forgave white lies that preserved pride. She also wondered if the bell for the next class had rung and how she was going to face a roomful of pitying stares.

Last, she wondered what she was going to do with a pretty pair of shoes that now had nowhere to go.

SATURDAY NIGHT was clear and cool, the perfect night for a party.

From her studio, which consisted of the entire second floor of a small warehouse, Claire stood at the floor-to-ceiling windows and stared out. She had first seen the warehouse on a sunny day and had known the moment she'd entered the spacious upstairs that it would be an ideal place to paint. For the next few months, she'd worked diligently to convert the downstairs into living quarters. She had bought the building because of the way the sun gloriously spilled into it, but she'd gotten a bonus she hadn't bargained for: the way the night, sprinkled with billions of bright stars, pressed lovingly, nurturingly against the glass panes. There were times she could believe that she could pluck those stars, bring them to earth and make them shine especially for her.

"Wonder how she's doing?" Claire whispered, squatting beside Smudge and stroking her sleek black fur.

The dog, as though she understood perfectly, gave a half bark that said she wondered, too.

"Wonder what this boyfriend is like?"

Again, Smudge gave a responsive sound.

Wonder what it would be like to be hopelessly in love on such a perfect night?

The query laced itself so gently with the ones that had gone before that Claire found herself more than a little surprised when she realized the turn of her thoughts. She recognized the sudden restless feeling within her. It was one she'd felt often of late. As al-

ways, the days, filled with hard work, flew by. It was
the nights that had become longer, the perfect ones in
particular, for they emphasized just how alone she was.
She had a supportive family, she had wonderful
friends, she had business cohorts, but she had no one
at the end of the day to take her in his arms and love
her. She had no one with whom she could share the
star-studded night.

As though reading her mistress's mood, Smudge
whined a "You've got me."

"I know," Claire whispered, burying her face in the
dog's silken ebony hair.

Woman and dog had been together for nearly four
years, ever since Claire had found her on the side of the
road with a broken leg. Assuming she'd been struck by
a car and left to die, Claire had swallowed her outrage
and taken her to a veterinarian. Actually, she'd had
little choice after she'd gazed into the animal's be-
seeching golden-colored eyes. Once the dog's broken
bone had mended, Claire had sent her to school to
learn how to be a hearing-impaired person's companion. Claire's family had been delighted with her decision, since they'd long tried to get her to accept such
help. Because she considered herself independent
enough, Claire had always resisted the idea. She, however, had never regretted keeping the dog. The love
she'd gotten from the animal had been immeasurable,
as had been the help. With a gentle lick, Smudge woke
her each morning when the alarm sounded. She also
alerted her to the buzzing of the doorbell, the ringing
of the telephone, the beeping of the microwave—along
with a dozen other things. The dog would have awak-
ened her even at a baby's cry...if Claire had had a

child, but she didn't, which was another reason the nights were long...and perhaps destined to remain so.

"C'mon, Smudge, we're getting maudlin," Claire said, rising. "How about we go stuff ourselves on sunflower seeds...or maybe granola bars...or...okay, okay, Doggie Chewies."

They were halfway down the stairs when Smudge barked and raced for the front door. Claire frowned. Who could it be? She looked at the clock, which read a few minutes after eight, and glanced in the mirror, which hung near the door as a last checkpoint for any paint she might unknowingly be wearing. Sure enough, a streak of citron yellow blazed across her cheek. Moistening her finger with her tongue, she wiped the paint away, though there was little she could do for the paint-encrusted jeans.

The woman who stood on the other side of the door was slender with a slim build. She wore little makeup—only a smidgen of mascara and a hint of lip gloss—and her hair, somewhere between silver and blond, had been styled in a simple but becoming pageboy. Her age might have been anywhere from mid-thirties to mid-forties. Claire realized with a start that the woman was AmyAnn's mother. When the two met at Claire's first meeting with AmyAnn, she had noticed Sharon Williams's worn, weary eyes. The same eyes, however, could seem incongruously youthful and trustingly naive.

"I'm sorry to bother you," the caller said softly, "but I was wondering if I could talk with you."

Claire now could see clearly the similarities between AmyAnn and her mother—the same high-cheeked bone structure, the same apricot coloring, the same tall, trim build.

"Of course. Won't you come in?"

Sharon Williams stepped inside and slid out of her thin all-weather coat. Claire noted that she was dressed tastefully but inexpensively.

"Let me have that," Claire said, taking the coat, hanging it on a rack and motioning toward a clump of furniture that constituted the living room.

Like the upstairs studio, the first floor had no walls but was sectioned off into functional areas—kitchen, dining area, living room and, toward the back, a bedroom. The bed was a huge four-poster festooned in yards and yards of a white gauzy fabric. Everything in the warehouse was a shade of white and a sea green so pale it was virtually neutral. Accessories of glass and crystal dotted the serenity of the unwalled rooms, as did lush green plants. Boldly colored paintings hung on any available space.

Sharon seated herself on the white-on-white herringbone sofa and glanced up. An apologetic look crossed her face. "I'm sorry to bother you," she repeated, "but I simply didn't know where else to turn." Her eyes seemed deeply troubled.

Claire eased herself into an adjacent chair. Smudge lay down on the rug, stretched out her front legs and laid her head on her big paws. "Is something wrong with AmyAnn?" Claire asked.

Sharon took a huge breath, as though that action might help stifle a torrent of tears. "I don't know how to reach her. She's my daughter, the person I love most in the world, but I can't reach her. She's shut me out." At this, a tear slipped from the corner of the woman's eye. As though embarrassed by its presence, she quickly wiped it away.

"I don't understand," Claire said. "Earlier in the week AmyAnn seemed better than I'd ever seen her. She was looking forward to the party tonight."

"She didn't go to the party," Sharon announced.

In her mind, Claire could see an excited AmyAnn finally finding the right shoes—an AmyAnn so excited that she'd signed *pretty* without even realizing it. "Didn't go? Why? I thought everything was arranged."

"She wouldn't tell me anything except that there had been a change of plans." At the look on Claire's face, a look that said maybe there *had* been a change of plans, maybe the party had been postponed, rescheduled, or a dozen other legitimate things, Sharon said, "I think she and Curt broke up. It's the only thing that makes any sense."

Claire sighed.

"I've seen it coming," Sharon said. "AmyAnn's pulled away from her friends, not so much from Curt as from her girlfriends, but AmyAnn's so resentful and so angry that I wondered just how long Curt would put up with her." Without malice, she added, "Curt has never struck me as long-suffering."

Claire's heart constricted at the pain she knew AmyAnn must be feeling. "Where is she?"

Sharon's eyes once more filled with tears. She reached inside her purse, removed a tissue and dabbed at the betraying moisture. "I'm sorry," she said at the emotional display. She sniffed, seemingly regaining her composure. "AmyAnn's at home...playing the stereo. She's just sitting before it, watching the lights on the dials jump."

The vision that leaped into Claire's mind threatened to break her heart. She could imagine it all too vividly—the young woman punishing herself for things she could no longer do, for things she could no longer hear.

"I didn't want to leave her," Sharon said, interrupting Claire's dark musings. "I had to, though. I work on Saturdays...until midnight. I'm on my break now. We need the money. It's that simple."

"I understand. Even with insurance, illness can be catastrophic."

"But it means leaving AmyAnn alone so much of the time," Sharon continued, adding, "Too much of the time."

Claire could understand the woman's all too common guilt. She was reminded of how a disability was really a family matter. Its consequences rippled outward until every family member was touched, until every family member had to make his own adjustment.

"Some things can't be helped," Claire said.

Sharon Williams gave a mirthless laugh. "Oh, how I've learned that. When the doctors told me she was deaf, my first thought was that that's no big deal. She'll just have an operation and everything'll be fine. I mean, medical miracles happen every day now, don't they? Surely there was something they could do for my little girl. There had to be." The woman gave an unsteady bitter sigh. "But there wasn't. There wasn't anything the doctors could do, and there wasn't anything I could do."

"None of this is your fault," Claire said quietly. "Don't punish yourself for crimes you haven't committed."

"No, the spinal meningitis wasn't my fault, her losing her hearing wasn't my fault, but I keep telling myself that I should do something to help her adjust, but I can't even manage to do that." She laughed—again without humor—and tore at the tissue in her hand. "I didn't even know what to say when they told her she'd have to give up cheerleading . . . or when they told her she'd have to give up the lead in the class play." She smiled, a tight little grimace that twisted her mouth. "I said something totally trite like, 'I'm sorry.'"

This news of what AmyAnn had sacrificed came as a surprise to Claire. "AmyAnn never mentioned that she'd given up being a cheerleader or about the play."

"I don't think being a cheerleader really mattered. I mean, she enjoyed it, but she didn't live for it. But acting's different. From the minute she could talk, she told me she was going to be an actress." This time when Sharon smiled, the smile was genuine. "She used to play-pretend *Cinderella*. She'd play all the parts from Cinderella to the wicked stepsisters. She'd even make up songs and dances and . . ." She stopped, as though it hurt too much to go on.

When silent second bled into silent second, Claire asked, "Would you like me to check on her tonight?"

"I have no right to ask you to do that. You're already doing so much, but I can't tell you what it would mean to me if you would. Frankly, I'm worried about her."

Claire smiled in understanding. "Then I'll check on her."

A look of relief passed across Sharon's face, but it was instantly replaced by a harsh look that seemed totally contrary to this woman's obviously gentle character. "None of this should have happened to AmyAnn," Sharon said bitterly, angrily. "She was so pretty and so bright, and she had the whole world before her.''

In that moment, Claire realized that Sharon Williams was as angry as her daughter—maybe even more so. Perhaps AmyAnn was reflecting the feelings she was picking up from her mother. But how did you tell a mother that she was negatively affecting her child? How did you tell a mother that her attitude was vital to that of her child's well-being?

Slowly.

Carefully.

A hint at the time.

''AmyAnn is still pretty,'' Claire said softly. ''She's still bright. And she still has the whole world before her.''

LESS THAN THIRTY MINUTES later, Claire pulled the van into the driveway of AmyAnn's house. Except for a dim light in what she assumed was a bedroom, the house was dark. Even as she unfastened Smudge's seat belt, she wondered what she would say to AmyAnn. True, they were both deaf, but beyond that they had little in common. She had never had to make the adjustments that AmyAnn was struggling to make. She had never had to compensate for things suddenly lost to her. As a child, her nonhearing world had opened up to her slowly, revealing her limitations in manageable portions. More importantly, no one had ever walked out of her life because she was deaf.

As Claire rang the doorbell, she prayed for inspiration. *Please let me find the right words to help AmyAnn.* In the dark, without the ability to hear, Claire had to rely entirely on Smudge's reaction to determine when the door opened. At least Claire thought the door opened a crack. She was certain that Smudge's ears peaked.

"Hi," Claire signed into the darkness, though she knew she couldn't be seen.

If AmyAnn made a response, Claire failed to see it.

"May I come in?" she asked, still unable to determine if she was being seen any better than she was seeing, but hoping her presence would elicit an invitation.

Abruptly, the door opened wide. There was silence for a few seconds, then, "Mother came to see you," AmyAnn's voice sounded like an accusation.

Because of the darkness and because AmyAnn had already turned away, Claire couldn't read her lips. Stepping into the house, she turned on the light. When AmyAnn glanced around, Claire said, "I didn't understand you."

"Mother!" AmyAnn snapped, effectively communicating what she'd previously said, as well as her irritation.

"Your mother's worried about you."

"Yeah, well, I just wish everyone would leave me alone."

Claire ignored her young friend's rudeness. Without an invitation, she followed AmyAnn into her bedroom. The small room, filled with a collection of clutter, looked like any teenager's room, except for the bare walls. It was obvious that posters had once hung there. Claire wondered why they'd been removed—and why so hastily if the pieces of left-behind tape, even a ripped corner of a poster, were any indication. The posters had been piled in the bottom of the closet, as though they were now no longer wanted. As interesting as the posters were, however, Claire was more interested in the stereo, which she discreetly searched out. She was relieved to discover that it was turned off.

AmyAnn crawled onto the middle of the bed and folded her legs Indian-style. Textbooks, like a small village, rose around her.

"I have a research paper due Tuesday," AmyAnn announced, indicating that Claire was wasting her valuable study time. Most of the books, Claire noted, looked undisturbed, as though there hadn't been as much studying going on as AmyAnn wanted her to believe.

"I thought you were going to a party," Claire signed.

"My plans changed," AmyAnn answered verbally. Claire could feel the curtness in the reply. It felt sharp and piercing like a temple-pounding headache.

"That's a shame."

"It's no big deal," AmyAnn said, adding as she opened a book, "I needed to study."

Again without being asked, Claire seated herself on a chrome and velvet stool in front of the vanity table. Smudge hunkered down beside her. "Was the party canceled?"

AmyAnn looked Claire squarely in the eyes. "No."

"You just decided not to go?"

"Yes."

Each was waging a battle: Claire to get her friend to talk, AmyAnn to say nothing. It was a battle neither was winning.

"It's a shame," Claire repeated. "I mean, that you went to the trouble to have your mother make a new dress and you to buy new shoes, then you decide not to go."

"A lot of things are a shame."

Claire could see AmyAnn's pain. It was as obvious as her sassy blond curls and winter-brown eyes. AmyAnn needed to reach out to someone—perhaps *wanted* to reach out to Claire—but couldn't, because she couldn't find her way through the maze of her anger.

"A lot of things, like the fact that you can no longer be a cheerleader?" Claire asked, looking over at the pom-poms.

AmyAnn shrugged, repeating, "It's no big deal."

"And what about your having to give up the lead in the class play? Is that a shame, too? Or is it just no big deal?"

Claire thought that she might have finally found the key to unlocking AmyAnn's silence. The young woman opened her mouth but closed it without saying a word. She merely shrugged.

Talk to me! Claire wanted to scream. Instead, she sighed in abject frustration. As she did so, her gaze roamed back to the floor of the closet and the cast-aside posters. It suddenly crossed her mind that teenagers were teenagers were teenagers. Would AmyAnn have had on her walls what Claire's nieces had on theirs? Claire's heart beat just a note faster as she realized that TV and movie screen idols would have even more significance for AmyAnn than for the average teenager. AmyAnn's dreams for an acting career—her shattered dreams—would be a perfect reason for tearing the posters from the walls.

Sliding from the stool, Claire walked to the closet and stooped down. She could feel AmyAnn's eyes on her as she unfolded first one, then another of the discarded posters. She'd been right. Even though she herself wasn't a movie buff, she knew that all were of

TV or movie stars: Ken Wahl, Michael J. Fox, Mel Gibson, Nash Prather.

Still holding a poster, Claire stood. Her gaze meshed with AmyAnn's. AmyAnn looked . . . defiant.

"You know," Claire said, "being deaf doesn't have to end your dreams of an acting career."

"Yeah, sure, name one deaf actress."

"Who's the one who played in *Children of a Lesser God*?"

"Marlee Matlin."

"Right. Marlee Matlin."

"Name another," AmyAnn ordered.

"AmyAnn Williams."

AmyAnn snorted and looked away. When Claire tapped the bed, she looked up.

"There's also the National Theater of the Deaf—"

"No!" AmyAnn shouted. One would have thought that Claire had said something vile and ugly.

Claire let the poster in her hand fall gently back onto the closet floor. Just as gently, she signed, "You're deaf. You're going to have to accept that fact."

Defiance once more swaggered across AmyAnn's face. "I know I'm deaf. Even if I could forget it, nobody will let me."

"Curt, too?" Claire prodded.

AmyAnn laughed, though there was no joy in her eyes. Only pain. A pain that Claire wanted desperately to ease, because she was beginning to care for this tormented child-woman. But would AmyAnn trust her enough to share her heartache?

Finally, and in an emotionless voice that Claire could hear with her heart, AmyAnn said, "He told me he thought I wouldn't want to go to a party where there'd

music and dancing." She smiled, again sarcasti-
lly. "After all, I *am* deaf."

"I'm sorry," Claire signed.

"I guess he thought that deaf people didn't even hear
mors," AmyAnn added. In explanation, she said,
He's been dating someone else. He's taking her to the
arty."

"I'm sorry," Claire repeated.

"It doesn't matter," AmyAnn said with sudden
avado as she slipped from the bed and walked to the
creo. "Besides, he's right," she said, flipping on
vitches that set the stereo to playing. "You can't
ince when you don't hear the music."

Claire saw the red lights flash. From their frenzied
otion, she suspected that the stereo was blaring. She
dn't hear a thing, however. Any more than did
myAnn. Claire would have preferred her to cry, to
sh out at the stereo, to send it crashing to the floor—
nything to vent her anger. Instead, AmyAnn sat qui-
ly, with disturbingly dry eyes. With each unheard
ote, she pulled deeper and deeper into herself.

As Claire watched, she knew one thing with uncom-
romising certainty. She had to find a way to reach
myAnn. And soon. Or else the young woman was
oing to drown in a sea of silence.

EVERAL MILES AWAY, another stereo blared, sending
agan notes into the party-filled air. Curt Knight, who
ave AmyAnn only an occasional fleeting thought,
anced with Heather Blakely to the song ricocheting
ff the walls.

A few hundred miles away in Beverly Hills, a simi-
ir song was being shouted from a stereo. This party,

if possible, was even wilder, louder than the one C[
and Heather were attending.

He no longer fit in with this kind of clamouro[
crowd, thought the tall, dark-haired man who sto[
alone with a Scotch and water in his tanned hand. [
hadn't wanted to come to the party, but it was bei[
hosted by a movie mogul, a producer with a half do[
Academy Awards to his credit. No one refused t[
man's invitations, not even someone like him, who,[
and of his own right, seldom heard the word [
Though he himself was royal by Hollywood sta[
dards, he nonetheless played the prince to this ma[
king.

Prince. Depraved prince. Profligate prince.

He was tired of playing the role of Hollywood's b[
boy, the man thought. He was simply tired of playi[
roles, period. He was tired of guarding his priva[
tired of women pawing him, tired of... tired of t[
damned music! As unobtrusively as possible, the m[
slipped through the sliding glass door and out onto t[
balcony. A stillness and solitude immediately engulf[
him. The silence was more priceless than precio[
gems.

Silence.

He needed silence in his life—the kind of silence th[
represented not only the absence of noise but also t[
kind that meant a peace in his soul. Discontent, like [
uninvited guest who would not leave, had settled in. [
could not go on the way he was. Because of that, [
would be traveling to San Francisco the next day [
search of that silence he so desperately needed—at le[
a temporary slice of it. He was going on a pilgrima[
of self-discovery. He just hoped to heaven there w[
something left of him to find.

The sliding glass door opened and the movie mogul said, over the din of the crowd, the roar of the stereo, "What the hell are you doing out there? The party's in here."

Nash Prather downed the drink. He said nothing. He didn't think the man would understand his need for silence. Instead, he stepped back inside, where he instantly drowned in a deep sea of loud, indifferent sounds.

CHAPTER THREE

CLAIRE HAD ONCE READ that there was no such thing as coincidence, only fate-directed occurrences. The day following her visit with AmyAnn, she was inclined to agree after skimming the script for the upcoming play to be staged at the community theater. Because she and her art students would be responsible for the scenery, she had taken a quick look to determine the nature of the project. What she'd discovered was possibly a way to help AmyAnn.

"Can I talk to you a minute?" she asked the theater director the next afternoon. She had gone by the playhouse after her three o'clock Monday class at the university to make some sketches of the proposed scenery.

"Sure," Gary Evans, who'd been knee-deep in preproduction problems ever since Claire's arrival, answered.

Claire had liked Gary from the first time she'd met him, nearly seven years ago. Their paths first crossed at the university. Gary had been teaching a drama course, which he still occasionally taught, and had been assigned the classroom next door to Claire's. Out of sheer proximity, a relationship had developed from a "Hi, how are you?" in the beginning to friendship by the end of the semester. What Claire liked most about Gary was that he gave 110 percent of himself on every occasion. He handled each play he directed with respect, understanding that some playwright had worked long and hard on it. He also treated people as though they were inherently worthy.

"What an afternoon," Gary complained, walking across the stage, which was now empty except for Claire. Using a high wooden stool as a worktable, she was making copious preliminary sketches.

Tall, too thin and not even remotely handsome, although the latter didn't seem to keep women from his doorstep—Claire thought it had something to do with the way he respected women, even his ex-wife—Gary bent and scratched Smudge behind the ear. The dog wore her usual kerchief, this one blue and black.

"Had a chance to look at the play?" he asked.

"Yeah. I glanced over it yesterday."

"See any problems scenerywise?"

Claire shook her head. "A school gym, a New York restaurant, the school gym again twenty-five years later at a class reunion—should be pretty straightforward and simple. What do you think about a mural painted with bleachers on this wall?" she asked, indicating the side of the stage she meant with a wave of her hand.

The two of them spent the next few minutes discussing possibilities for the setting, concluding with Gary's, "Do whatever you think best. You know I trust you implicitly."

Claire grinned, wriggling her patrician, paint-speckled nose. "That's going to get you into trouble someday, Mr. Director. I'm just waiting to splash nudes all over the walls and the ceiling."

Gary laughed—Claire could feel the humor radiating from him. "Save it for *Oh! Calcutta!* okay?"

Claire's grin widened, then began to fade. "Has the role of the deaf character been cast?"

The play, entitled *Two Queens and the King of Bur*
wick, centered around three people—two teenage girl
and a teenage boy—and followed them from hig
school through the next twenty-five years of their lives

Gary seemed more than a little surprised by th
question. "No, we haven't even had auditions yet
Why? You thinking of giving up the paintbrush for th
greasepaint?"

Claire's grin danced back. "Hardly. Besides, n
amount of makeup, no matter how cleverly applied, i
going to make me look like a teenager."

"I don't know about that."

"I do," Claire said, threading back one of the man
wisps of hair that had slipped from her casual chi
gnon. "Listen, I know someone I'd like to have read
for the part. That is, if you have no objections to au
ditioning a young girl who's really deaf."

"I don't see why that would be a problem. Is she a
friend of yours?"

"Yeah—a special friend. She's just recently lost he
hearing and is having some problems adjusting." *Some*
problems was an understatement, Claire thought, bu
said, "This might be just what the doctor ordered."

"Tell her that tryouts are this Saturday, at one til
however long it takes to finish. Oh, by the way, I won'
be making the final casting decisions."

Claire's raised eyebrow asked eloquently, Why not?

"A friend of mine is casting and directing this play."
Gary smiled. "I'm just the assistant director this
time—the gofer."

Claire's eyes twinkled. "Think this friend wants
nudes splashed all over the walls and ceiling?"

Gary laughed. "Knowing this guy, he probably
would."

The remark was cryptic and . . . well, downright interesting. Claire might have actually enquired who this debauched individual was—she could feel the question taking shape on her tongue—had fate, in the form of a pizza delivery, not intervened.

"Ah, my lunch," Gary said, motioning to the man who appeared suddenly.

Claire glanced to the back of the theater, then down at her watch. It was nearly six o'clock. The fact that she had a seven o'clock class drove all other thoughts from her mind, including those of Gary's perverted friend. "I've got to go," she said, adding, "I don't know how to tell you this, but it's dinnertime. Lunch was hours ago."

"It's been that kind of day. And it *ain't* over yet."

"Tell me about it," Claire said, gathering up the sketches and reaching for her purse. Recognizing the signs of departure, Smudge stood and began to move toward the side steps leading from the stage. Claire signed, "See you."

Gary had seen the gesture often enough to interpret it. His response was "Bye. And tell your friend to stop by on Saturday."

"I will," Claire said, wondering how AmyAnn would react to the suggestion.

Even as she wondered, she suspected she knew. AmyAnn would fight it just the way she was fighting everything these days. But then, Claire thought, she, too, knew a little bit about combat. She was prepared to handcuff, hamstring and otherwise hog-tie her if she had to. Come hell or high water, AmyAnn Williams *would* attend the audition.

THE PARKING LOT of the theater was deserted except
for Gary's car and Claire's van. It was toward this last
that Claire, Smudge trotting alongside her, hastened.
A brisk, chilling wind blew off the bay, chastising
Claire for having left her jacket in the van.

"Why didn't you tell me I needed a jacket?" Claire
asked Smudge.

Smudge barked as if to tell her she was on her own
when it came to predicting the weather.

Claire plopped the stack of design sketches onto the
hood of the van. She anchored them with her purse,
which she opened to search for her keys. When it became apparent that the keys were playing hide-and-
seek, Claire shifted the purse, which slipped from the
stack of papers, leaving them vulnerable to the wind.
A breeze fluttered the papers' edges, tentatively at first,
then brazenly whipped some of the sketches from the
pile, whirling them like dervishes and scattering them
in all four directions at once.

Panic slammed through Claire at the thought of losing the work she'd slaved over for the past few hours.
Muttering something decidedly unladylike, she threw
her purse on top of the remaining sketches and took off
after the rest. She snatched one from here, one from
there, with such concentration that she didn't even see
the sleek BMW pull into the parking lot. Of course she
didn't hear the driver blow the horn when it became
obvious that she was going to step in front of the car.
At the blaring sound, Smudge, a snarl at her lips, raced
toward her mistress. The dog reached her just as brakes
squealed and a bobbing bumper brushed Claire,
knocking her to the ground.

Claire's backside connected none too gently with the
hard, grating concrete. Air whooshed from her lungs

as an involuntary cry leaped from her throat. How badly was she hurt? the practical part of her brain asked, though she got no immediate answer because her attention was suddenly riveted on the man spilling from the silver car. He was gesturing frantically, obviously hollering. Though proficient at lipreading, Claire couldn't understand a word he was shouting.

Over the roar of her heart—stepping in front of the car was an inexcusably careless thing to have done—Claire said, "You'll have to speak slowly and look directly at me."

Calmly, she noted the man was dressed entirely in white—tight white jeans hugged long, lean legs, and a bulky white turtleneck highlighted his suntanned, handsome face. His hair, sable brown and slightly curly, rippled over the sweater's collar, while his eyes, thickly lashed and more turquoise than blue, seemed designed for a single purpose: to grab one's attention...and hold it.

Some part of Claire registered and admitted freely, for it would have been foolish to deny something so apparent, that the man was incredibly good-looking. In fact, he was more than merely good-looking. He was perfect. Physically perfect. Quite possibly the standard by which all other males were judged. Another part of Claire, in a similarly detached manner, thought there was something vaguely familiar about him. But she had no time to ponder her observation, for the man was still hollering and her backside was beginning to throb. More importantly, a couple of papers still fluttered across the parking lot.

Claire managed to lip-read some of what the man was saying. "...stupidest thing...damned fool... What's wrong with you, lady? Are you deaf?"

"Yes, I am," Claire replied matter-of-factly, as though being struck and knocked to the pavement were an everyday occurrence.

When her response finally penetrated, the man stopped talking abruptly. He studied Claire as though seeing her for the first time. Sprawled out as she was, her black skirt at midthigh, she appeared all legs. All shapely legs. All shapely legs with a grotesque tear in one black stocking. A copper-colored, oversize sweater snuggled next to her hips, while the neckline plunged recklessly but stylishly onto one shoulder. Her hair, raven black and vibrantly shiny, was slicked back from her face and knotted at the nape of her neck. The knot now sat askew, with tendrils of hair flying in the breeze. The man had the feeling that her hair might have been somewhat mussed even before the accident. One thing was certain. Actually two. Firstly, there was a smudge of paint on her nose, and secondly, the severe hairstyle drew attention to her wide, saucerlike brown eyes. Eyes so dark that they were almost black. Eyes that were intently watching his lips even as she began to scramble to her feet.

He reached out to help her up. "I'm sorry—" he began, but was cut off.

"Forget an apology and get my sketches," Claire said, unabashedly dusting off her backside.

Now that he was no longer hollering, the man could hear the discordance in Claire's voice, leaving no doubt that she was indeed deaf. Though her speech was certainly intelligible and not unpleasant, it was different.

"My sketches...please," Claire commanded, brushing back her hair even though it fell right back into disarray. With dignity and deliberate movements, she straightened her hose, as though they bore not a single run.

At Claire's simple aura of authority, the man couldn't escape the crazy feeling that he was in the presence of bedraggled royalty, royalty that wore its privileged coat of arms as a dab of paint on the nose. He found himself doing as he'd been bade.

Claire watched as the stranger's long legs covered the area, snatching one sheet from a greedy shrub, another from just beneath the edge of Gary's car. In no time at all, he walked back to Claire, gathering the papers she'd dropped and handed them to her. She put them with the others, which she had miraculously managed to hold on to.

"I'm sorry for hitting you . . . and for the tactless remark," he said.

"No apology is necessary for the latter, and the former was my fault," she said, her shoulders back, her head high. "I shouldn't have been so careless."

"Are you all right?"

"Yes, except for my bruised dignity."

The stranger still looked unconvinced. "Are you sure you shouldn't have something X-rayed? I'll pay for having it done."

"I'm fine."

"Or for having your clothes cleaned. Or for the stockings—"

"I'm fine. Really."

"Then how about if I offer you my firstborn child, which I don't have yet, but if you're willing to take an IOU—"

Claire smiled. "That won't be necessary."

Somewhere along the way, the man's lips had curved into a grin. Claire realized that the grin was as perfect as the man's looks. And altogether as mesmerizing as his eyes, which were boldly watching her. The chill that had been in the air only minutes before seemed to have been replaced by an inexplicable warmth. Claire was also aware of the surreal feeling that time, if it hadn't exactly stopped, had at least hesitated.

"Your dog," the paragon said finally, though his eyes didn't leave Claire's, nor hers his. In fact, hers seemed just as bold.

At last, Claire forced her gaze away. She found Smudge, with teeth bared, snarling at the front tire of the sporty BMW.

"She doesn't like cars," she explained, calling, "C'mon, girl!" Then, glancing at her watch, she muttered, "Oh, no, I'm late!" Turning back to the man, she said, even as she started running for the van, "Sorry. I've got to go." In seconds, Smudge joined her and the two of them disappeared inside the vehicle.

The man had the feeling that he'd just been summarily dismissed. "Hey!" he called as the van door was closing.

After he said it, he realized that she couldn't hear him, which was probably for the best. What in heck had he been about to say, anyway? He had no idea, though he was certain he'd never met anyone quite like the woman pulling out of the parking lot. She had mentioned bruising her dignity in the fall, but, despite the paint on her nose and the run in her hose, it seemed intact to him. Her proud carriage, her self-assured walk and the unselfconscious delivery of her off-pitch speech exuded confidence. No, he was certain that this was a woman who knew who she was and where she was going in life. And not even being knocked on her keister could sidetrack her.

He, on the other hand, had not only been sidetracked from his lifetime journey, he'd completely
forgotten where he'd been headed, the man thought as
he parked the sports car and walked, frowning, toward the theater. And the truth was that he had no one
to blame but himself for the detour. The stars in Hollywood had shone so brightly that they'd blinded him.
His friend, Gary Evans, hadn't had the same problem, however. Gary had known from the start that he
wanted to devote his life to drama through community
theater. On the other hand, he, Naughty Nash Prather
as the tabloids loved to call him, had opted to... To
what? It was a question he asked frequently, and as always the answer stuck in his throat. The truth was he'd
exploited drama to become one of the most recogniz-
able movie stars of his day, in the same bankable company as Kevin Costner, Mel Gibson and Tom Cruise.

Remembering what one critic had said of him, Nash
Prather grinned, tilting his lips into the smile that
melted women's hearts. The critic, whose acerbic wit
was legendary, had described his personality as somewhere between good-time Don Johnson and Mel Gibson's Mad Max. Nash's smile faded. Interestingly, he
himself had bought into that evaluation for a while,
living too hard and too fast. Now, at thirty-five, he was
just too old to play games. Or, more to the point,
maybe he'd played them all and had realized that that
was just what they were—games. Maybe he'd realized, too, that games were designed as momentary di-
versions but were hardly something to base one's life
on. They weren't part of any journey leading to somewhere significant, but were merely distracting joy-
rides.

But did he have what it took to travel the road he wanted? Where did a kid from Brooklyn, who'd flunked out of high school and barely kept himself out of jail, get the audacity to think he could succeed where other, brighter people had failed? He knew, and all too well, that his good looks had bought his ticket to fame and fortune. It was a fact he resented. Just the way he resented how he'd been exploited personally. Talent be damned, his own wants and needs be damned! All Hollywood wanted was for him to wear his pants tight enough to give every woman in the movie audience a cheap thrill.

As he mounted the steps to the theater, Nash wondered what Hollywood would say if it knew what he was going to be doing for the next six weeks. Whatever the outcome, he would always be grateful to Gary for believing in him—even if he himself had trouble mustering up the same faith. A thought crossed his mind. Maybe it hadn't been the Hollywood stars that had blinded him. Maybe he'd been blinded or, more aptly, paralyzed by his own fear, his own lack of confidence.

Confidence.

His thoughts raced back to the woman in the parking lot. He'd wager that nothing could dent her self-confidence. He'd wager that she had the silence in her soul that he craved in his own. It was too bad that confidence and peace couldn't be loaned.

The theater was dark except for the stage lights, which silhouetted his longtime friend. Gary sat on the edge of the stage, his feet dangling into the orchestra pit. He held a slice of pizza in one hand, a pencil in the other. A copy of what looked like a script rested on his lap. Occasionally, as he read, he jotted something down.

As Nash moved down the center of the carpeted aisle, he imagined that he could hear the roar of the audience in the tiered seats. Before him, on the stage, he could see the ghost of every character that had ever been performed there. The world of make-believe. It was the only thing that had gotten him through a troubled youth. When the real world had caved in around him, when it had been too painful to live his own life, he'd created another in his mind. Then came Hollywood, which paid him decadently large sums of money to be only a body, to suppress any thoughts or feelings. Was it now too late to find the real Nash Prather?

"Hey, goombah," Nash called out quietly in an exaggerated Brooklynese-Italian accent.

Gary jerked his head upward and peered into the shadows. The man in white stepped into view. Gary smiled and said, "Well, it's about time, you Italian son of a sea cook."

Nash grinned and for a moment speech was unnecessary as the two exchanged the wordless communication of friendship. Both were remembering a shared apartment years before; Gary plugging away at a drama degree, Nash struggling to find any kind of work that would put food in his mouth. They'd met in a supermarket in the pasta aisle, which Gary had once said was an apt place for two Italian kids to meet. When Nash had pointed out that Gary wasn't Italian, Gary had feigned surprise, stating that next he supposed Nash would say he wasn't handsome. In reality, their relationship hadn't proved that odd. Their friends called them both Oscar Madison slobs. They called themselves lucky, lucky to have found each other.

Bounding up the steps that led to the stage, heedless of what a dirty floor would do to white jeans, Nash slapped Gary on the back and then plopped down beside his friend. "So, how's it going?"

"You want the bad news first or the good?"

"Geez," Nash said, "gimme a break. I just got here."

"You asked."

"Hit me with the bad."

"I think the ending of scene 2 needs work, the bank that pledged sponsoring for the opening night gala went under, and the woman in charge of costumes quit."

Nash groaned. "What's the good news?"

"There isn't anymore bad." Before Nash could say anything, Gary added, "Welcome to the wonderful world of directing." At that, he passed Nash the script, the pencil and a stack of messages. He also shoved the pizza in his direction. "Oh, and you'd better eat some lunch. It's the last decent meal you'll get today...and maybe for the next six weeks."

"Lunch? It's time for dinner."

"Have I made my point?" Gary asked with a crooked grin.

He had. Despite the grueling schedule he knew lay before him, excitement raced through Nash's veins, an excitement he hadn't experienced in years. He was going to work his tail off for the next six weeks, and win, lose or draw, he wasn't going to regret what happened. And somewhere along the way he might even find the real Nash Prather.

"YOU ALL WANT to settle down?"

Gary Evans's question heralded the end of the break

he'd announced five minutes before. It was ten after two on Saturday afternoon. Auditions had been going on for more than an hour. So far, four young men had read for the role of Eric, the play's only male character. AmyAnn had commented, "He's good" following the reading of the last young man—Lance Randle. Claire wondered on what AmyAnn had based her opinion since she'd obviously heard nothing. She decided it must have been gestures, expressions, the way he worked the stage. Other than those two words, AmyAnn had said nothing since they'd arrived at the theater. She'd simply sat like a bird poised for flight at the slightest provocation.

Considering AmyAnn's initial reaction to the suggestion that she try out for the part of the deaf character—the reaction had been an adamant no—Claire was surprised that she'd finally agreed. Claire had left her copy of the play with AmyAnn, begging her to at least read it before rejecting the idea. Nothing more had been said on the subject until last night, when AmyAnn had casually asked, as they'd eaten hamburgers at McDonald's, what time the auditions began. Claire had taken the question to be a form of assent. She'd even sensed a subdued excitement in her young friend. Claire suspected, however, that at the moment AmyAnn was regretting her decision.

"We're going to read next for the role of Lindy," Gary said from his midstage position.

Claire could almost feel every muscle in AmyAnn's body tense. Smudge must have sensed it, as well, for she looked up at AmyAnn and whined some words of comfort.

"You will do fine," Claire signed.

AmyAnn said nothing. She didn't even object to the open signing, which was a clear indication of just how nervous she was.

As the minutes passed, AmyAnn's tension mounted. The first teenager who read for the part was good, the second, excellent. With normal hearing, both responded to all the cues and adjusted their performances to fit Gary's direction. At those times, AmyAnn's anxiety soared. For a person who couldn't hear and was only learning to lip-read and sign, Gary's instructions appeared formidable. The probability of AmyAnn making a fool of herself loomed large.

Occasionally, Gary would confer with the shadowy figure who sat at the back of the theater. Was this the friend whom Gary had spoken of? Claire wondered. The one who was casting and directing the play? Out of curiosity—after all, it was only normal to wonder about a man who'd had such an interesting buildup— Claire glanced back a couple of times but couldn't make out any of the man's features. AmyAnn looked around a couple of times, too, but Claire thought she was searching for the nearest exit.

At last, Gary sought out AmyAnn from the dozen or so people sitting in the first few rows. He crooked his finger for her to come up onstage. She panicked. As though she'd been catapulted from the seat, AmyAnn bolted for the side door. She'd just thrown it open and was about to flee out into the warm sunshine when a hand closed around her arm. AmyAnn turned.

"Wait!" Claire begged.

AmyAnn lifted her gaze from Claire's lips to her eyes. Silently, she pleaded with Claire to understand.

"I can't," AmyAnn whispered. "I can't go back in there."

Claire didn't have to be able to hear to know that the words had been torn from her young friend. She could see the way the ragged words trembled on AmyAnn's lips, the way their deliverance paled her.

Releasing her hand from AmyAnn's arm, Claire began to sign. Even though Claire was signing slowly, AmyAnn could not follow her. At the teenager's frown, Claire reached inside her purse and pulled out a pen and a used envelope. Across the white surface, she wrote, "Being deaf is one thing—being a coward is another." Claire knew that the accusation was harsh, but she knew, too, that this was not the time for mincing words. Whatever happened in the next few seconds would have an effect on the rest of AmyAnn's life.

AmyAnn's face didn't give a clue as to what she was thinking, yet Claire knew that fear was battling with pride. It would take courage for AmyAnn to walk back into the theater, courage to ignore the curious stares, courage to mount the steps to the stage. Claire recalled her belief that people with grit always managed to mend their broken lives. She was about to see just how much grit AmyAnn Williams possessed.

Slowly, after what seemed like an eternity to Claire, AmyAnn's chin tilted upward. Without a word, she walked back into the theater and toward the stage. Claire gave a deep sigh of relief. She also felt a deep sense of pride in the young woman who hadn't taken the easy way out.

"Louder," Gary said a few minutes later. "Tell her to speak louder."

AmyAnn glanced over at Claire, who stood at the edge of the stage. Clair signed, "Speak louder." Claire saw AmyAnn's hesitation and knew that she was worried about the pitch of her voice. "Gary will tell you if you're speaking too loudly."

Nodding, AmyAnn began again.

Claire watched closely. Though she knew little about acting, she could sense that AmyAnn was good, which was what she'd suspected all along. One rarely had a passion for something without being good at it. A curious thing had happened when AmyAnn stepped onstage. An undeniable confidence had swarmed around her. No longer was she an emotionally insecure AmyAnn; she had become the character of Lindy Boyd. AmyAnn had literally breathed life into fictional lungs. What she did onstage was magical... and Claire sensed that Gary felt that magic, as well. She wondered if the shadowy figure at the back was equally enthralled.

"Good...good," Gary said, which Claire translated to AmyAnn. AmyAnn smiled—a genuinely happy smile. "Tell her to read the end of act 1, on page—" Gary plowed through the manuscript "—on page 37."

Claire relayed the message and AmyAnn began to read.

In minutes, though, frown creases in his forehead, Gary stopped her. Again using Claire as a go-between, he asked, "Why isn't she reading what's written in the script? Why's she winging it?"

AmyAnn anticipated the question. "It isn't what Lindy would really say," she explained.

The soul of tact and patience, Gary answered, "Well, that may be so, but please read the lines the way they're writ—"

Claire saw the word chopped off in midsyllable, saw Gary's gaze shift out into the theater, as though someone there had spoken to him. Claire followed Gary's gaze. By now there was a roomful of gazes all turned to the figure walking down the aisle. With a start, Claire recognized the man as the one whose car she'd stepped in front of. He was still the most handsome man she'd ever seen . . . and still annoyingly familiar.

Was this Gary's friend? The director of the play? Obviously he was. Claire couldn't believe the coincidence.

His eyes on Claire, the stranger said, "Ask her why the character wouldn't say what's written in the script."

Had Claire not been so stunned at seeing the man again and discovering that he was connected with the play, she might have seen AmyAnn's expression. It was one that said she could hardly believe she was staring at one of the hottest stars in all of Hollywood. As it was, Claire didn't notice but simply repeated the stranger's question, which ultimately had to be written down for a star-struck AmyAnn to understand.

"If Lindy had just gone deaf," AmyAnn explained, after finally finding her voice, "she wouldn't appear afraid of her friends' reaction. She'd brave her way through."

Claire watched the stranger sort through what he'd heard. His eyes then connected with hers once more. "Tell her to read it her way."

AmyAnn did read it her way...and brilliantly. There was even a round of applause when she'd finished.

Afterward, Gary announced another break. Those who'd already read were dismissed and told that a decision would be made within the week. Claire was just picking up her purse when she noticed the stranger walking toward her. He spoke to AmyAnn.

"You were right," he said. Claire interpreted the comment. "You're also good." Claire didn't have to translate this, for AmyAnn's smile told her that she'd understood.

"Thank you," AmyAnn said, a faint blush at her cheeks.

The stranger's eyes raised to Claire's. "Did you understand that a decision will be made this week?"

"Yes. I explained that to AmyAnn."

The stranger nodded, adding, "Either way, if she gets the part or not, Gary or I'll call."

This time Claire nodded.

Suddenly the stranger smiled. "So, have you stepped in front of any more cars?"

Claire grinned. "No. I try to limit my acts of stupidity to one per week."

It was obvious that both were well on their way to apologizing again for what had transpired in the parking lot, when Gary hollered to his friend, "Hey, what do you think about this?"

"Gotta go," the stranger said, smiling.

"Good luck with the play," Claire said.

"Thanks," the stranger replied, glancing over at AmyAnn, "and thanks for the reading."

AmyAnn, the color still high in her cheeks, grinned.

And then the stranger was gone, he and Gary lost in the script.

Claire signed to Smudge, who fell in beside her as she started for the door. AmyAnn, her excitement now bubbling over like champagne, started to speak both verbally and in the sign she had so stubbornly resisted before.

"Slow down," Claire said.

But AmyAnn didn't slow in the least. Instead, she asked a dozen rapid-fire questions. "Was my performance really all right?" Claire started to tell her that it was more than all right, but AmyAnn rushed ahead. "Did he—" there was no mistaking who "he" was "—really like it? Should I have asked for his autograph? No, that would have been tacky, wouldn't it?"

Autograph.

The blank expression on Claire's face told AmyAnn all she needed to know. Namely, that Claire had no idea who the man was. Giving an "I don't believe this" look, AmyAnn said, "Does the name Nash Prather mean anything?"

"Nash Prather? The movie star?"

"Nash Prather. The movie star. Oh, my gosh, isn't he gorgeous?"

Claire didn't answer. Instead, she whirled around. Suddenly, the man's familiarity made sense. Suddenly, his picture-perfect handsomeness made sense. Suddenly, she realized that it had been Nash Prather's car she'd stepped in front of.

Nash Prather.

The man women drooled over.

The man women dreamed of.

The man most women considered the sexiest in all the world.

CHAPTER FOUR

THE FOLLOWING WEEK at the grocery store, Claire saw Nash Prather again. This time his handsome face graced the cover of a popular magazine. After passing by the issue numerous times, the turquoise-blue eyes proved irresistible and Claire bought the magazine. Once home, before she'd even unpacked the perishable items, she reached for the magazine and turned to the article on Nash. Within a short while she'd learned that he had a new beach house in Malibu, that he'd recently been seen escorting the blond queen of a daytime soap opera, and that his last movie, now available in video, had netted an impressive figure at the box office. There was no doubt about it, Claire thought as she reached for a carton of eggs, Nash Prather was bigtime. Why, then, was he directing a play in a small community theater in San Francisco?

Later that afternoon, with a wag of her tail and a dash down the stairs, Smudge indicated that they had a visitor. Claire gave an exasperated sigh at the interruption. She had to finish this painting today, because she was falling further and further behind on the pieces to be exhibited at the one-woman show, now scheduled in Dallas in the spring. Laying aside the brush she'd just dipped in cobalt-blue paint, she grabbed a rag and began to wipe her hands as she descended the stairs. Not even bothering to look at herself in the mirror—she knew she looked a mess—she opened the door. At the sight of the man casually leaning against the porch railing, Claire's heart picked up its beat, though she would have been hard-pressed to explain exactly why.

As her gaze traveled over bronzed skin, sable-brown hair, pleated brown slacks and a butter-yellow sweater, Claire made the observation that, as always, Naughty Nash Prather—was he as naughty as the tabloids said?—looked perfect. The feminine side of her wished that he'd caught her in something other than paint-streaked clothes. The practical side of her asked, What did it matter? He was accustomed to hanging out with the most beautiful women. By comparison, she was bound to lose every time—paint-streaked clothes or Sunday best.

At the same time that Claire was assessing Nash, Nash was assessing Claire—in a lazy, languid manner. He noted her raven-black hair, which seemed to be neither up nor down but rather some wild state in between, her paint-spotted shirt and jeans and the dab of blue paint on the end of her nose. She looked...a mess. A delightful mess. But more importantly, she looked real. Not like the flawlessly beautiful women who played opposite him in movies. Not like the "Aren't I gorgeous?" women he'd often dated in the past but couldn't work up a whole lot of enthusiasm for these days. As far as he was concerned, that realness gave Claire Rushing an edge that most of the women he knew didn't have.

Nash pushed from the railing and, nodding to the rag in Claire's hand, said, "Hi. Did I interrupt anything important?"

Following the direction of his gaze, Claire looked at the rag and tried to remember just what she'd been doing before the doorbell rang. Suddenly, her memory came flooding back. Painting. She'd been painting.

"No, it was nothing important," she answered, forgetting the tight deadline she was working under.

As before, Nash noted the atonal quality of her voice. Even so, there was a particularly appealing softness to it. "If you have a few minutes, I'd like to talk to you... about AmyAnn."

"Of course," Claire answered, moving back to allow him entrance.

Patting a friendly Smudge on the head, Nash stepped inside. Claire took this opportunity to peek in the mirror. She grimaced. Not wanting to be caught looking at herself, she turned away from it at the same time as she quickly swiped at the paint on her nose. The result was that she merely managed to smear it. Likewise, the rush of her fingers through her hair only created more chaos.

"Please sit down," she said, putting the rag on the gilded white commode table near the door. She motioned toward the living room.

Recalling their first encounter, Nash was careful to face her when he spoke. "Thanks." He said nothing more until he sat on the sofa. Then, without preamble, he said, "I'd like AmyAnn to play the role of Lindy Boyd."

Clair forgot about how awful she looked. She forgot that a famous movie star was sitting in her living room. She forgot everything except how excited AmyAnn was going to be. She had pretended that getting the part didn't matter, but Claire could tell how important it was to her.

"AmyAnn's going to be thrilled," Claire said, her face beaming with a smile.

Real. The word scurried through Nash's thoughts again. This woman's smile was as real as everything else about her.

"There was never any question about AmyAnn getting the part," Nash said, adding, "She's very talented. Plus, she brings an authenticity to the role that I hadn't expected to find."

"She is authentic. She's also going through a period of adjustment right now. A rough period. Believe me when I tell you that this play, her getting the part, is a godsend."

Without betraying any confidences, Claire volunteered information regarding AmyAnn's illness, which had resulted in her deafness, and some of the problems she was having coping.

"Though the play has a deaf character, I had underestimated the isolation that deafness can create," Nash commented.

"The problem is one of communication. AmyAnn is having trouble communicating with her friends. She now feels alienated from them."

"Which she is to a certain extent."

"Exactly. She now has a disability. An invisible disability, but a disability nonetheless."

"So, how do you and AmyAnn know each other?" Nash asked. He'd wanted to ask about Claire's deafness, when it had occurred in her life, about the adjustments she'd had to make, but he didn't. He didn't feel the personal questions appropriate.

"She's my Little Sister." At Nash's surprised look, Claire explained, "Not in the biological sense. I'm a volunteer for the Big Brothers/Big Sisters of America. I was assigned to AmyAnn. Or she was assigned to me. Whichever way you want to look at it."

"I've heard of the organization but don't know much about it."

"I didn't either until a friend recruited me. The organization has been around since about the turn of the century, although the Hearing-Impaired Program was started in 1982. It's primarily for kids from single parent, low-income homes. The organization just wants to give kids the break they might not otherwise get in life."

"Yeah, kids deserve a break," Nash answered.

Something in his expression told Claire that the tone of his voice had changed, perhaps had even grown hard. She wondered about his childhood. Had he been one of those kids who'd needed a break but hadn't gotten it? He must have gotten the direction he'd needed somewhere. How else could you explain his success? After all, this was the man who owned a beach house in Malibu, drove a BMW and had women falling at his feet. The vision of a throng of women at his feet, a throng including the queen of a daytime soap opera, had just jumped into her artist's creative mind when she noticed that he was speaking again.

"Obviously AmyAnn's trying to learn sign language."

"Actually, the reverse is true. She's fighting tooth and nail against learning it," Claire said, glad to have her attention diverted from the unsettling image of the harem at his feet.

"I don't understand."

"It calls attention to her deafness. It's like waving a red flag for all to see."

Nash nodded, as though he hadn't considered this before, but now that he had, it made perfect sense. "How important is her learning to sign?"

"Very. It's the path to her future."

"Why don't we make her getting the role conditional on her signing skills improving. We can even adjust the play to accommodate signing."

Claire smiled. "I like your approach—out-and-out bribery."

Nash grinned. "I've always found it effective."

"Actually, we might not even need bribery in this case. I have a feeling that if you asked AmyAnn to fly, she'd try to. She's more than impressed with the fact that the famous Nash Prather is directing the play."

Claire was uncertain what she'd expected Nash's reaction to be to her comment, though she was certain she hadn't expected embarrassment. But how else could she explain why he suddenly seemed ill at ease?

"I'm sorry," she said. "I didn't mean to embarrass you."

"Look, I'm just like everybody else."

Claire didn't point out that that was hardly true. Instead, she said, a minxlike glint in her brown eyes, "If it's any comfort, I had no idea who you were when we first met."

Nash gave a lopsided grin. "Are you serious?"

She made a "cross my heart" sign. "I promise. AmyAnn had to tell me."

Nash's grin turned to laughter. Claire could feel its richness rippling toward her. "That's the nicest thing that anyone's said to me in a long time. You've no idea how tired I am of being recognized."

Her guest's sudden good mood was contagious. "If not recognizing you pleased you, you're going to love the fact that I've never seen any of of your movies."

Before Claire knew what was happening, Nash leaned toward her, as though he were about to share a deep, dark secret. "Neither have I," he said.

Claire knew that he'd lowered his voice. She could see the lacy whisper singing across his lips. She could see his smile dancing. Suddenly, inexplicably, she became very much aware of his mouth—its mobility, its fluidity. She excused her interest by reminding herself that lipreading demanded a kind of concentrated intimacy.

Nash, too, had become aware of Claire's mouth—its gentle curves, its easy familiarity with a smile. He was also aware of a faint smell emanating from her. It was the airy smell of turpentine or paint or something art oriented. It was not the fragrance of a "sell your soul for an ounce" perfume. He realized that those expensive perfumes were not for this woman, just as he realized that it was presumptuous of him to make such a personal observation. How could he possibly know what was right for this woman? Especially since he seemed to know so little about what was right even for him.

Standing abruptly, he said, "I won't keep you any longer. If I could just trouble you for AmyAnn's address. I have her phone number, but under the circumstances, I thought a personal visit might be better than a phone call."

Claire stood, as well. "Sure, I'll get it. It's upstairs on my desk."

Alone, Nash glanced around. He'd been right when he'd first seen the building. It *was* a renovated warehouse. Somehow all the unwalled, unconfined space suited Claire. Just as did the white and pale sea-green motif. Both space and color were restful, peaceful, the outward signs of a woman inwardly content. Unlike what his new, expensive mansion in Malibu revealed about him? The question had come out of nowhere, but now that it had, it begged to be answered. Actually, sad to say, the answer was simple. Yes, unlike what his new, expensive mansion in Malibu revealed about him. The house had been extravagantly built, luxuriously decorated, yet it reflected nothing of him, for there was nothing to reflect. The truth was that he didn't really exist. He was just some celluloid creation of Hollywood. Offscreen, he wasn't certain he'd even cast an image in a mirror. And even if he did, it certainly wouldn't be the peaceful, contented image that Claire reflected.

Allowing his gaze to roam, Nash took in everything in the huge room—the telephone equipped with a special telecommunication device for the deaf and a television obviously outfitted for closed-caption broadcasting. Beyond that the house looked as though it belonged to any ordinary individual. The woman's artistic talent was evident everywhere. Who but one with a creative, unregimented mind would have an elegant crystal chandelier over a simple white bamboo table? Or who else would have a huge four-poster draped in yard upon yard of silky fabric?

And then there were the paintings. Nash stepped closer to examine them, noting that all were done by Claire. She had a distinctive style, one that utilized bold shapes, bright colors and unique spatial concepts. The painting he was presently looking at was a montage of several figures superimposed upon another. Whether one liked her style or not, there was no mistaking the confidence with which the paintbrush had been wielded.

From there, Nash stepped to some framed photographs. They appeared to be of a protest at Gallaudet University. Nash vaguely remembered the uprising in 1988, something about the student body wanting a deaf college president. He recognized Claire in one photograph. Her placard said Deaf Prez Now. Her dog was also in the picture with a sign, Deaf Pride, hanging from her neck. Though Claire would probably have graduated from college by 1988, he recalled that nonstudents, including alumni, had arrived on campus to lend their support.

Somehow, he wasn't surprised that Claire had been part of the uprising any more than he'd been surprised that she'd talked AmyAnn into returning to read for the part when it was obvious that all AmyAnn had wanted to do was run away. Actually, little would surprise him about Claire Rushing. He was quite convinced, not only could she move mountains, she could make them apologize for being in her way in the first place.

Once more, he looked around him, inexplicably interested in what made up Claire Rushing's life, in what made up a *real* person's life. There were fresh flowers in a crystal vase, a bonsai tree on the sill of the kitchen window, magazines on the coffee table. A couple of steps and Nash was thumbing through the magazines. There were several dealing with art, one a popular women's magazine, another...

He stopped as his own face jumped into view. At the same time, a sound on the stairs drew his attention. He looked up. As Claire walked into the room, her gaze lowered to the magazine in his hand. For a moment, neither said anything. Finally, with a disdain that showed what he thought of the publication, Nash tossed the magazine back onto the coffee table.

"I'd like to ask two things of you," he said.

"Sure," Claire said, hoping he didn't suspect that she'd bought the magazine just for the article about him.

"I know you're busy with your own schedule and I know you'll be busy with the play's scenery, but I was wondering if you could sit in on some of the rehearsals. It's going to be a challenge directing a deaf participant. Plus, if we add sign to the script, you'll have to coach us." He grinned. "You may notice that I'm now bribing you... and that I've arrived at the real reason I stopped by."

It was impossible not to smile when he did, so she didn't fight it. Some part of her acknowledged that, though she'd never told him, he knew she was in charge of the scenery. It was logical enough to assume that Gary had told him. Had Nash been interested enough to ask who she was? she wondered. Not that it mattered, she hastened to add.

"As you said," she answered, her smile still in place, "bribery is effective."

Nash's grin dimmed. "If it would be a hardship—"

"No, I can work some time in."

"Good. I think AmyAnn would be less tense with you there."

Claire agreed, handing him AmyAnn's address. "I know AmyAnn's going to be thrilled to be in the play."

"I hope so." There was a few seconds of silence. As Nash viewed Claire's disheveled appearance, he thought again how real this woman seemed. Claire, meanwhile, was thinking how unreal Nash's physical perfection was. Finally, Nash said, ''Thanks for your time.''

''My pleasure,'' Claire said, following him to the door. There, he said goodbye and started to leave. Just as he stepped outside, however, Claire recalled what he'd said earlier. ''Hey!''

Nash turned.

''You said you wanted to ask two things of me. What's the second?''

Nodding back toward the house, he said with not a trace of a smile on his oh-so-mobile mouth, ''Don't believe everything you read.''

The magazine! Claire knew that he was referring to the magazine with the article about him. As she watched him climb into the silver BMW and drive off, she couldn't help but wonder which part of the article was false. Didn't he have a house in Malibu? Or wasn't he dating the beautiful blond soap opera queen?

REHEARSALS WERE ORGANIZED bedlam. Or so they always seemed to Claire. On the first Friday night of the month-long rehearsals, she watched as that organized bedlam went on around her. Some of her art students were working on scenery in the far corner of the stage. A group of four actors were practicing their lines in the middle of the theater. Others sat in front waiting to go over their scene. The three people playing the major characters—AmyAnn, Lance Randle and a young girl named Marjorie Davidson—were on the stage.

As was Nash.

Claire, sitting in the nearby stairs, with Smudge curled at her feet, allowed her gaze to settle on him. He

wore a pair of jeans that looked old enough to draw
Social Security, a gray sweatshirt torn at the shoulder
and ripped at the sleeve, and athletic shoes that had to
have belonged to several people before him—there was
no other explanation for their grunginess. His hair was
tousled from the innumerable times his fingers had
combed through it, while the stubble on his cheeks and
chin bore shadowy evidence that it was well beyond five
o'clock. Any other man would have looked like a
frazzled reject. But Nash looked gorgeous, like one of
the sexy studs he played in films.

And it wasn't just her opinion. Claire could tell that
every other female in the theater, both young and old,
thought the same thing. In fact, she could see downright awe on most of their faces. Some of that awe
came not from the way he looked, but rather from the
spicy gossip circulating about him. Everyone knew
he'd been romantically involved with movie stars, a
renowned ballerina and even a princess.

Claire remembered Gary saying his friend would
probably approve nudes for the wall and ceiling. It had
been she who'd thought of the word *debauched*. While
she didn't necessarily think it applied to Nash, she had
absolutely no trouble with the word *experienced*.
Thoroughly experienced, even if only half the gossip
she'd heard was true. She also would have readily admitted that he was dynamic, charismatic and that he
urged—no, demanded—the best from the cast. Intuitively, as she had from the beginning, she sensed how
important this play was to him.

"No, no!" Nash said, raking his fingers through his
hair once more. "You're reading the lines as if you
don't care what Eric thinks." This he said to AmyAnn.
At the blank look on her face, Nash said, "Tell her..."

Realizing that he wasn't facing Claire, he turned and repeated what he'd said.

Claire signed the message.

"But I don't want him to know I care," AmyAnn said, fumbling to sign as she spoke orally. Nash had insisted on the first day of rehearsals that AmyAnn had to at least make an attempt to sign. He'd told her that it was for the sake of the play now that sign language had been added to the script. AmyAnn hadn't argued.

"Fine, but . . ." Nash turned again to Claire. "Fine, but you're also telling the audience that you don't care." He waited for Claire to translate this, which took several attempts. "You've got to show your vulnerability to the audience. Not to Eric, but to the audience." The word *vulnerability* stumped AmyAnn completely, and it was Lance who finally wrote it in the margin of her script. AmyAnn nodded that she understood, and Nash said, "You've got to show the audience, not Eric, that you care despite what you're saying."

Far from his critique upsetting AmyAnn, she seemed eager to absorb everything Nash had to teach her about acting. "How do I do that?" she asked.

Claire noticed, as she had all week, that her young friend was becoming more and more comfortable speaking out loud. At least onstage. Offstage, however, she remained selfconscious.

"By hesitation," Nash explained. "Hesitate before you say your line."

Claire could see AmyAnn digesting what she had just been told.

"Okay, let's try it again," Nash ordered. The line was read. At its finish, he said, "Better. One more time." Again, the line was read. "Louder." The message was conveyed, the line repeated. "Excellent!" Nash said, adding, "Take five."

Everyone sighed in relief. As though she hadn't the strength to take a step, AmyAnn crumpled into a sitting position right where she stood on the stage. Marjorie collapsed beside her and started writing something on a tablet for her to read, while Lance headed for the water cooler. The young man brought back cups of water for both girls. Claire watched as the three conversed about the play. It was just this interaction that AmyAnn needed, though it was obvious that she grew frustrated when she couldn't follow what was being said. Even so, it was a normal frustration, the kind that came from being involved. And it was preferable to denial and withdrawal.

Claire felt a sudden movement and realized that Nash had plopped down beside her on the steps. He carried two foam cups of steaming coffee. Without even asking if she wanted any, he handed her a cup and asked, "Am I being too hard on her?"

It had been an unusual week. On the one hand, Nash had treated Claire professionally. After all, they were both involved in the play. On the other hand, out of the clear blue he would do something personal. Like join her for a coffee break. Or ask for her opinion . . . just as he was doing now.

She took a sip of the coffee and asked, "Are you worried about being too rough on Lance and Marjorie?"

"No, but—"

Claire interrupted gently with, "Deaf people don't want to be treated differently. AmyAnn doesn't want to be treated differently. It's part of what she fears."

A slow smile drifted across Nash's lips. "You've made your point." Taking a swallow of coffee, he braced his back against the top step and stretched out his legs. The pose was one of relaxed casualness as he tweaked a drowsy Smudge behind the ear. Nash had managed to charm the dog just as he had every other female. "So, am I being too hard on all of them?"

"I think you're being hardest on yourself."

Startled by her observation, he halted the cup on its way to his lips. Claire had the oddest sensation that, though he still sat beside her, he had scurried away to some hidden place within himself. It wasn't the first time she'd felt that way. Several times during the week she'd come to the conclusion that Nash was good at retreating. Though in a high-profile job, he was nonetheless quiet and very private. There was also a broody side to his nature.

"The play's important to me," he said, and Claire felt the defiance in his words.

"I know," she said. "I can tell."

"It's my first job of directing."

Claire smiled. "You don't have to defend yourself. I'd feel the same way. I think most everyone would. I just said that I thought you were being hardest on yourself."

"Yeah, well," Nash answered—sarcastically, she thought, "I have to be twice as good as everyone else. I'm Nash Prather."

Yes, there was definitely an undercurrent to this man's personality. She sensed dissatisfaction, frustration, even hostility. To his comment, she answered simply, "Then you'll be twice as good."

Suddenly, unexpectedly, Nash laughed and shook his head. "You're unbelievable."

"What do you mean?"

"You're so darned confident."

Claire shrugged. "If you believe you can, you can."

"And it's that simple?"

She started to elaborate, then said, "Yeah, it's that simple. Of course, I suppose it helps to come from a family who doesn't understand the word *failure*. My father and sister are medical doctors, my mother has a Ph.D. in English, one brother is a criminal lawyer, the other a test pilot for an aviation company. We children were taught that we could do anything we wanted to, be anything we wanted."

"Even you?" Nash asked pointedly.

"Within reason. Some things my deafness won't allow me to be." She smiled. "I can't be an orchestra leader, for example. But, beyond certain limitations, the sky's the limit."

"You were lucky," he said, and though she couldn't hear, she could sense the wistfulness in the statement. The comment made her wonder again about his youth. She was on the verge of indulging her curiosity when, as if he sensed what she were about to do, he said as he stood, "Let's finish up here so we can call it a night."

"Nash," she called. He lowered his gaze to hers. "You're going to do great."

He said nothing. He just stared at her. She fleetingly wondered if the movie stars, the ballerina and the princess appreciated the amazing color of his eyes, a shade somewhere between sea and sky, green and blue, profane and sacred. Those extraordinary eyes darkened as he said, "Are you ever wrong?"

She smiled—a beguiling, bewitching smile, Nash thought. "Hardly ever...and never about anything as important as this."

Nash couldn't help but smile, too. In the back of his mind he thought that her confidence could become addictive.

In the hour that followed, AmyAnn, Lance and Marjorie repeated the scene they'd rehearsed earlier. On the heels of that, the three people who played the characters as adults gave a quick run-through of their first scene. The play was a sensitive, evocative story of three friends who grew up together, then went their separate ways. The last scene picked up the trio twenty-five years later. Thematically, the play was a study of perfection versus imperfection. Each character had failed to achieve his life goal because he'd asked too much or too little of himself. He'd either demanded perfection in an imperfect world or used that imperfect world as an excuse for not striving to be the best he could be. Claire thought the play excellent. She also wondered who the playwright was, since no name appeared on the script.

At last, to the delight of all, Nash called a halt to the rehearsals. Claire could imagine the chatter that erupted. Several people waved goodbye to her. She waved back. Her students made a few comments to her about the scenery. She responded to them. Out of the corner of her eye, she saw Lance hold AmyAnn's jacket for her and thought that maybe she had been correct in thinking that the young man had been giving AmyAnn more than the usual share of attention. AmyAnn, she noticed, was polite but nothing more. Now that she was walking offstage, she was no longer the play's character; she was back to being herself.

"You don't know anyone who needs a job, do you?" Gary Evans asked Claire, suddenly appearing from the back of the theater. He'd been absent for most of the rehearsal. "We need someone to be in charge of costumes. Everyone we hire quits."

At that moment, Nash walked up and asked his friend, "Did you find anyone?"

"No," Gary answered. "I've called everyone I know."

Claire thought that Nash uttered a profanity.

"Sorry, I don't know anyone," Claire said in response to Gary's question. "But I'll keep my eyes open."

"Thanks. What about..."

Claire could no longer read Gary's lips, for he'd turned toward Nash, the two men forming a private huddle. Picking up her purse, Claire signed to Smudge. Both started for the door, where AmyAnn waited for them. Suddenly, Claire felt a tap on her shoulder. She turned.

"Have a nice weekend," Nash said.

Claire had certainly been wished that countless times, but suddenly she couldn't recall a single other time. Her memory loss had everything to do with the intensity of Nash's blue eyes. That intensity suggested that he'd never meant anything any more sincerely. It also suggested that she was the only person on the face of the earth at that moment—no movie stars, no ballerina, no crowned princess from any kingdom existed. Just she. That singularity was heady stuff. So heady that she barely managed a reply.

"Thanks. You, too."

PINT-SIZE PEGGY PANNELL had a heart as big as all outdoors. With flaming red hair and forest-green eyes, she had been in charge of the Hearing-Impaired Program of the Big Brothers/Big Sisters agency in San

Francisco since its inception. To date, she had supervised twenty matches—twenty volunteers, many of them hearing impaired themselves or able to communicate with those who were, and twenty needy, hearing-impaired children, many originally from Third World countries. According to the guidelines of the program, each couple met once or twice a month, at least in the beginning, with a caseworker. Because Claire and Peggy were friends, Peggy opted to personally supervise AmyAnn and Claire.

"AmyAnn's doing better," Peggy signed that following Saturday morning. Earlier, she'd met with both AmyAnn and Claire together, then with AmyAnn alone. It was now time to get Claire's unguarded perspective.

The only hearing person in her family, Peggy had had to learn sign to communicate with her parents and her siblings. Claire accused her of signing the way she did everything else in life—at double time—but it proved the point that Claire often made, which was that signing was as individual as verbal speech. No two people spoke alike; no two people signed alike.

"Play," Claire signed, leading with the subject, which one often did in sign language. When talking with people within the hearing community, she tried to use the syntax of verbal communication. With experienced signers, however, she often used the syntax of sign, omitting the verb "to be" and articles. "Turning point."

Ball-of-energy Peggy nodded. "Thank heaven the play came along."

Claire explained how AmyAnn assumed a more confident persona on the stage, how she interacted with the other characters in the play. Claire concluded with,

"Now if only I can instill that confidence in the off-stage AmyAnn."

Peggy smiled, displaying the braces that had been her present to herself on her thirty-fifth birthday. "Why do you think I wanted you to be AmyAnn's Big Sister? No one dishes up confidence like you."

It was the second time in a matter of hours that she'd been accused of being confident. The first accusation had come from . . .

"Nash Prather," Peggy signed.

"What?" Clair asked.

"AmyAnn tells me that Nash Prather is directing the play."

"Yes."

Peggy grinned—lustily. "So? What's he like?"

"What do you mean?"

"Is he gorgeous? Is he sexy? Does he really have those infamous blue eyes?" The questions came so quickly that Claire, for all her experience, could hardly follow them.

But follow them she did . . . to the extent that a pair of blue eyes flashed in her memory. Actually, she realized that they'd been burned there, branded there, ever since yesterday.

"Is he?" Peggy asked impatiently.

"Is he what?"

"Gorgeous, sexy, blue eyed?"

"I suppose he's gorgeous. Yeah, he's sexy. I guess. And yes, he does have blue eyes. I think. I haven't really paid that much attention."

With that, Claire knew that she'd just entered the liar's Hall of Fame. Peggy's spritelike green eyes, twinkling a mile a minute, said that she was well aware that Claire wasn't telling the truth. And furthermore,

Peggy wasn't the only one who knew. The pair of sexy
blue eyes that blazed in Claire's memory—the ones she
couldn't shake—were just as perceptive . . . and just as
accusing.

CHAPTER FIVE

As Claire walked toward the theater Monday night, she realized with a start that she'd actually been looking forward all weekend to resuming rehearsals. She wasn't sure exactly why. Her enthusiasm no doubt came from the pleasure of seeing AmyAnn beginning to blossom. The young woman, who walked beside her, had bubbled and burbled ever since Claire had picked her up a half hour before. It was the play this, the character of Lindy Boyd that, and on and on until Claire could have easily believed that this play was the only one ever written.

The only sour note had been AmyAnn's revelation that her mother had lost her job with the interior decorators. The shop's need to make financial cutbacks had taken its personal toll on Sharon Williams. Claire could tell that AmyAnn blamed herself for her mother having to work two jobs. If she hadn't gotten ill, the financial pressure wouldn't be so great. Claire longed to ease both AmyAnn's guilt and Sharon's burden, but she didn't know how to do either.

A blend of fresh coffee and stale greasepaint wafted around Claire as she stepped into the theater, and she felt the bustle of activity already under way—people scurrying back and forth, groups chattering like magpies, someone motioning for someone else to come onstage. She realized that part of the reason she was glad to be back at rehearsals was simple. It posed a distraction. Despite talking to her family, the weekend had seemed long, the nights lonely. Work—people—filled the emptiness that she sometimes felt, or at least they helped to mask the hollowness. As she thought this, her friend Gary waved as he mounted the stairs to the stage. A smile streaked across his lips, transforming his homely face. Claire waved back.

It was then that Claire saw the familiar broad shoulders, the familiar worn sweatshirt, the familiar rumpled hair. Though his back was to her, she instantly recognized the man Gary was approaching onstage. Gary's wave to her caught the man's attention, for he turned to see whom Gary was greeting. His gaze, stunning and infamous, immediately merged with Claire's.

In that second she knew. While there might well be several reasons why she'd been looking forward to getting back to rehearsals, at least one of those reasons had something to do with seeing Nash Prather again.

IT WAS CRAZY.

Absolutely crazy, with not one whit of sense to be made from it, but there it was. The sight of Claire was like an unexpected jab in the middle of Nash's stomach. Her jeans, over which she wore red high-top boots, bore the usual dots of paint, while red suspenders crawled over her shoulders. Tendrils of traitorous hair peeked from something ridiculously masquerading as a ponytail. While Claire was pretty—unquestionably she had the largest brown eyes he'd ever seen—he nonetheless had dated more beautiful women. Scores of them. In every case, they had been wearing something more stylish than paint. In every case, they had looked as though they'd been dressed by something other than a whirlwind. Why, then, hadn't the sight of one of them kicked him in the solar plexus?

And why did he suddenly have the strangest feeling that the reason he'd wanted the weekend to end and rehearsals to begin again had something to do with this woman? He'd worked long and hard on rewrites to the script, plus he'd done all he could—to no avail—to find someone to handle the costumes. Even with his time so thoroughly consumed, he'd nonetheless felt . . . lonely.

Being lonely was a new feeling for him . . . though, perhaps it wasn't new at all. In a way, he'd always been lonely, from his childhood to the present. He'd often crammed his life with people to compensate for that loneliness, yet those same people had only seemed to exacerbate the feeling. The larger the crowd, the louder the crowd, the more alone he felt, which, in turn, caused him to seek even larger and louder crowds. The greater the number, the more he retained a singularity that was both sad and safe—sad because it meant he was still alone, safe because it meant nothing was demanded of him. And, if you had no demands placed upon you, how could you fail?

Yet the loneliness was growing stronger, more painful. He was simply tired of living life in a solitary lane with no one there to share the dark moments or to celebrate the bright ones. For all that, though, he felt a vulnerability he could never remember feeling before. Had he just forgotten what it was like to be a real person? Wasn't vulnerability a part of being human? Had he sacrificed that part of him, along with so many other parts, when he'd assumed the glamorous role of Nash Prather? He knew with a certainty that surpassed understanding that the woman with the rich brown eyes would settle for nothing less than real. He knew, too, that she deserved something more than a forty-carat fraud like him.

AMYANN GLANCED AROUND the theater, feeling herself come alive again. She'd waited all weekend for Monday to come...Monday and rehearsals. When she was onstage, she no longer felt the pain of her life. She no longer felt the anger, the bitterness, the fear. It no longer mattered that she was different, because the truth was that she was no longer herself. She was Lindy Boyd, complete with Lindy Boyd's personality and Lindy Boyd's problems.

Onstage, she didn't have to worry about lessons she couldn't follow, about friends who tried too hard, about a boyfriend who had betrayed her. She didn't have to worry about anything except her lines...and all the things Nash Prather was teaching her. Moreover, for the duration of this play at least, her drama dreams and hopes weren't lost.

What would happen to her, though, when the play was over? What would happen to her when she had to go back to being AmyAnn Williams? Alone. She sometimes felt so alone, as if no one had ever endured what she had. And yet, she knew that wasn't true. Claire's life hadn't been easy, either—it couldn't have been—and, if Claire could find her way, maybe she could, too? AmyAnn heard the silent question. She had no answer. But then, she didn't need one. At least not now. For now, she had the play. For now, she could be Lindy Boyd.

"THAT'S IT FOR TONIGHT," Nash announced three hours later.

Claire wasn't sure, but she thought she saw some-one shout out a "Thank heavens!" She knew for cer-tain that it was the sentiment she felt. This rehearsal had been particularly grueling, with Nash demanding more and more each time a line was read. He seemed unwilling—no, unable—to accept anything but per-fection. Gary had tried to soften the tone of the re-hearsal by throwing in a couple of breaks, which it appeared Nash, if left on his own, would have forgot-ten to take. During those short breaks, Nash had stayed pretty much to himself. The only times he'd spoken to Claire were in the line of duty—when he'd asked her to translate for AmyAnn or when he'd asked her to add some sign language to the script.

Slipping into her jacket, she glimpsed AmyAnn out of the corner of her eye. Lance had detained her. The young man was saying something, to which AmyAnn shook her head, said something in return, then hur-ried from the stage.

"Ready?" AmyAnn signed.

In view of AmyAnn's sudden haste, Claire couldn't help but wonder what Lance had said.

"Yes," Claire signed back, looking around for Smudge. As though she, too, were ready to call a halt to the exhausting night, the dog was already waiting at the door with an impatient look in her golden eyes. Claire and AmyAnn started in her direction.

"I was awful tonight," AmyAnn said.

"You were not."

"I missed two cues."

"Marjorie forgot her lines. You had no way of knowing she wasn't finished."

"I'm never going to learn to sign," AmyAnn wailed.

"Give yourself time."

"I haven't got time. The play's in three weeks."

Claire thought how drastically things had changed. Until recently, AmyAnn had fought signing; now, for the sake of the play, she couldn't learn it fast enough. Not for the first time, Claire wondered what would happen when the play was over. AmyAnn was channeling all of her frustration into it. Would her anger and bitterness reappear once the play was finished?

"What was wrong with Nash tonight?" AmyAnn asked.

Claire shrugged. "I don't know."

"He almost snapped my head off," the young girl said. It was obvious that her idol's censure had hurt.

Claire recalled the incident AmyAnn referred to. It was one of the times that Gary had called a break.

"The play's important to him," Claire answered, wondering why Nash had invested so much emotional energy into something that would run for only two short weeks. Now, instead of worrying about Amy-Ann, she wondered what would happen to Nash once the play was over. He would hardly turn back into a frog, she reassured herself. How could he when he was clearly every woman's prince?

"Oh, I forgot," AmyAnn said suddenly. "Mom said that she could drive me to rehearsals now that she isn't working nights."

"I don't mind the driving," Claire said.

"It's out of your way."

Claire stopped abruptly. "Wait a minute. Nash said that they needed someone to help with the costumes."

AmyAnn had stopped, too. Her face lighted up. "You think Mom—"

"Why not?" Claire interrupted. "If they haven't found someone."

"Go ask," AmyAnn said, more than excited at the prospect.

"Come with me."

"Uh-uh," AmyAnn balked. "If he snaps, it's going to be your head this time."

"He won't snap—"

"Smudge and I'll wait in the van."

Before Claire could say another word, AmyAnn signed to Smudge and the two were fleeing out the door. "Chicken," Claire signed after both of them.

Claire found Nash still onstage. He was alone, making notes on a clipboard. In the noise created by everyone's hasty exodus from the theater, he obviously didn't hear her approach.

"Nash?" she called quietly.

As though startled, he jerked his head up.

A stubble of beard charcoaled his cheeks, while his hair tumbled around wildly. She'd seen him this rumpled, but never before had she seen him this tired. No, he wasn't just tired. He looked like a man driven to the point of exhaustion. Suddenly, he no longer looked like the picture-perfect Nash Prather. Suddenly, he looked like any ordinary man who'd had a bad day. His imperfection, his ordinariness, spoke to her in a way his perfection, his extraordinariness, never had. Something deep inside her wanted to offer comfort—human being to human being.

"Ah, fools step in..." he said with a slight smile. He then added, "Haven't you noticed that everyone's trying to get out of here? No one's hanging around to talk with the crazed director."

A smile slipped to Claire's mouth. "Like you said, I'm a fool."

No more than I, Nash thought. He hadn't really known how to explain what had come over him that evening. He'd felt the pressure of making the play a success from the very beginning, but he'd panicked tonight. It was as though he realized that somehow this play's success would validate his life. He'd needed that validation from the moment he'd stared into Claire's brown eyes this evening. He'd needed that validation from the moment her realness had reminded him of what a fraud he was.

"How do you sign *fraud?*" he asked, wondering why he'd thought that staying away from her would make him feel better when, in truth, he thought it had only made him feel worse.

His question took Claire totally by surprise. "Fraud?"

"Yeah. How do you sign it?"

She showed him. He repeated the sign, the way he had much of the sign language that had been added to the script during the rehearsal. He was like someone learning a foreign language—he moved slowly around the word, feeling it, repeating it, committing it to memory. As he spoke with his hands, Claire couldn't help but notice his slender, tanned fingers, the dark hair scoring his knuckles, the expensive gold watch at his left wrist. The word seemed strange tripping from his hands, for his hands didn't in the least look fraudulent. To the contrary, they looked strong and capable. And gentle?

This last thought troubled her a bit—why should the gentleness of his hands even come to mind—and so she distracted herself by asking, "Why do you want to know how to sign the word *fraud?*"

Nash's grin was somewhere between sad and sarcastic. "Never mind. Did you want to see me about something?"

"I was wondering if you'd found someone to be in charge of costumes."

Nash threaded his fingers through his already disheveled hair. "No, I haven't, and I wish to heaven..." The relevance of Claire's question hit home. Nash's hand stopped in midjourney. "Do you know someone?"

"AmyAnn's mother is looking for a job. She has a day job, but her night job was terminated. She's a seamstress."

"Do you think she'd be interested in working here?"

"AmyAnn seems to think she might."

"The job doesn't pay a lot—it's minimum wage."

"I suspect anything would be a help right now. AmyAnn's illness left a lot of medical bills."

"I'll call her tomorrow," Nash said, and Claire thought he looked a little less tired, as though one burden might have been removed from his shoulders.

Claire nodded. "Good, I hope it works out. For both of you."

For moments, they just stared. Neither could have said exactly why.

"Well," Claire said finally, motioning toward the side door. "AmyAnn's waiting for me."

"Tell her I'm sorry I was such a grouch." No sooner had he spoken than he amended what he'd said with, "Never mind, I'll make my own apology. And thanks." He brought the tips of the fingers of one hand to his lips and then forward and down to form the sign thank-you. It was one of the sign symbols that had been added to the script.

The gesture sent a sweet emotion purling through Claire. "For what?" she asked. She could feel her voice fluttering.

"For telling me about Sharon Williams, for adding sign to the script, for being a fool that steps in."

Claire knew it was ridiculous, she knew it was every woman's reaction to Nash, but, nonetheless, she felt her heart jump with an uneven, foolish beat.

THE NEXT MORNING, Sharon Williams gratefully accepted the job of coordinating the costumes for the play. That evening, when AmyAnn arrived at the theater for rehearsals, Nash presented her with a dozen long-stemmed red roses. They were his way of apologizing for his curtness the previous evening. From AmyAnn's reaction, one would have thought she'd just been given a million dollars. Actually, what she'd been given was more valuable than that. She'd been given roses by Nash Prather. By *the* Nash Prather!

By the end of the rehearsal, which was intense but not as uptight as the one the evening before, the weather had taken a turn for the worse. The gray, angry clouds that had fretted the sky all day had finally ripped apart. Sheets of rain, driven by a harsh wind, slashed earthward, reducing visibility to zero and putting a prayer on every driver's lips.

"We're almost home," Claire said to Smudge, who kept dodging the rain pounding the windshield of the van. Occasionally, if a car moved too swiftly past them, the dog would whine and bury her eyes. It had been a rainy night when Claire had found her. As a result, Smudge didn't trust inclement weather any more than she did cars.

As though she understood Claire's comment, Smudge whimpered a "Good! Please hurry."

In minutes, Claire and Smudge stood in the middle of the kitchen, with Claire running a towel over Smudge's wet fur. "There, that'll do," Claire said, and the dog shook in agreement.

Within a short while, Claire had changed from wet jeans into a dry jogging suit, had put on a pot of coffee and was sitting at the kitchen table towel-drying her hair. It was ten minutes to eleven. The drive home had taken almost twice as long as usual. The last thing Nash had said to her was, "Be careful." Without a doubt, he'd given the same caution to everybody, for it made no sense that he would have singled her out. It would have been nice, though, to have someone—some man—worry about her. That she didn't was part of the loneliness she felt.

Standing, she walked to the window. If possible, the rain was falling at an even faster tempo. Grimacing, Claire whispered, "Thank heaven I'm home. I can't see a thing in this."

"I CAN'T SEE a damned thing!" Nash muttered as he wended the silver BMW along the narrow, uphill-downhill streets.

He should have asked himself why he was out in this instead of safely indoors. Gary's apartment, where he was staying for the run of the play, was located only a few blocks from the theater. He could have been there in minutes. Yeah, he should have asked himself why he was out on an evening that not even a duck would have been out on, but he didn't. Instead, he squinted, trying to see through the windshield. He hoped he'd recognize the house again. Heck, he just hoped he could see enough of it to recognize it!

The expression on Smudge's face said that she was as startled as Claire to discover the doorbell was ringing. Startled wasn't even close to what Claire was when she opened the door. The man who stood before her, his shoulders hunched in a jacket, his hands buried deep in its pockets, looked like a drowned rat. Hair that when dry was slightly curly was now coiled in tight wet ringlets all over his head. One ringlet, weighted down from the moisture, curled like a corkscrew onto his forehead. Rain dripped from it and ran down the center of his nose. The man made no effort to swat at it. Nor any of the other raindrops beading his bronzed face. He did, however, blink at the moisture glistening from his long, spiked lashes. He also spoke, thereby ending Claire's speculation that maybe the man was only a figment of her imagination.

"I just wanted to see if you got home all right," Nash said.

He was aware of hoping that she didn't ask anything more about why he was standing on her doorstep, because he honestly didn't know what to tell her. Why he was there was a mystery even to him.

"I got home all right," she answered.

She was aware of wondering if her response seemed as stupid to him as it did to her. She also wondered if he was stopping by every cast member's house to see if he or she got home all right. Suddenly, she became aware of the rain splattering off the eves of the house and onto the two of them.

"Come in," she said.

"No, I couldn't. I'm wet. I don't want to track up your house. Besides, it's getting late."

Lightning flashed, thunder rumbled and Claire grinned. "I just brewed some coffee."

One corner of Nash's mouth quirked upward. "Don't offer that kind, tempting reed to a drowning man unless you mean it."

Claire stepped back in invitation. Even Smudge wagged her tail in welcome. Leaving his wet jacket and shoes to drain on the entryway rug, Nash followed Claire into the kitchen. She threw him the towel she'd just used on her hair. He caught it without even being warned that it was coming.

"It's damp," she apologized, removing two mugs from the cabinet.

"It's fine." He realized that she hadn't seen him speak and was about step into her view when she looked up.

"Cream and sugar?" she asked.

"No, just black," he answered, adding, "Thanks." He indicated that this last referred to the towel he was drawing through his wet, curly hair. He was aware that the towel smelled faintly of Claire's hair—a clinging, sweet fragrance.

As she poured the coffee and carried the mugs to the table, where he now sat, Nash allowed his gaze to roam over Claire. He'd never seen her hair down before, and he was surprised at its length. It brushed her shoulders, giving the impression of an ebony veil drawn around her. Because it was damp, the hair had rippled into waves, which reminded Nash of the way the sea etched itself on the beach near his Malibu home.

Again, like the sea and the shore, there was a naturalness about Claire. Her inexpensive jogging suit fit in a totally unpretentious way, and he was certain from the soft, natural movements of her breasts that she wore no bra. She also wore no makeup. Perhaps she'd wiped it away or maybe the rain had run it into obscurity. Whichever, her face—her life—was clear and clean, like the dawn of a brand-new day.

What was he doing here? he thought abruptly, painfully. Wouldn't his very nearness taint her? Didn't all the women he'd known rise up in mockery of this woman's naturalness? Wouldn't those same women have insisted on designer jogging suits? Wouldn't the silicone breasts of those women have risen with provocative deliberateness? Wouldn't those women have rather died than be caught without their makeup? And wasn't he as vain, as shallow, as meaningless as they? What was he doing here? The question came again, but this time there was an answer. He was here because Claire's natural simplicity, her implicit confidence in who she was, drew him like a pilgrim to a shrine. He was here because he was lost, and she was a light in his endless darkness.

"... roses."

Nash came out of his reverie and noticed that Claire's fingers were wrapped around her warm mug. She was awaiting a reply to something she'd said.

But he didn't know what she'd said. He'd been too busy watching her to listen to her. "I'm sorry. I guess I wasn't listening."

"I said that AmyAnn loved the roses."

"I'm glad," he said, then asked, because he suddenly needed to know everything—every small and large thing—that comprised this woman's world, "How do you sign *rose?*"

Removing her hand from the mug, Claire drew the fingers of her right hand together until they resembled a bunch. She then passed the fingertips under first one nostril, then the other. "This is the sign for flower," she explained. "If you wanted to specify rose, you'd spell the word out." She then fashioned her hand into the appropriate letters of the alphabet and spelled as she spoke. *"R-o-s-e."*

Nash attempted the sign for flower.

"Most everything in sign language has its origin in logic," Claire said. "The sign for *flower* is simple. You smell flowers."

"Sign is a pretty language," Nash commented, thinking that maybe it was Claire and her inherent grace who made it seem so.

"Yes, it is. It's also very expressive."

"You're good at it."

Claire smiled. "I've had a lot of practice."

"Have you been deaf from birth?" He'd wanted to ask this a dozen times but had never felt the moment was right until now. Maybe he was simply believing the moment right because he wanted so desperately to know all about Claire.

"Yes."

"And no one else in your family is?"

"No, no one."

"Why you?"

She grinned impishly. "You mean physically or philosophically?"

Nash grinned back, and Claire wondered if the rumor was true about the ice-skating star who'd dramatically threatened to kill herself over him. Somehow Claire could imagine such a thing being true. She could imagine women killing themselves for a mere glimpse of the smile she was now viewing.

"Both," he said.

"Physically, the doctors haven't much idea. It may have resulted from medication my mother took while pregnant, but no one really knows. So, I suppose that answers the philosophical question of why. It appears to have been my karma."

Nash's expression grew pensive. "Do you think one can change one's karma?" he asked as he idly slid his finger over the rim of the mug.

What Claire thought was that the conversation had taken a surprisingly serious turn. She hadn't meant her reply about karma to be anything more than flippant.

"I'm not a philosopher," she said. "I'm an artist."

"Doesn't one have elements of the other? Don't you have to see the truth to be able to paint it?"

"Yes, I suppose, but couldn't that be said of everyone? Don't you as an actor have to be able to see the truth in order to recreate it on film?"

"So, the question becomes, what is truth?" This Nash said as he brought the mug to his lips.

Claire agreed with a nod. "No two artists see life in the same way, no two actors see life in the same way, so that must mean that each of us sees truth in a different way."

"So truth is subjective," Nash said. "Reality is subjective. Which means that whatever one thinks about his karma is true. Likewise, if you believe you can change it, then you can. If you believe you can't, then you can't. Which is, more or less, what you told me once before."

Claire remembered the conversation well. He had told her that he had to be twice as good as everyone else, because he was Nash Prather. She'd told him that he would be twice as good then. Next had come a discussion on confidence, which had ended with her saying that confidence was simply a matter of believing that one could do something.

"Whose karma do you want to change?" she asked softly. It was a highly personal question, yet she felt no qualm about asking it. The sudden heavy, even dark mood that had descended upon them had tilled the fertile ground for such an inquiry.

Nash studied Claire, trying to gauge how much to say, how much of his soul to lay bare. He wasn't good at baring his soul. He found that too many people wanted to pick at it like vultures at prey. Ultimately, he answered her question with another. "Did you ever hear of Vincent Pratatorri?"

Claire shook her head. "No."

Nash grinned—self-deprecatingly. "No, I didn't think you would have."

When he said nothing more but just sat staring into the steaming coffee, Claire prompted with, "Should I know him?"

Nash glanced up, as though coming back from somewhere far away. "No, there's absolutely no reason you, or anyone else, I might add, should. He was just this dumb Italian kid," he said.

Claire was struck by the past tense. "Is he dead?"

Nash looked thoughtful. "I don't know," he answered, then said, "His mother is. She died when he was twelve, and his old man was a drunk who beat him up on a regular basis."

Claire sensed that Nash was speaking matter-of-factly, tonelessly. That very fact lent a macabre element to his grim statement.

"But the kid was nobody's fool," Nash continued. "He figured if he didn't come home, his old man couldn't beat him, so the kid split from home at fourteen and lived on the streets of Brooklyn, doing what he had to to survive. He quit school, mainly because no one cared one way or the other. And when no one else cared, neither did the kid. School was a drag, anyway. So he just hung out on the streets—being tough and being bad.''

Nash took another slow swallow of coffee. As he set the mug back on the table, he said, ''No one can be tough enough, though, to weather a New York winter on the streets. But, like I said, the kid was nobody's fool. By day, when he had the money, he'd hang out at the movies. By night, he got real clever at hiding himself in the city library. That's where he'd spend most of his nights—reading and sleeping and reading some more. He'd never had much time for books before. Books weren't cool, you understand.'' Nash gave a faint smile. Claire watched as the smile faded slowly.

''Those uncool books changed his life, though. In them, he found worlds he'd never known existed. In them, he found people—good people, bad people, scared people, people like him. He began to write his own stories in his head, hundreds of them, thousands of them, all ending just the way he wanted life to be— happy ever after. By now, the stories on the shelves, the stories in his mind, coupled with the hundreds of movies he'd seen, had given Vincent a dream. So off he went to Hollywood to make that dream come true.''

''Vincent Pratatorri became Nash Prather,'' Claire said, taking a guess that wasn't all that wild.

''Yeah.'' Again, his expression, his gestures, were rich with sarcasm.

''I don't understand,'' Claire said. ''This sounds like a success story, but I have the feeling you think it's not.''

"Let's just put it this way. You've done more with your imperfection that I've done with my perfection."

This last Claire understood to be an irreverent reference to his looks. What she didn't understand was his attitude. "How can you think you've done so little when you're a major star?"

"But only because of my looks. Hollywood isn't the slightest bit interested in what I have in the way of brains. It's only interested in how sexy I look in jeans. It's only interested in how much I can stimulate the hormones of the women in the audience."

Claire could not keep her eyes from lowering to his jeans—his damp, clinging jeans. A thought popped into her mind. Nash Prather and denim could jump start the heart of a devout nun. Realizing this was probably not a good time to mention it, she said, instead, "Obviously, you want meatier roles."

"No, what I want is Vincent Pratatorri's dream. I want to be on the other side of the camera—writing, producing, directing. That's all I ever wanted to do—to create worlds of my own. I never wanted to act out someone else's world. I never wanted to speak someone else's lines."

The simple truth hit Claire like a ton of bricks. Now it all made sense—the subject matter of the play, Nash's obsession at rehearsals, his driving himself to the edge to make the play perfect. "You wrote the play, didn't you?"

His gaze merged with hers, brown to blue green. "Yeah," he answered finally, "and if you listen, even *you* can hear Hollywood laughing."

Neither said anything. Claire was wondering what she could say to ease his pain. Nash was wondering why he'd dumped his personal life at the feet of this

stranger. Suddenly, he wished with all his heart that he
hadn't, for he could never remember feeling so vulnerable. Suddenly, he just wanted to get away, to be
alone—the way he'd always been alone.

"I shouldn't have stopped by," he said, scraping
back his chair and rising. He headed for the door. He
already had his jacket and shoes on and the door wide
open when she reached him.

"Nash, wait!" she said, touching his arm.

He looked first at her hand, then into her eyes. The
rain, still coming down with a vengeance, fell harshly
upon him—his shoulders, his hair, the face that melted
women's hearts.

"Why is it too late to realize Vincent Pratatorri's
dream?"

"Maybe if you ignore a dream too long, it dies."

"Then again, maybe it just grows stronger," Claire
added.

"Maybe...but what scares me is that maybe it's always been Vincent Pratatorri's karma to be Nash
Prather."

"Then change the karma."

"What if I can't? What if I'm stuck being Nash
Prather?"

"Is it so bad being Nash Prather?" Claire asked, still
puzzled that he could think himself such a failure.

"You don't get it do, you?" Nash said softly. That
very softness was compelling, telling. "It's not a question of being bad or good. It's a question of existing at
all. Nash Prather isn't real. He never has been—he
never will be."

Nash Prather isn't real...real...real...

As she got ready for bed, Claire pondered Nash's
parting remark. She always came to the same conclu-

sion. Whether Nash Prather was real or not, the man who'd stood framed in her doorway, the rain spilling onto him, had been real—as real as any man she'd ever seen. She'd felt the realness of his pain. But most importantly, she'd felt the real warmth of his skin beneath her hand. It was a warmth that had burned to the very core of her being.

CHAPTER SIX

CLAIRE'S TEACHING schedule kept her away from the theater until Friday night. During those couple of days she tried not to think of Nash Prather. She tried not to think of the conversation they'd shared. The professional persona of Nash Prather, the heartthrob of the silver screen, intimidated her, while at the same time the vulnerable private side of the troubled man drew her to him. The moment their eyes connected Friday night, she could tell that he regretted their conversation. Perhaps for that reason, or perhaps because, with the play scheduled to start in a couple of weeks, every moment was needed for rehearsal, he only spoke to her occasionally, always in connection with the play. Inexplicably, Claire felt a loss.

She also worried about AmyAnn. Though the young woman continued to shine on the stage, Claire wasn't certain that her personal life was improving. After more than a little cajolery, Claire got her to admit that Lance Randle had asked her out—several times. Each time, AmyAnn had refused. When Claire asked her why, AmyAnn insisted that Lance only pitied her, that she knew for a fact that no boy would be interested in her. Claire told her that not every male was like Curt Knight. As far as Lance pitying AmyAnn, Claire suspected—though she tactfully kept the suspicion to herself—that it was more a case of AmyAnn pitying herself. It was a reaction she understood, but one she had no patience with.

By the time Friday's rehearsal ended, everyone was more than willing to call it a night. As Claire, heavy with fatigue, prepared to leave, she noticed Lance moving toward AmyAnn. The girl, who obviously had seen his approach, as well, made a beeline for Claire. Ordinarily, Lance would have given up there. Tonight he didn't.

"Hi, Ms. Rushing," he said. The teenager stood only inches above AmyAnn, but his sleek black hair and his sharp, almost bladelike facial features gave him an imposing look that seemed to add to his height.

"Hi, Lance," Claire answered.

Not wasting time on anything other than what he had on his mind, Lance turned to AmyAnn. "You want to go get a Coke?"

Claire admired his spunk just as she sympathized with AmyAnn's discomfort. In what Claire recognized as a distancing ploy, AmyAnn clutched her purse to her chest.

"It's late," the girl said.

"It's not that late," Lance said, insisting, "Ah, c'mon, AmyAnn. I'm not gonna bite, and I'm not gonna take no for an answer tonight."

Something in the jut of his hawklike chin told both Claire and AmyAnn he meant what he said. As clearly as if AmyAnn had shouted the fact, Claire could feel the young woman's fear. It was a palpable thing that shuddered in the silence. AmyAnn clasped her shield more closely to her. Glancing toward Claire, she begged her to intercede. The intercession came from an unexpected source, however, and it wasn't in the least what AmyAnn had in mind.

"C'mon," Nash said, stepping forward, "the four of us'll double-date." Before anyone could say anything, Nash directed his attention to the stage. Gary and Sharon stood discussing the costumes. "How long are you all going to be?" Nash called out.

Gary glanced down at his friend, then up at Sharon. "About an hour?" he asked AmyAnn's mother.

"At least," she agreed.

"The four of us are going to get something to drink, then," Nash said, giving Sharon the opportunity to object to her daughter coming along. When no objection was forthcoming, he added, "See you all in an hour." With that, he placed his hand at the small of Claire's back and nudged her forward. "Let's go."

At the word *double-date,* Claire's heart had skipped a beat, though she told herself that it wasn't a date in the conventional sense, that Nash had only been trying to encourage AmyAnn to socialize. At the feel of his hand at her back—his strong and certain hand— Claire's heart skipped another beat.

Sensing that the walk to the parking lot might be awkward, Nash immediately began discussing the play. Did Lance and AmyAnn think that the end of scene 2 was stronger? And what did they think about their characters' consistency throughout the play? Both Lance and AmyAnn made comments, though Claire thought that AmyAnn would have liked to run away at the first opportunity. There was no such opportunity, however, and within seconds the four of them were seated in Nash's BMW. Smudge, who, out of principle, had snarled at the front tire, rode at Claire's feet, though it was clear she'd have preferred to be belted in.

Starting the engine—it purred like a playful cat— Nash looked over at Claire. In the semidarkness, their gazes brushed before he slid the gear into place and backed from the parking space.

During the drive, Claire noted how quietly AmyAnn sat in the back seat and how Lance tried, not always successfully, to engage her in conversation. She noticed, too, how casually Nash spoke and drove ... and how good he looked even at the end of a tiring day.

To avoid being recognized, Nash chose the back booth of a small diner. Even so, he wore sunglasses until he was seated in the shadows. For the first time, Claire considered what an invasion of privacy stardom could be. Did Nash resent this aspect of his success the way he seemingly resented all the others?

"What'll everyone have?" Nash asked when they were seated. He'd allowed Claire to precede him into the booth. Again, Smudge curled at Claire's feet.

"I'll just have coffee," Claire said.

Nash looked in AmyAnn's direction.

"I'll have a Cherry Coke," the young woman responded—begrudgingly.

In seconds the order was given, and a short while later the drinks were delivered to the table. The interim was spent discussing the safe subject of the play. Claire thought that AmyAnn was just beginning to relax a little when Lance grabbed her arm and dragged her from the booth.

"Let me show you what a whiz I am at pinball."

As she had from the very beginning of the outing, AmyAnn had little choice but to follow.

"Maybe I shouldn't have pushed AmyAnn into coming," Nash said when he and Claire were alone.

"Actually, a push is exactly what she needs at this point."

"I guess I felt sorry for Lance," Nash said. "He's done everything but fall to his knees and beg."

Claire smiled as she stirred a dash of cream into her coffee. "I wouldn't have been surprised if he'd tried that next." Claire's smiled faded. "AmyAnn's boyfriend broke up with her several weeks ago. It shook her confidence pretty badly."

"Why did he break up with her?" Nash asked.

Nash could feel the slight stirring of Claire's shoulder as she shrugged, just as she could feel his thigh. Neither one felt the actual flesh of the other, but rather, the promise of body touching body if either one moved a fraction of an inch. Nash thought it interesting that he'd never been this keenly aware of a woman's touch. How was it possible then to be so aware of just the suggestion of it? Claire simply ignored the tingling feelings that sprang to life. If she didn't acknowledge them, then they didn't exist, did they?

In answer to his question, she said, "Maybe he was looking for an excuse to break up, anyway, and AmyAnn's deafness simply gave him that excuse. Then again, maybe he couldn't cope with the chip on her shoulder. Whichever, his timing couldn't have been worse."

"My money's on Lance," Nash said. "He seems persistent enough to wear down the devil. He also seems like a darned nice kid."

Both Claire and Nash looked over at the couple. Lance was motioning for AmyAnn to take his place at the machine. She did—reluctantly. He pulled back the lever, releasing the metal ball, then patiently settled in to guide AmyAnn through the game. In time, as the natural movements of the game demanded it, he stepped behind AmyAnn, loosely caging her in his arms. AmyAnn didn't seem to notice. She was too caught up in making the metal ball go where she willed it.

Claire noticed, though, and wondered why such a small thing as AmyAnn standing within Lance's arms should catch her attention. Curiously, she felt an ache as she watched the young couple. Perhaps they simply reminded her that she was single in a couple's world.

Nash also observed the two teenagers and felt pangs of regret. He wondered what it would be like to belong to someone. Not the shallow kind of relationships he was accustomed to, but the real kind—the kind where you belonged to someone heart and soul.

"I'm sorry about the other night," Nash said. His apology came abruptly, so abruptly that Claire realized he'd obviously wanted to make it for a while but was only now finding the courage to bring up the subject.

"There's nothing to apologize for," she said.

"Yes, there is. I had no business dumping my problems on you."

"You didn't. We were just talking."

Nash snorted. "I was doing all the talking, all the complaining."

"You weren't complaining."

"I was."

"You weren't."

Nash grinned. "Don't argue with me. I was complaining."

Claire thought how truly potent this man's smile was, potent enough to banish clouds on a stormy day. "Okay, so you were complaining," she said. "So what?"

Nash's grin thinned. "So I'm sorry."

"I just wish there was something I could do." She looked up into his blue eyes. "I wish there was something I could say or do to convince you that you are real. It doesn't matter what name you use—Vince Pratatorri or Nash Prather—you *are* real."

"Am I?"

"Yes. You're very re—"

Claire stopped in midword as Nash's hand covered hers on the table. She felt a dozen things at once. She felt her heart slamming against her chest. She felt the warmth of his slender, tanned fingers cupping hers. She felt the very definition of the word *real*.

"You said that you wished you could do something," he said, adding, "You can." He spoke softly, sincerely. This Claire would have staked her life on.

"W-what?" she managed to say.

"Loan me some of your confidence."

"How much do you need?" she whispered.

"As much as you can spare."

Claire told herself that his taking her hand meant nothing, that he probably wasn't even aware he had. At the same time, Nash was aware of wanting to remove his hand—in fact, he *needed* to remove it, because Claire's skin was burning his—but he couldn't pull his hand away. It was as though he'd found an anchor and couldn't let go for fear of sinking to the bottom of his life.

Claire was uncertain how long they sat, his hand molding hers—seconds, minutes, eons. Suddenly, as though a noise had distracted him, Nash jerked his head in the direction of Lance and AmyAnn. Claire's gaze followed. The kids were laughing as the pinball machine flashed the impressive number of points they'd scored. As Claire watched, AmyAnn, her eyes sparkling, ran her fingers through her short, curly blond hair and said to Lance, "Let's play again."

Before Claire knew what was happening, Nash was meshing his fingers with hers. "C'mon," he said, pulling her from the booth and towing her toward a second pinball machine.

"But I don't know how," Claire protested.

"I'll teach you. It's easy."

Nash played the first game, with Claire standing beside him, watching. The ball bounded from one area to another, collecting points along the way. More than once, with some fast hand movements, Nash snatched the ball from the jaws of defeat and sent the silver sphere back into play. Occasionally, Claire's gaze drifted to the muscles rippling across Nash's back. She'd read that he did most of his own movie stunts. She could believe it, for his body looked in top physical condition.

"All right!" Nash said, pleased with his performance when the game ended.

Claire checked her thoughts about rippling muscles and said, "You're good."

"One of the advantages of a misspent youth," he answered. "C'mon, you try it."

"I don't—"

"C'mon," he said, encircling her waist and hauling her to the machine.

"It's easy," AmyAnn encouraged her. She signed the remark. She was signing more and more without realizing it.

"Yeah, sure," Claire said, signing back and looking down at the surface of the inclined board. Just how big a fool was she about to make of herself?

"Here, pull back on this lever to release the ball." After he said this, Nash realized that Claire hadn't understood, because she hadn't been looking at him. He tapped her shoulder. She looked up, and Nash repeated his instructions.

"Pull this?" she asked.

"Yeah," Nash answered, but realized that it was going to be difficult, if not impossible, to talk to Claire when necessity demanded she turn her back on him. To compensate, he stepped behind her and placed his hand on hers. Pulling back, they both released the ball, sending it into play.

The ball arched onto the board, then pinged, pinged, pinged as it hit here and there before it began to drop to the slanted bottom of the machine.

A competitive excitement burst to life inside Claire. "No!" she cried in protest of the game ending so soon.

"Here," Nash said, but, instead of hearing him, Claire saw his left hand snake out, move a lever and tilt the ball back into a scoring position.

"Okay!" she said at the last minute save. She could feel the adrenaline pumping through her now and idly wondered how anyone could get so worked up over a silly game. Even Smudge, who'd moved to stand beside Claire, wagged her tail with bold enthusiasm.

The next time the ball threatened to plunge out of play, Claire did as Nash had and, using her left hand, rescued the ball by flipping it back into the upper portion of the board. Though she couldn't read what he said, she could feel Nash's praise. Inexplicably, it sent the adrenaline pumping faster, harder.

As the game progressed, Nash continued to stand behind her. Occasionally, his thighs brushed against the backs of Claire's legs. Each time this happened, she was aware of the muscle-toned strength of his thighs. She was also aware of a tiny fluttering in her stomach. She convinced herself that this latter was nothing more than game jitters, for the ball was still rolling, rolling, pinging, pinging...

Abruptly, the ball zipped past despite her best efforts, and the game ended. Even so, she and Nash had scored high. Exhilaration surged through her as she turned to confront her partner.

"We did...good!"

The word died in her throat. At the same time, her heart thudded to a stop, then burst into a frenzied beat. Nash stood directly in front of her, his chest only inches from hers and his thighs almost touching hers. His face was so near that his breath fanned against her cheek. His hair-dusted hands rested against the pinball machine, creating a cage identical to the one Lance had earlier formed around AmyAnn. Just as she had then, Claire felt an ache, the consuming, overpowering ache to have this man step closer and closer and...

Closer. Nash fought the overwhelming urge to move closer. He fought the urge to bring his thighs against hers, to send his fingers tunneling through her attractively disheveled hair, to brush at the tiny smear of paint on the underside of her chin. He fought the urge to lower his head and kiss her...

Lips. Claire's gaze lowered to his lips, his sensually curved, sexy-looking lips. Her own lips began to move, to say something, but it was now Nash who couldn't hear above the loud pounding of his heart. Finally, he forced himself to listen, forced himself to concentrate.

"Shouldn't we be getting back?" she whispered.

Getting back? To where? From where? Nash glanced around as though he'd just landed after soaring to another world. He was in a diner—a plain, ordinary diner with a most extraordinary woman almost in his arms.

"Yeah," he answered hoarsely, stepping from her, "we need to get back."

The drive to the theater would have been deathly silent had it not been for Lance. Even AmyAnn seemed to have become uncomfortable. As for Claire and Nash... neither had much to say. Both were too busy trying to figure out what in heck had just happened.

NOTHING.

Nothing had happened, Claire thought as she lay restlessly tossing back and forth in bed. Smudge, rolled into a furry ball at her feet, glanced up, as though inquiring what was wrong now. The same roll and toss and jab the pillow routine had been repeated a dozen times in the past hour and a half. With each repetition, Claire reaffirmed, and more strongly each time, that nothing had happened.

It was obvious—actually, more than obvious—that everything she'd felt in Nash's arms—well, she hadn't really been in Nash's arms; his hands had just been braced against the pinball machine and she'd been caught between Nash and the machine—anyway, everything she'd felt had been nothing more than the rush of excitement at playing the game. That was all. Plain and simple. Simple and plain. She hadn't really been that aware of him. Why, she'd barely noticed the alluring, almost wicked stubble on his face, nor had she really paid much attention to the breadth of his chest or the firmness of his thighs or the faint masculine cologne that clung to him. And his lips...

At the vision that flashed in her mind, Claire once more turned to her side, then to her other side, then jabbed the dickens out of the pillow. Smudge rolled her eyes in a "please not again" expression.

Of course, Claire thought, even if his nearness had sparked something in her—which it hadn't!—even so, surely she could be forgiven the emotional transgression. Or would that be a physical transgression? Either way, surely she could be forgiven. After all, Nash Prather was one of the sexiest men on the face of the earth.

Which was the very reason she must have been mistaken about his reaction. His eyes hadn't darkened and his gaze hadn't lowered to her lips. Of course not! Why, it was downright laughable—as in the hoot of the decade—that one of the world's sexiest men had reacted to her. True, she'd never lacked for self-confidence, but neither did she lack for brains. This man could have any woman he wanted and, if rumor were true, he'd wanted a lot including the blond soap opera bimbo—Claire overlooked the fact that the woman had now assumed the proportions of a personal adversary. Why then, Claire asked, summing everything up in one tidy question, would a man like Nash be the slightest bit attracted to a woman like her? Simple. He wouldn't. Which meant that nothing—absolutely nothing—had happened between them. She and Nash were just friends.

There, that was settled!

Thank goodness!

Now she could sleep!

Claire pushed once more onto her elbow and jabbed her pillow before settling back into the bed's softness.

Smudge whined. It was going to be a long night.

NOTHING.

Nothing had happened, Nash thought as he lay wide-awake in the bed in Gary's guest bedroom. His hands were stacked beneath his head, the cover draped only to his waist despite the room's slight chill. It was a chill he relished for no other reason than its distraction. Yet, even at that, he found his mind too singularly occupied with thoughts he wished weren't there—thoughts of Claire's eyes, thoughts of Claire's subtly scented perfume, thoughts of Claire's lips.

He groaned.

So he'd noticed her eyes, her perfume, her lips! So what? It was no big deal. He was a man; she was a woman; he'd noticed. It was that simple. It was not the stuff of commitments. It wasn't even the stuff of one-night stands. Hell, it was a man's job to notice women! It was what a man did best.

And he hadn't really longed to kiss her—he'd simply *noticed* her. Just the way he'd noticed the pleasure radiating from her face. She'd been having fun. Interestingly, her fun had spiked his own. He could never remember a woman's pleasure spilling over to become his. There was a headiness to that phenomenon that he'd never experienced before.

Had she noticed him, too? There was a second when he'd thought she had, but he'd quickly subdued his ego. He was so accustomed to women throwing themselves at him that he'd jumped to the conclusion that Claire had been moved by his nearness. What a joke! What would someone like Claire want with someone like him? She'd want a man of substance, not some flimsy legend that Hollywood had spawned.

This last thought brought another to his mind. Did she have a man in her life? He'd always assumed no, but what right did he have to assume that? And what difference did it make to him if she had a dozen? He and she were friends. Nothing more. Which led him back to exactly where he'd started.

Nothing had happened that night.

Absolutely nothing.

NOTHING.

As always, she heard nothing, AmyAnn thought as she lay awake staring in the darkness of her bedroom. In the beginning, she'd been certain that the doctors had made a mistake, that someday she'd hear again. She knew now that she never would. She knew now that she was doomed to spend the rest of her life in silence. That realization made her angry and sad, yet sometimes when she was around Claire, the despair she often felt gave way to a feeling less than hope, but more than hopelessness. If Claire could survive, if Claire could succeed, then perhaps she could, as well. There were even times, unguarded moments, when she forgot to be angry and sad.

Like tonight.

A small smile drifted around AmyAnn's lips. She hadn't wanted to go, yet, once at the diner, she couldn't say she hadn't had fun. At least while she and Lance played the pinball machine. Lance. He was nice. A cross between Michael J. Fox and Lou Diamond Phillips—kinda clean-cut but with a raw sexiness. Sorta like—

The name Curt came to mind, destroying AmyAnn's smile. His betrayal still hurt. She was never going to let anyone hurt her that badly again. No one. She'd be Lance's friend but nothing more. She wouldn't give him the chance to betray her. More importantly, she wouldn't let him patronize her with pity.

She hated pity!

Turning onto her side, she withdrew into herself, to that private place deep within where nothing or no one could hurt her. She fell asleep listening to the sound of silence.

FOUR WEEKS AFTER rehearsals began, they ended—on a Saturday night in February.

"That's a take," Nash announced, borrowing the vernacular of the movie industry.

A chorus of hurrahs and hallelujahs rose to the theater rafters. Someone sent a script sailing into the air. The dress rehearsal had gone on and on and on, with Nash demanding everyone's last ounce of energy. Claire wondered what Nash, who'd pushed himself far beyond the ragged edge of perfection, was running on. Her guess was caffeine and adrenaline—not necessarily in that order.

"Before you go..." Nash began, but stopped when he realized he couldn't be heard above the chatter. "Hey, could I have everyone's attention for just a minute?"

Someone whistled and the noises began to fade—one note, then another, until everyone, both onstage and off, waited for Nash to speak.

From the steps leading to the stage, he said, "Give me a minute more of your time. I just wanted to say how much I appreciate all your hard work. I've never been associated with a more talented group of actors... or with a nicer group. You all are the best."

"So are you!" someone shouted.

"Even if you have worked our tails off," someone else added.

Laughter erupted.

"Thanks," Nash said, adding, "I think. Anyway, enough of this sentimentality and on to a more practical matter. Be here Monday night at least an hour before the curtain call and—" Nash smiled "—break a leg."

"Hear, hear!" someone shouted.

"Go for it!" another voice called out.

"Oh, and remember," Nash tacked on, "that an opening night party follows the performance."

"At the Brighton home," Gary added. The Brightons, patron contributors to the theater, had volunteered to host the party at their lavish hillside home.

"That's it!" Nash hollered in dismissal, and everyone began to scatter.

AmyAnn, who'd caught enough of what Nash had said to at least make sense of the sentiment, waved to Claire, who stood offstage. Claire waved back and watched AmyAnn disappear backstage, where her mother was collecting the costumes.

Claire had just slid her arms into her denim jacket when she felt a hand on her arm. She recognized the hand immediately. In reaction, her heartbeat picked up its pace.

"Hi," Nash said.

"Hi," Claire answered.

It was the first time they'd spoken privately in several days. While neither had planned it thus, both had been relieved that last minute play details had kept them apart. Even though she'd decided that they were nothing more than friends, that nothing extraordinary had happened between them, Claire couldn't shake the memory of being trapped between Nash and the pinball machine. The same memory haunted Nash. Since neither knew how to deal with this memory, it was easiest to ignore it, though that really wasn't effective, either, for the more they tried to forget, the more they remembered.

Claire smiled. "Well, how does it feel for everything to be over but the shouting?"

In spite of his dog tiredness, Nash grinned. "Scary."

"It's going to be a huge success."

"From your mouth to the audience's ear. Look," he said, as though he were about to get to the reason he'd stopped her, "I want to thank you personally for all you've done."

"I haven't done—"

"Yes, you have," he interrupted. "Not only have you made it possible for AmyAnn to perform, but you've added something to the script itself. The sign language has given it depth, scope."

"Both were my pleasure."

"I want to repay you—"

"That isn't necessary," Claire interrupted.

"Perhaps it isn't necessary, but I still want to. Have dinner with me tomorrow night." Before Claire's heart could do more than quicken its already quick rhythm, Nash grinned, and Claire felt as if her feet had been knocked out from under her. "Actually," he said, "I have an ulterior motive. I need to hang out with your confidence until the play opens."

Up to a point, Nash knew he was lying. While he could most certainly use a strong dose of Claire's confidence, her company was something he needed more. He was tired of analyzing what had or hadn't happened the last time they were together. The fact remained that he'd missed her and that right this moment he didn't give a royal damn about defining their relationship—or about the fact that someone like him was totally wrong for someone like her. The truth was that he just wanted to be with her.

Claire was more direct with herself. She didn't bother with all the fancy emotional footwork. In fact, she had grown tired of sparring with the events of that Friday night at the diner. She had no idea what her feelings meant, but rather she simply gave in to them. She wanted to be with him. What woman wouldn't want to be with the sexiest man on the face of the earth?

"Yes, I'll have dinner with you," she said without the slightest hedging.

"Good," the sexiest man on the face of the earth answered, "then it's settled."

CHAPTER SEVEN

"MAKE YOURSELF at home," Nash said as he took Claire's purse and jacket the following evening. He laid both on the table in the entrance to Gary's apartment. Smudge, a red bandanna at her throat, was already smelling her way around her new surroundings. "You're sure you don't mind eating in?" Nash asked again—for the third time.

He'd first brought up the subject as he'd settled Claire into the BMW. She'd assumed that they were going to a restaurant, which was, indeed, what he *had* meant by his dinner invitation. It had only been when he'd realized Gary would be out for the evening—Gary, who didn't know a needle from a thimble, was helping Sharon put the finishing touches to the play's wardrobe—that Nash had altered the plans. Hating the public eye, the lure of a private dinner had been more than he could resist.

"No, I don't mind eating in," Claire answered—for the third time.

Actually, she wasn't at all certain how she felt about an evening alone with Nash, but then, for that matter, she wasn't too sure of anything she was feeling these days. What was one more uncertainty among so many?

"Something smells good," she said, fighting the urge to run her damp palms—she could never remember her hands perspiring from nervousness!—down the legs of her black trousers.

As it had a hundred times since he'd picked her up, Nash's gaze traveled over Claire. She wore a pair of men's pants with wide black suspenders. Beneath the suspenders was an ordinary white T-shirt—again a man's—with the sleeves rolled up in a James Dean rebel-like fashion. The high black heels that she wore, however, were decidedly feminine, as were her enormous gold disk earrings and the dozens of thin gold bracelets jangling at her wrists. Her hair was fluffed around her shoulders in unruly but blatantly sexy curls.

"...famished...not a bite since breakfast..."

Nash dragged his reluctant attention back to what Claire was saying. "Yeah, well, if I don't check on dinner, we might be eating out, after all," he said as he started for the kitchen. "Just make yourself at home...or have I said that already?"

Claire smiled. "You have."

Nash grinned back. "Then do it."

Claire watched as he disappeared. With him gone, she tried to erase the image that had been indelibly etched on her mind from the instant she'd opened the door to him. The image was that of a man so unbelievably handsome that he'd taken her breath away. Literally. Never before had a man's appearance had such a visceral effect on her.

Crisp and pleated, his white slacks fit as though the gods had handmade them for him, while a sweater, exactly matching his blue-green eyes, appeared to have been knitted by adoring angels. It crossed Claire's mind that he looked so handsome he didn't even seem real, which, ironically, was what he kept telling her—that

Nash Prather wasn't real. But he was. He had to be. It would be too great a tragedy if such perfection wasn't.

Noting that the image, if anything, grew sharper when he was out of sight, Claire tried to ignore her thoughts by calling out, "Is there anything I can do?"

"Uh-uh," he answered, then realized she couldn't hear him. He stuck his head around the door. "No...just make yourself—"

"At home," Claire finished.

He grinned. "Right."

Taking him up on his offer, Claire prowled around the room, realizing this was the first time she had been in her friend's apartment. By and large it was done in rust and moss green, with only marginal attention to any decorating scheme. The most effort had gone into simply making the room, the apartment, comfortable. Smudge found herself just such a comfortable spot beside the sofa and lay down. Noticing the pictures on one wall, Claire, her moist hands stuffed in her pants pockets, stepped forward and scanned them. Most were photos of Gary and various members of the innumerable casts he'd been a part of. Several of the pictures, however, were of him and Nash—when both were very young. Even then Nash was picture-perfect.

Unexpectedly, she felt a tap on her shoulder. She turned, and Nash offered her a glass of ruby-red wine.

"Thank you," she said, taking the glass, then commenting, "I didn't realize that you and Gary have known each other so long."

"Yeah, we go way back. We used to room together...back in the good ol' days." Nash's eyes roamed to the photos. Claire had the feeling that he'd stepped back into time, back into those good ol' days.

"How did you two meet?"

Nash looked over at Claire, as though a little startled to find himself in the present. "In a grocery store. We were both trying to live off nothing, so we pooled our nothing and moved in together."

"Was Gary in college then?"

"Yeah."

"And what about you? What were you doing?"

"Anything, everything, nothing—that was before the great Nash Prather existed." This last he said with obvious sarcasm, then washed the bitter taste of the name from his mouth with a swallow of wine. "Lord, was I stupid in those days!"

"How?"

"I honestly thought Hollywood would want the stories in my head. I had this script I'd written—now, mind you, I was only seventeen and hadn't even finished high school, so you know how good it was, but I was certain the script would make a smash movie if I could just get it to the right people."

When he said nothing more, Claire prompted, "And?"

Nash gave a snort of laughter. "What do *you* think? Not only didn't anyone want to read the script of a seventeen-year-old kid who hadn't finished high school, no one even wanted to talk to the kid about it. One producer, who I managed to meet by lying my way into a party, did congratulate me on my spunk. Unfortunately, I had little else. I especially had little money."

"So how did you . . ." Claire started to ask how he'd gotten his big break, but, considering how he felt about his career, she amended her question to, "So how did you end up in movies?"

"Via a commercial," he said. "Gary and I were down to two fish sticks and a half package of frozen English peas when I tried out for an after-shave lotion commercial and got it. The rest is history, as they say." He took another swallow of wine, then said remorsefully. "I never did get back to that script."

"What happened to it?"

"Gary has it somewhere. I threw it away after it was obvious Hollywood wasn't interested, but he rescued it. Said he'd give it back to me someday—after I'd shown Hollywood what a mistake it had made by rebuffing my writing skills."

"Sounds like he has faith in you."

Nash glanced once more at the photos of him and Gary. "Yeah, the stupid jerk."

"Friends are like that," Claire said. "They believe in you during those times when you don't believe in yourself."

"Actually, Gary's my one real friend but he's much more than a friend," Nash said with feeling. Claire could see that feeling in the intensity of his gaze as he stared at the photo. "He's family. The only family I have."

Claire studied Nash, ferreting through the subtleties and nuances of this complex man. What she saw, what she felt, was a loneliness she'd never noticed before. How odd that a man who was recognized by millions considered one man his only friend, one man his only family. She'd never thought of it before—had never had occasion to—but being a star was emotionally draining. You gave yourself to millions of fans but received nothing in return except an impersonal, distant adoration. And in Nash's case, there was no family to fill the void in his life. Claire suddenly felt guilty for having such a large, loving family. She suddenly wanted to share her vast riches.

"Maybe sometime you can meet my family. I think you'd like them. They're—"

She stopped abruptly when she realized the grandeur of her presumptuousness. She had presumed that the two of them—she and Nash—had a relationship, when, in truth, only the play held them together. In two weeks the play would be finished. Then they would go their separate ways—Nash back to Hollywood, where dozens of women, one blonde in particular, would be more than willing to ease his loneliness. Who in the world did she—Claire Rushing—think she was, to assume that the famous Nash Prather would be interested in meeting her family.

Nash read her thoughts as clearly as if she'd spoken them out loud. "I'd love to meet your family," he said.

"Well, maybe sometime," Claire said, embarrassed by her rashness. "If you're ever back this way. If the occasion permits. I mean, I know you'll be going home soon. And I know how busy you are. I'm sure the public makes too many demands as it is. I'm sure—"

"Would you do me a favor?" Nash interrupted. Before Claire could say anything, he said, "Would you forget that I'm Nash Prather? Would you please have dinner this evening with just plain ol' Vincent Pratatorri?"

His plea was genuine. There was no doubt in Claire's mind as to that. Just as there was no doubt that she couldn't refuse him, not when he stood there looking for all the world as if his life depended on her answer. The depth of his need spoke to her as little else ever had. She'd once said about AmyAnn that if Nash asked her to fly, she'd try. Claire now understood that kind of emotional aviation.

A slow smile sauntered across Claire's lips. "So, Vincent Pratatorri, where is this dinner I keep hearing about?"

Undeniable relief flickered across Nash's face, and he, too, grinned. "I believe you did say you were famished."

"Actually, that was a gross understatement."

"Are you in luck, then! I just happen to make the best lasagna you've ever eaten."

"Prove it," Claire demanded.

Nash did precisely that. In addition to the wonderful lasagna, he served fresh green salad, buttered French bread and a Bordeaux with a rich bouquet. His culinary expertise surprised her, for she had visions of his life being filled with cooks and housekeepers and servants who performed even the most mundane of rituals for him. She envisaged his life as bigger and better than that of mere mortals. In truth, though, Nash was turning out to be quite normal. Disturbingly normal, as a matter of fact, for Claire found herself drawn to this ordinary man. She sensed a very real threat in Vincent Pratatorri, perhaps a danger that far exceeded that of Nash Prather. Vincent Pratatorri had the ability to make her forget about Nash Prather entirely—which she couldn't afford to do, because, even though he insisted that Nash Prather wasn't real, he was real enough to belong to a glittery world that bore little resemblance to her own.

Claire felt the gentle touch of Nash's hand upon hers and glanced up. "Hey, where are you?"

She tried in vain to remember what he'd been talking about, some anecdote about him and Gary. She had only one option: to own up to the fact that she hadn't been listening.

"I'm sorry," she said. "I guess I wasn't listening."

Nash grinned. "Is my conversation that boring?"

"Oh, no," she countered. "I was just..." She trailed off as she realized the corner she was painting herself into.

"You were just what?"

It crossed Claire's mind to wonder if the color of Nash's eyes had grown more vivid, which seemed an impossibility, but they did appear somehow bigger or wider or more intense as they awaited her answer. Something in their turquoise clarity demanded she tell the truth.

"I was thinking how normal you really are," she said, trailing her finger over the stem of her wineglass.

Nash's lips curved into a mischievous grin. "You mean as in contrasted against abnormal?"

"No, I mean as in contrasted against...against..." The words eluded her.

"Homo starus?" he supplied.

Claire's look clearly said that she didn't understand what he meant.

"Homo starus is a species of man. You have, among others, *Homo erectus, Homo habilis, Homo sapiens, Homo starus.* We've evolved to the point that we walk erect and assume, on film, the identity of other *Homo sapiens."*

Claire smiled. "That's really rather clever."

Nash picked up his wineglass and lazily swirled the liquid within it. "Oh, we're a clever species. Or maybe we're not clever at all," he amended, as though he'd had a change of mind. "How clever can you be always living your life as someone else?"

"That's just it. You don't seem at all like Nash Prather. At least not the Nash Prather in the tabloids. You seem..." She tried to find just the right way to express what she was thinking. "You seem like any ordinary man."

For long seconds, Nash simply stared at Claire...as though surprised by what she'd said. When he spoke, Claire was certain that his voice had softened. She'd have guessed that it was barely audible to the human ear. "The truth is that sometimes even I don't know who, or what, I am. How come you can see what I can't?"

"I haven't seen it. I've heard it."

It was Nash's turn not to understand.

"Sometimes being able to hear hampers one's ability to listen. When I listen to you, I hear only a man."

Even as she watched, Nash's eyes darkened, shade by shade, hue by hue, until the color was one of... the word *sultriness* came to Claire's mind.

"I promise you I am a man, Claire. Who that man is, I may not always be certain, but I'm quite certain I *am* a man."

His statement was thoroughly provocative. As was his gaze, which dipped to her lips, where it lingered for the span of an erratic heartbeat—his and hers. A sense of déjà vu settled around Claire. She was reminded of being pinned between him and the pinball machine. As swiftly as lightning, she felt the same breathlessness, the same hollowness in her stomach, the same feeling that the world had turned upside down. Would she later be able to dismiss this feeling as she had before? Would she be able to convince herself that nothing had happened? And in fact, was anything happening? Was she simply imagining the look in his eyes? Had she simply misunderstood what he'd said about being a man?

"More lasagna?" he asked suddenly, casually.

His question landed her squarely back in the middle of reality. "No...no...it was delicious, but...no...." Did she sound as flustered as she felt?

"More wine?"

"No," she answered. "I've had enough." Quite possibly too much!

"Shall we?" he asked, indicating that they return to the living room since dinner was over.

Claire folded her napkin and stood. She could feel the feathery presence of Nash's hand at the small of her back. His hand seemed inordinately hot, like a fire passing too close. Smudge, who'd spent the meal napping near the sofa, looked up as the two entered the room. Claire stopped to scratch her behind the ears. There was something comforting in the familiar gesture—at least for Claire, whose world only moments before had seemed altogether foreign.

"How about watching a video?" Nash asked, going to Gary's extensive collection and browsing through it. It had been decided on the drive over that there'd be no talk about the play, although Claire sensed it wasn't far from Nash's mind.

"You'll have to interpret for me if I can't lipread."

Nash glanced up. "Did I just make a faux pas?"

Claire smiled. "Of course not. Deaf people watch movies."

"Then come choose something," Nash ordered. "How about *Top Gun* or *An Officer and a Gentleman* or—"

"How about *Sonora Sunset*?" Claire asked, plucking one of the videos from the rack.

At the mention of his latest film, Nash looked instantly uncomfortable. He hadn't even realized Gary had a copy.

"No, c'mon, let's watch—" Nash began, only to be cut off.

"Indulge me. I haven't seen any of your movies."

"Let's keep it that way. How about *Lethal Weapon*—"

Claire waved the video in her hand. She was uncertain why she was pushing so hard. Part of it had to do with plain curiosity—she wanted to see a Nash Prather movie. There was more to her insistence, though, and she knew it. She needed to remind herself just who this man was. For all that she'd said he was just like any other man, the fact remained that a part of him, a significant part of him, wasn't. A part of him belonged to Hollywood and scores of lusting female fans.

"You really want to see *Sonora Sunset?*" he asked, giving her one last chance to change her mind.

"I really want to see *Sonora Sunset.*"

On a deep, resigned sigh, Nash conceded.

Claire seated herself on the sofa in front of the fireplace. As the credits rolled at the beginning of the film, Nash started a fire, which sputtered to life before spewing its warmth around the room. Smudge stretched out only inches from the hearth, basking in the fire's soporific glow. Giving the dog a pat, Nash settled on the sofa and ran his arm along the sofa's back. He did not touch Claire, yet she was vividly aware of his nearness.

In reaction, she fitted herself into the far corner of the sofa and, removing her shoes, tucked her feet beneath her. "So what's the movie about?"

"Wait and see."

"C'mon, give me an idea."

"All the plots of the movies blur together. I'm not even sure what the plot is in this one."

Claire knew that couldn't be true, but she let it pass as she reached for the video box and read the summary paragraph. After she had, she laid the box once more on the coffee table and said, "It's about a guy—you—who sets out to prove that his buddy wasn't a traitor during the cold war with Russia. Now do you remember?"

"Vaguely," Nash answered.

Seconds into the movie, Nash appeared on the screen. When he did, Claire could hardly believe her eyes. She'd of course known that sooner or later he'd make an appearance—he *was* the star of the movie—but she was totally unprepared for his entrance. He filled the screen to emotional capacity with his dynamic presence. Claire turned to the man beside her. Had she not been so caught up in what she was feeling, she might have sensed that he was painfully waiting for her reaction.

"It's you," she said, as though just realizing he was indeed *the* Nash Prather.

"Who were you expecting? Mel Gibson?" Nash said, but his attempt at humor came across exactly like what it was—a feeble attempt.

"No, but... it's really you."

Nash was once more on the verge of explaining that the man on the screen wasn't him at all, when Claire rushed ahead with, "Quick, tell me what you're saying."

Nash translated what his character, dressed in a black leather jacket and looking meaner than a pack of wild wolves, was saying.

No sooner had he answered than she asked a dozen more questions. Who were the other actors? What was he saying now? Did Nash really do his own stunts? Were they dangerous?

In response to this last, he said, "I dislocated my shoulder when I threw myself on the hood of the car. After that, they brought in a stuntman. If you look real close, you can tell it isn't me."

"Like where?" Claire asked, totally caught up in the movie.

At her enthusiasm, Nash began to relax despite himself.

"Like there," he said minutes later, but she didn't see his lips move. He touched her arm, drawing her attention. "There," he repeated, freezing a frame of the film, "you can see where a double took my place."

Even though the stuntman's physique did remarkably resemble Nash's, there would have been no fooling Claire even if Nash hadn't pointed out the substitute. The stunt man simply did not have Nash's impressively wide shoulders.

Fifteen minutes into the movie, the woman playing opposite Nash, the woman who would eventually be his character's love interest, made her entrance. If Claire had been unprepared for Nash's appearance, she was doubly unprepared for this woman's. She was physically as beautiful as Nash was handsome, as fair as he was dark, with the blondest of blond hair and the palest of green eyes. She reminded Claire of sparkling sequins, of icing on a party cake or a frothy umbrella-decorated drink too pretty to consume. She also annoyed her. Greatly. It had something—okay, everything—to do with the way she was looking at Nash in

he movie . . . as though she were about to devour him
and make him love every minute of it.

"She's very pretty," Claire commented grudgingly,
tucking her feet even further beneath her.

Something in the tone of Claire's normally off-pitch
voice corralled Nash's attention, but then he told himself he'd just imagined it. "Yeah, she is."

"Who is she?" Claire asked casually, trying not to
show her sudden urge to punch out the starlet's lights.

"Kathleen Dumond."

Claire wondered if Nash had had an affair with this
Kathleen Dumond. The tabloids had him having af-
fairs with all his leading ladies. The question of
whether he'd had an affair offscreen was soon lost in
the realization that he was about to have an onscreen
affair with the woman. As Claire watched, Nash began to unbutton Kathleen Dumond's blouse. Claire
was torn between wanting to avert her eyes and not
being able to if her life had depended on it.

Nash was in no such way torn. He knew precisely
what he wanted. Or rather, what he didn't want. He
didn't want Claire seeing what was on the screen even
if it was make-believe.

Nash's mouth lowered to Kathleen Dumond's as her
blouse slithered over her Nordic-goddess shoulders and
onto the floor.

Claire's mouth went absolutely dry—primarily at the
prospect of what Kathleen Dumond must have felt
when Nash's lips had closed over hers. For all of
Claire's wild imaginings of late, she couldn't even begin to imagine what his lips would feel like.

Nash's mouth went absolutely dry, as well—primarily because he wished he could disintegrate on the
spot.

When the woman's tongue sensually sought Nash's, Claire's heart was instantly filled with an emotion she'd never experienced before—the urge to kill.

Nash just groaned.

Smudge looked up, as if to say "Hey, you're waking me here."

And then came the wench's—the word had just sprung to Claire's mind—unbuttoning of Nash's shirt. Before Claire could do more than swallow deeply, Nash's shirt fell open. A broad chest jumped into view, along with a dark thicket of hair.

Claire's reaction was instantaneous and unguarded. What would it feel like to run her hands through Nash's hair the way the woman on the screen was?

Nash's reaction came just as swiftly and was remarkably similar. What would it be like to feel Claire's fingers trailing through the hair on his chest?

Before either could arrive at an answer, Kathleen's skirt fell into a puddle at her feet, and Nash's jeans were unzipped by fingers with mile-long nails.

Oh, my! Claire thought.

Oh, hell! Nash thought.

Uh-oh, Smudge yawned.

And then it was happening—with the aid of a lot of camera trickery... or what Claire hoped was camera trickery—the couple, who'd fallen to the floor, were making wild, passionate love. For one brief, fleeting moment, Claire very clearly saw Nash's backside. It was just as perfect as the rest of him. So perfect was it that Claire was barely aware that Nash jumped from the sofa and fled into the kitchen. Claire would have fled, as well, but she was too mesmerized by the sight before her.

When she finally came to, as though she'd been knocked out for a while, she realized that the two lovers were clothed and having coffee . . . and that she was still alone. Walking into the kitchen, she found Nash making coffee. She knew that he must have heard her coming, but he didn't turn around, didn't acknowledge her entrance in any way. He just kept heaping coffee into the container.

What was he thinking? Feeling? And why had he left?

Nash had heard her walk in, but he didn't look up. He didn't want to see her face. He didn't want her to see his. And so he just kept heaping coffee as though heaping coffee were the most important task in the world. But obviously it wasn't. He felt an acute sense of embarrassment at Claire viewing the scene she just had, even though it was far from pornographic; actually, it was standard fare for a modern movie. He also felt angry at Hollywood all over again for the roles they had foisted on him. He also kept wondering what Claire was thinking. Was she censuring him, condemning him? And what in hell difference did it matter what she thought? Still avoiding her eyes, Nash jammed the container, now laden with enough coffee crystals to make even Juan Valdez caffeine crazy, into the coffeemaker.

"You left," Claire said.

Nash didn't look up. " . . . coffee," he mumbled.

"I can't read what you're saying."

Out of necessity, Nash glanced at Claire. Their gazes meshed, each trying to divine what the other was thinking. "I wanted to make some coffee," he repeated.

Claire nodded. "That sounds good."

Neither spoke, though they continued to stare. Claire could feel the awkwardness surrounding Nash. She wanted to say something to ease his discomfort, but didn't know what.

"The love scene was really very tastefully done," she said grudgingly, but found that she meant it, though she couldn't understand why she still felt this gut-raw ache. "It was really very pretty. I mean, you and she...you look good together."

Nash said nothing. He just continued to consider Claire.

Claire smiled—nervously. "I don't think I could ever perform something that intimate, though, with everyone watching.... I mean, with the cameramen and all." Her palms were suddenly damp again. The moisture had something to do with the concentrated way Nash was looking at her. "I mean, it looked so real...like it was really happening...like..." She stopped when she realized that she was rattling on. Why didn't he say something? Anything!

"It isn't real, Claire," Nash said, and she could tell he was speaking softly. "It's all good angles and wide shots and close-ups and finding everyone's best side. It's all doing it over and over and over until you think you'll scream if you have to do it one more time. You feel nothing because it's all pretend."

"But it looks real," Claire insisted.

"How something looks doesn't make it real," Nash said. "It's how it feels that makes it real."

Somewhere along the way, Nash had pushed from the opposite cabinet and walked slowly toward Claire. He now stood so near that, even though she wore heels, she had to tilt her head back to maintain eye contact. Curiously, her heart had begun to pound. It did even

more so when Nash reached out and brushed an ebony strand of hair from her cheek. He'd intended to
pull his hand away, but he couldn't. Instead, as though
it had every right, his hand splayed against her cheek.
Not to be denied, his other hand captured her other
cheek. Under the prompting of his thumbs, her head
angled upward . . . at the same time that his head began to lower.

He was going to kiss her. The realization spread like
wildfire through Claire's senses, through her body.
Some part of her insisted that this was Nash Prather.
Surely, Nash Prather wasn't about to kiss *her*. Another part of her said that Nash Prather or not, in seconds she would feel his mouth on hers.

He was going to kiss her. The realization rocked
through Nash with all the force of an earthquake.
Some part of him told him that he shouldn't be doing
this, that the last thing Claire needed was someone like
him in her life. Another part of him said that the whole
thing was beyond his control, that he'd wanted to kiss
her for what seemed like an eternity and that, God help
him, he was going to!

His mouth closed over hers. Warmly. Sweetly. With
all the delicacy of shadows slipping before the moon.
Claire felt that warmth, that sweetness. She felt as
though she were free-floating in the most beautiful of
moonlit skies.

Nash, too, felt the innate beauty of her lips pressed
against his. Never in his life had he felt such beauty,
such rightness, such realness. "This is real," he mur-
mured. "Not what was on the screen."

In her world of silence, all she felt was the patter of
his breath, his unsteady breath, against her lips. It was

all she needed to convince her of the kiss's authenticity.

Slowly, Nash raised his head. His hands remained at her cheeks, where his thumbs sensually circled her skin in a caressing motion. His gaze burned into hers.

"Gary said you broke up with someone several months ago," Nash said.

Claire was uncertain whether she was more surprised at this unexpected question, and it was a question, or at the fact he'd actually bothered to ask Gary about her private life. She thought it best not to consider the implications of the latter, for fear of reading too much into it.

"Yes," she answered. It crossed her mind to wonder about his past, but Claire found that she didn't have the courage to ask. She was frightened at what she might hear. But there was something she had to ask him, something she needed to have an answer to. "Are you as naughty as the press claims?"

Both thumbs stilled at Claire's cheeks. The unexpected question cut through Nash as sharply as though he'd been pierced by a rapier. He wanted to lie—God, he wanted to lie!—but he knew that he could not. Not to this woman.

"Yes," he answered roughly, even harshly. "In the past I've deserved everything that the press said about me. And possibly more. I'm not a saint, Claire. I'm jaded and cynical, and if you have any sense, you'll run like hell from me."

But she didn't run. In fact, with a brazenness that she could hardly believe, she tilted her head in a seductive invitation for him to kiss her again. Her invitation was more than Nash could resist. Moaning softly, he once more eased his mouth onto hers, even

as his body edged closer until he had her securely
pinned against the cabinet. This time the kiss was tentative, innocent, as though he had wiped the slate clean
and was starting over. This time both would have
sworn that they'd never kissed, nor been kissed, before.

CHAPTER EIGHT

FROM BACKSTAGE the following night, Claire watched as the audience rose to its feet for a standing ovation. Pride swelled deeply within her, filling her chest with a warm, glowing feeling. AmyAnn, standing onstage with the rest of the cast to receive their accolades, had been superb, magnificent, the clear hit of the play. The young woman was smiling as Claire had never seen her smile.

Nash, too, beamed with pride and pleasure as the audience demanded the playwright's appearance. Walking to the center of the stage, he waved an acknowledgment, then fell back to allow the performers the prominent place they deserved. He joined in the audience's applause, giving his own personal approval to the outstanding job the cast had done.

Claire kept her eyes trained on Nash. They hadn't spoken all evening, in fact not since he'd taken her home and kissed her good-night the night before. He'd spoken little even then. He'd simply kissed her again, as gently and tenderly as earlier, and silently disappeared into the dark. Tonight both of them had been too busy to speak, she with the scenery, he and Gary with a myriad of little chores. When Nash wasn't scurrying, he had seemed to pull into himself, to some safe haven where he wouldn't be hurt if the play was badly received. Claire had respected his privacy. Besides, she didn't really know what to say to him. Was he as baffled as she by what had happened between them?

No matter how many times she went over the evening before in her mind, she kept coming back to one thing: the man who'd kissed her was no ordinary man, however ordinary he'd seemed last night. There was no forgetting that he was a famous person. Or an infamous person, if the tabloids and Nash himself were to be believed.

I'm not a saint, Claire. I'm jaded and cynical, and if you have any sense, you'll run like hell from me.

She hadn't run, though, and she had no idea whether that was out of bravery or extreme foolhardiness.

With the final lowering of the curtain, the cast rushed offstage amid what Claire knew had to be a whirlwind of noise. Claire saw AmyAnn coming straight for her. The young woman threw herself into Claire's arms, almost crushing the breath from her.

Claire hugged her close, releasing her only to sign, "You were wonderful."

"I missed a cue." AmyAnn signed back.

"No one knew but you."

"Was I really okay?"

Claire smiled. "Okay? Are you kidding? You were wonderful!"

"What about the end of scene 3? Do you think I spoke loudly enough? What about—"

Her cheeks filled with apple-red enthusiasm, AmyAnn began her usual barrage of questions as she started for the dressing room, dragging Claire behind her. Claire gave one quick look over her shoulder, only to see a clutch of people swarming around Nash. Some she thought were press, who'd obviously learned that *the* Nash Prather was directing a play. She thought

Nash looked decidedly uncomfortable with their presence.

"The end of scene 3 was great," Claire assured, giving her full attention back to AmyAnn. She didn't see Nash glance toward her.

Nash heard the bulletlike questions being fired at him, or more to the point, he half heard them. The evening had been the scariest one of his life. He'd arrived at the theater long before curtain time, thinking that there was something he should be doing. But all he'd done was pace—back and forth, over and over—and worry. Oh, brother, had he worried! By the time the cast had arrived, he had thoroughly convinced himself that the play was a travesty of scriptwriting, with not a single scene, act or word to redeem it. By the time the curtain rose, he had further convinced himself that he was on the verge of making a complete fool of himself. He'd looked for Claire, but she'd arrived late, which he'd been glad of after he'd reached his hellish conclusions. Strangely, what he hated most was failing in front of her. Now, however, with the exhilaration of success pumping through his veins, Claire was the only one he wanted to share that exhilaration with.

But he couldn't. Not now, at least. Not with a hundred half-heard questions being hurled at him. Later, though. At the party. This promise was the only thing that got him through the madness of the next few minutes.

THE PARTY WAS HELD at the posh home of Benton and Sarah Brighton, a couple as charming as they were rich. Claire took in the beautiful surroundings and wondered if Nash's beach house was as grand and if he was as wealthy and when, if ever, she'd have a moment to

speak to him. Since arriving nearly an hour ago, she'd
still said nothing to him...simply because she couldn't
fight the crowd. The press had shown up at the party,
as had, seemingly, all of San Francisco. Even Smudge,
who wore a red kerchief to match Claire's elegant red
wool jersey jump suit, seemed intimidated by the crush
of people.

Claire bent and whispered a few words of assurance
in the dog's ear. Smudge thanked her by licking the
back of her hand. As Claire straightened, she glanced
around the room. Gary and Sharon, with whom she
and Smudge had ridden to the party, were standing in
a far corner. It seemed that Gary was spending—and
had spent—an inordinate amount of time with the
costume director. Was something going on there?
Claire hoped so. Gary was a great guy, and more and
more, Claire was getting to know and like Sharon Williams. On the other side of the room, Claire saw
AmyAnn decked out in a darling dress and the pretty
shoes they had bought together. Even at a distance
Claire could see the girl bubbling from all the praise
being bestowed upon her. She was not so lost in the
moment, however, that she still wasn't wary of Lance.
This Claire had sensed several times during the evening. AmyAnn was willing to be friends with the young
man, but not a thing more. This troubled Claire, as did
the question that kept roiling in her mind. What would
happen to AmyAnn once the play was over?

It was a question she didn't get to dwell upon, for at
that moment Peg Pannell stepped forward and signed,
"She's radiant."

Claire knew immediately whom she was talking
about. She knew, too, that Peg wouldn't have missed
AmyAnn's opening performance for anything in the

world. It was the kind of caring gesture Claire had seen all of the caseworkers involved in the Big Sister-Little Sister program display. All were more than willing to go that extra mile for the children in their care.

"Yes, she is radiant," Claire agreed.

"And her mother seems just as radiant," Peg said. Something in the look on Claire's face caused the woman to add, "You don't agree?"

"Yes. Sharon is pleased. There's no doubt about that. It's just..." Claire trailed off, remembering the conversation she'd had with Sharon Williams a short while before.

"It's just what?"

"I've sensed from the beginning that Sharon's having problems adjusting to AmyAnn's hearing loss. Earlier when I praised AmyAnn's performance, I had the feeling that, while Sharon was unquestionably proud, the success had only served to remind her of how the deafness had jeopardized AmyAnn's future. The woman is bitter, and I'm sure AmyAnn is picking up on that bitterness."

"What can we do about it?" Peg asked, as concerned as Claire.

"I don't know," Claire said reflectively, "but I do know that AmyAnn doesn't need that kind of negativity."

Nor did Claire need the negativity she herself began to feel as the party progressed. She wasn't exactly certain when the thought that Nash was avoiding her first came to mind. In truth, it didn't just plunge into her consciousness. It sort of slinked and slithered and slowly came to mind in scraps, like when the evening wore on and he didn't approach her, like when she never found him looking her way, like when she remembered that he had warned her about him. Maybe he truly was the womanizer he said he was. Maybe she was good enough to kiss in private but not good enough for him to be seen with in public. The thought hurt. Badly. It also made her angry at him and at her own gullibility.

When Claire felt the gentle tap on her shoulder, she was grateful for any distraction. She turned to find herself looking into the familiar face of Bill Gaensehal. It was the first time she'd seen him since they'd broken off their relationship some ten months ago.

"Bill!" she signed, her dark eyes glittering with surprise. "I had no idea you were here."

"I just arrived," he answered. "I brought some kids from school to see the play, and somewhere along the line we got invited to the opening night party."

Several thoughts passed rapidly through Claire's mind. One, that whoever had invited them knew the PR value of inviting deaf students to a party celebrating the success of a play partially dealing with deafness. Two, that Bill hadn't changed at all, that he still looked staid and dependable in his three-piece pinstripe. Three, that not one of this man's many kisses had ever made her feel the way Nash's kisses had.

"You look great," Bill signed, thankfully scattering this last unwanted thought of Claire's.

"Thanks. I'm well. How about you?"

"Can't complain. I've got a full schedule of classes at Fremont."

"I'm busy, too—classes and my painting and the play."

Bill's eyes rose toward the other side of the room. "I understand you all have had a celebrity directing this one."

At the reference to Nash, Claire's gaze settled once more on him. Dressed entirely in white, he was still surrounded by people. He was also still gorgeous. Claire felt her stomach flutter—just the way it had when he'd kissed her the night before, just the way it had when his virile body had pressed against hers. She smiled with as much nonchalance as she could muster, thinking that she was glad Bill wouldn't be hearing her voice. It would be sure to reveal her feelings.

"Yes," she signed, "he's a friend of Gary's."

From there, thankfully, their conversation moved into the realm of friends they had in common. Bill asked about her family, she asked about his...and tried not to look across the room.

Nash had wanted to speak with Claire a dozen times, but each time he'd started to, someone—usually a member of the press—had distracted him. In the end he'd decided it was best that the reporters didn't see him speaking to her. They had a way of smelling out a story with the barest of scents to follow, a way of linking him with someone based on speculation and wishful thinking. He didn't want Claire's privacy invaded. He also didn't want to speak to another reporter.

All in all, with his frustration mounting—he wanted to share the success of the play with Claire!—Nash knew he wasn't in the greatest of moods. Watching the exchange between the strange man and Claire—the smiles, the signing, the ease that existed between the two—wasn't improving that mood. He wasn't really certain which he disliked more—the signing that excluded everyone who didn't understand that specific

anguage, which most definitely included him, or the
private smiles. No, that wasn't true. He disliked the
miles more. They were the kind of communication
hat said these two people knew each other well. Just
how well? Nash wondered.

"Who's the guy?" Nash asked casually, at least as
casually as he could.

Gary, who'd sauntered over minutes before, glanced
up and followed the direction of his friend's gaze. "Bill
Gaensehal. He brought some of his deaf students up
from Fremont to see the play. I invited him to the party.
That, uh...that was all right, wasn't it?"

"Why shouldn't it be?" Nash asked, taking a drink
of champagne, which he hoped would quench the sudden fire-hot and very negative sensation that had
flamed within him at the mention of Claire's former
boyfriend. Somehow he'd known that was who the
man was.

"He's the one Claire used to go with."

"So?"

Gary fought the smile that wanted to jump to his
lips. "Well, they were a pretty hot and heavy item.
And, well, you did make her dinner."

Nash took another swallow of the chilled wine. He
knew Gary was good-naturedly baiting him, razzing
him, trying to see what his feelings for Claire were.
How could he tell him what he himself didn't know?
All he knew was that he didn't like the way he was
feeling—like the savage, primitive Mad Max he'd once
been accused of being, as if he'd feel a whole lot better
if he just punched out the stranger's lights!

"Dinner was just my way of saying thanks," Nash
repeated.

Gary's lips twitched despite his best efforts. "Yeah. Sure. Right. So, she does look pretty good in that red outfit, doesn't she? I mean, who could blame Gaensehal for maybe wanting to pick up where things left off? I always did think he was crazy about her."

The mention of the red outfit caused Nash's eyes to take in, for the thousandth time, what Claire was wearing. The fabric, sewn into a one-piece pants outfit with a bow on the left side of the waist, clung sexily to her every curve, while her hair, piled atop her head, threatened to tumble at any moment. The threat was extremely provocative. Nash rushed the drink back to his lips...and wondered what Claire and Bill were signing so intimately about.

Claire tried to keep up her end of the conversation, but her eyes kept darting across the room. She saw that Nash had been joined by Gary. What were they talking about, Nash with lips that moved so enticingly? Enticing. Why couldn't she forget just how enticing those lips could be? Why did their softness haunt her every waking moment? And would it hurt Nash to at least look in her direction? Even as this last question formed, she noticed that several members of the press gathered once more around Nash. Interestingly, Claire felt as though they shut her out, forcing her yet again to realize that her life was vastly different from Nash's. She felt angry—at the press for making her feel like an outsider, at Nash for ignoring her, at herself for caring.

Nash stole a quick glance across the room as he answered the reporters' questions. Through the years, he'd become skilled at fracturing his attention. Presently, though a part of his attention remained with the reporters, another part noticed Bill Gaensehal's laugh,

Claire's smile and the way the two of them kept signing as though there were no one else in the room, perhaps in the world. Once more Nash experienced that
shut-out feeling, as though the couple shared something that he could never be a part of. No matter how
much he tried, he could never really share Claire's
deafness. He felt angry—at the press for bugging him,
at Claire and Gaensehal for shutting him out, at himself for caring.

And then came the final straw.

Bill Gaensehal leaned forward and kissed Claire on
the cheek before walking away. Nash entertained vio-
lent thoughts. He also knew that he had to get rid of
the press or make a scene. He smiled the smile he was
so famous for, directing it at the only female reporter
in the group.

"This is the guy who had faith in the play. This is the
guy who really went out on a limb," Nash said, throwing Gary to the lions. "He's the one you ought to be
interviewing." With a "good ol' buddy" slap to Gary's
back, Nash excused himself.

Gary barely had time to do more than catch a quick
view of his friend crossing the room with what could
only be called purposefulness before the press descended. How long had he and Nash been friends?
When had he first learned of Nash's play? What did
Gary think of the play?

Claire watched Bill walk away. Even though she
knew she had done the right thing months before by
breaking up with him, she still experienced a wave of
longing. She wanted to belong to someone, she wanted
someone to belong to her, she wanted—

Suddenly, fingers curled around Claire's arm. Claire
jerked her head upward.

"Let's go," Nash said softly, directing her toward the nearest door. Claire was so stunned at his abrupt appearance that she didn't even protest. Neither did Smudge, who wagged her tail in grateful thanks that someone was at last taking her away from all the racket. "Do you have a wrap?" Nash asked.

"What?" Claire asked, aware that they were moving toward the front door. She was also aware that Nash seemed angry. But what did he have to be angry about? He's the one who'd ignored her!

"Do you have a wrap?" he repeated, looking her fully in the face so she could see his lips.

"Yes."

When she said nothing more, he asked in a voice she knew was exasperated, "You want to tell me what kind, or am I gonna have to guess?"

She felt her own temper rising several notches but controlled herself for the sake of the nearby servant. "A red-and-black paisley shawl."

The servant produced the black-fringed garment in seconds. Nash took it, draped it around Claire's shoulders, and marching across the vast foyer, Claire in tow, opened the front door. A velvet-thick fog rolled off the sea and across the San Franciscan landscape.

"Where are we going?" Claire demanded.

"Home," Nash answered.

"Don't you think it's a tad rude leaving without a word to the hostess?"

"Yes, but we're doing it anyway."

"I need to tell Gary—"

"He'll figure it out," Nash interrupted, yanking open the door of his sports car. At his urging, Claire eased inside, while Smudge, after her usual growl at the front tire, settled quite happily into the now familiar back seat. Without even thinking, Nash fitted the seat belt around the dog. In seconds, he sat beside Claire, revved the car to life and none too gently shoved it into gear. The car went from zero to seventy in a fast arc of the speedometer. Claire catapulted back against the seat, while Smudge's paws gripped the plush leather. A whine was frozen in the dog's throat.

"Are you crazy?" Claire shouted, her voice sounding unusually dissonant to Nash's ears.

"No, I'm angry!"

"What?"

"I'm angry!" he repeated, this time looking toward her.

"No joke! I never would have figured that out," she responded, adding angrily, "What in heck have you got to be angry about? I'm the one who should be angry!"

"*You* should be angry?" Nash shouted, though he realized that shouting with Claire was useless. She couldn't hear the tone of his voice. She couldn't hear his voice at all, which only reminded him of all the signing that she and Gaensehal had engaged in and how excluded he had felt.

"What did you say?" she asked. "And why are you shouting?"

"I like shouting!" he shouted, despite the futility.

"Will you look at me? I can't understand you."

Nash brought the car to an abrupt halt, partly because of the inanity of the conversation, partly because the fog prohibited the fast pace at which he was driving, partly because of Claire's demand. The second that he looked fully into her face, the second that his gaze lowered to her lips—lips he vividly recalled meshed with his—he realized just how difficult, if not downright impossible, it was to fight with Claire. Shoving his fingers through his hair, he gave a defeated sigh as he realized that her accusation had some validity. Maybe he was crazy.

"Is your van back at the theater?" he asked quietly.

"Yes. I rode with Gary." She knew from Nash's expression that he was no longer shouting. He also suddenly looked tired, as if the evening had taken an emotional toll. She longed to stretch out her hand and cradle his cheek. At the same time, his ignoring her still hurt. And what was he angry at her about? She glanced away. She suddenly felt as weary as Nash looked.

Nash eased the BMW forward, this time at a reasonable speed. Smudge whined a "thank you" and eased back into the seat. Her expression seemed to say that, for the life of her, she couldn't understand people.

Fog, as white and gossamer as the purest of clouds, swirled around the city, creating an ethereal wonderland. From the peaked hilltops, through the patchwork of fog, the bay looked like a sleeping black giant. Boats glittering with lights, like streaks from an artist's brush, bobbed in the glass-smooth water.

"Why are you—" Nash stopped and lightly touched Claire's arm. She turned toward him. "Why are you angry?"

Claire wished he'd asked anything but that. Minutes before, when tempers were raging, it would have been easy enough to answer the question. In fact, she'd longed to hurl an accusation at him. Now, her emotions more settled, she realized just how revealing that accusation was. The bottom line was that the accusation said she cared, that it mattered to her that he hadn't paid her any attention.

"It was nothing," she said, unwilling to lay herself so open to this man.

"No, you said you were angry. Why?"

"You said you were angry. Why?" she asked, putting the ball back in his court.

"Stop avoiding the issue."

"I'm not—"

"Claire...."

Something in the way he said her name, something in the way it tripped from his lips—like the gentle motion of a springtime breeze rustling the most fragile of wildfowers—tore down her resistance. She could not refuse him, not when her name looked so pretty on his lips.

"I was angry—" She glanced away, once more to stare straight ahead. "I was angry because you ignored me all evening." The moment it was said, Claire wished that she could take back the words. It was as if she had stripped herself naked emotionally, and she didn't like the feeling. She particularly wished she'd said nothing when silent second after silent second passed away. At long last, Nash's fingers hooked her chin and turned her head to him.

"Is that what you think? That I ignored you?" Claire said nothing. Pain flashed across Nash's face and he released her chin. "You honestly thought that last night meant so little that I'd willingly ignore you the next time I saw you?"

"I—I didn't know what to think." She longed to ask him exactly what last night had meant—to him, to her.

Claire could see him swallow, as though what she'd said was bitter and difficult to get down. She knew that she had hurt him. That fact hurt her.

"You're right. At least in part," he said finally, glancing over to see if she'd understood him. She hadn't, so he repeated what he'd said, adding, "I did purposely stay away from you, but I didn't ignore you."

"I don't understand the difference."

"You saw the press, Claire. Do you have any idea what they'd print if they even suspected that we..." He didn't know how to finish, because he didn't know how to define their relationship, because he didn't know what *was* happening between them. "They'd have been all over you like ants on honey. How would you like to be on the cover of next week's *People in the News*?" When she didn't answer, he said, "I couldn't let that happen to you."

"You couldn't have even spoken?" she asked, touched, even humbled by his protectiveness, but still very much aware of how long and lonely the evening had been.

"No," he said, and quite decisively. "I couldn't trust myself not to give anything away."

Claire knew that his voice had lowered, just as clearly as she knew that his eyes had darkened. She knew, too, that she suddenly felt as if all the air had been sucked from the surface of the earth. That feeling only increased when she saw his gaze lower to her lips. It stayed there only a fraction of a second, for necessity demanded he return his attention to driving. It was long enough, though, to make her want his lips on hers more than she wanted another breath.

For a while neither spoke. Nash negotiated the car through the fog-soaked streets, finally entering the section of town where the theater was situated. They would be there in only minutes. Claire suddenly realized that she still had no idea why Nash had been angry.

"Why were you angry?" she asked.

Nash glanced over at her. "I was ticked off with the way the press monopolized my time. I was ticked off with wanting to speak to you but being unable to. I'd wanted to share the play's success with you. I was ticked off with..." He stopped, weighing if he wanted to tell the truth. After all, the truth would expose him to this woman. But hadn't he already exposed himself to her? Hadn't the kisses they'd shared been like none he'd ever experienced before? He heard himself say, "I was ticked off with Bill Gaensehal."

Bill's name on Nash's lips startled her. She hadn't been expecting it. And she didn't understand it. Why should he be angry with Bill?

"Why?" she asked, aware that Nash had pulled into the theater parking lot alongside her van. Security lights burned, giving a hushed glow to the car's interior.

Nash shut the engine and angled his body toward Claire. His thigh brushed against hers. Powerful volts of emotion passed through both Claire and Nash.

"How do you sign *jealous?*" Nash asked.

The question took Claire by surprise. But she complied by folding her hand into a fist except for an extended little finger. This she placed at the corner of her mouth and twisted it, bringing her fist forward.

Nash repeated the gesture, saying, "I was jealous." Jealous.

Claire could hardly believe what she was seeing. Why in the world would Nash be jealous of Bill? Except if... She could not finish the thought.

"I felt like an outsider," Nash said.

"An outsider?" Claire repeated.

"Yes. The two of you were signing. I couldn't understand a thing you were saying. I felt angry at that exclusion, angry because I couldn't share your non-hearing world."

"That's—" She started to say that what he had said was ridiculous, but the truth was that she could understand the feeling perfectly. "I know," she said instead. "I felt the same with the press. They made me feel like an outsider. I'm not a part of your world, either."

Nash considered what she'd said, then, slowly running his arm along the back of the seat, he said, "You're right. You're not a part of my world. I'm not a part of yours. But then—" Claire sensed his voice had lowered again; she could also feel his finger drawing tiny, sexy designs on her fabric-covered arm "—maybe that's not so important. Maybe only one thing is important."

"Like what?" she asked, barely able to mouth the words for the sensations rampaging through her.

"Oh," he said, dallying with a coil of her hair that had jumped from its loosely regimented confines, "like creating our own world. Could we do that, Claire? Could we create our own world, where my being famous and your being deaf didn't matter a tinker's damn?"

"H-how could we do that?"

"Right now, it seems very simple," he replied, drawing his crooked finger along the side of her cheek...down...down...down...until it toyed with the corner of her mouth. With a maddening lack of haste, he rubbed his finger across her full bottom lip. The rush of her breath fanned against his hand. Nash moaned and whispered, "Oh, yes, it would be so simple."

"Simple...." Claire repeated, unaware that she, too, moaned.

Her moan was Nash's undoing. Slowly, but with more intent than he'd ever done anything, he lowered his mouth to hers, replacing his finger with his lips. At the same time, he pulled her into his arms.

Claire felt the sweet pressure of his arms and the sweeter pressure of his mouth. Had it been only twenty-four hours since they'd kissed? It seemed like forever. How was it possible to miss something, someone, so much in such a short time? Some part of her logical self asked if she was getting in too deep. Another part said she'd worry about that later. Now she simply wanted, needed, his kiss. Now, she simply wanted, needed, this exquisite and private world he was offering her.

Opening her mouth to the insistence of his, Claire felt his tongue tenderly probe, then gingerly penetrate. She let it; she even encouraged it. As it curled sensuously with hers, Claire thought she would die from the heat swelling within her. Somewhere flashed the memory of the movie they'd watched the evening before. The actress playing opposite Nash had made love to him with her tongue. That in mind, Claire took the initiative, sending her tongue to dance with his—tentatively at first, then more boldly.

Nash groaned and let Claire take the lead. After too many pleasing minutes, however, he wrenched his mouth away. He rested his forehead against hers. His breath, uneven, unsteady, beat a wild tattoo upon her lips.

"Nash?" she whispered.

Nash heard the plea in her voice, the plea to somehow explain what was happening between them. But he didn't know what was happening. He knew only that what was happening had never happened to him before, which perhaps explained his lack of reference.

"Sh," he whispered, threading her now love-mussed hair from her face and unhurriedly rolling his mouth back onto hers.

Both were aware that what seemed so simple tonight might seem inordinately complex by the light of day. Both were equally aware, though, that tonight it didn't matter. Tonight they were lost in their own lover's world.

CHAPTER NINE

`TWO WEEKS LATER, the play ended as it had begun—to have reviews. Afterward, Nash treated everyone—the cast, the crew, anyone who'd had even the smallest part in the play's production—to a late dinner. There were toasts and laughter and giggles galore, all adding to a gaiety that rose in volume until it was a wonder they weren't thrown out of the restaurant. Claire laughed, too, though she was keenly aware that, for the most part, her merriment was fake. No matter how much she tried to forget it, she knew that Nash was leaving bright and early the next morning for his home in Malibu. Was their whirlwind courtship about to end? Neither had spoken of the future. Both had lived only for the precious moments they had shared.

That night, Nash drove her home amid a thick silence. Even Smudge seemed aware that something out of the ordinary was in the air, for she sat quietly in the back seat of the BMW, her attention alternating between the driver and the woman beside him. Later, still without speaking, Nash walked Claire to the door, stepped inside the house and immediately, as though propelled by desperation, pulled her into his arms. He kissed her passionately, gently. He kissed her in every way, in every sweet angle and wild degree, that a man can kiss a woman.

When both were breathless, when Claire's hair had fallen victim to his ravaging fingers, he whispered, "I'll be in touch."

And then he left—wordlessly, without looking back, with nothing for Claire to cling to but his promise. And cling to it she did, as she undressed and climbed into bed. She tried to sleep, but sleep was an elusive shadow that hid behind a thousand memories: warm memories, hot memories, memories that simply would not settle down. She thought of Nash's lips, she thought of Nash's arms, she thought of the way Nash's body felt pressed against hers. Somewhere around three o'clock, having not had a minute's sleep, she thought herself the most consummate of fools.

How stupid could one adult woman be? She was acting like a besotted teenager mooning over a movie star. She couldn't honestly believe, regardless of what she and Nash had shared for two weeks, that he was going to go home and pine over her. She'd be lucky if he gave her a second thought. By his own admission, he was no stranger to the ladies.

And yet...

And yet what? And yet, the truth was that she would swear that what had happened between them—just what that something was she wasn't able to say—had been real, genuine, something felt equally by Nash. Surely she couldn't have misjudged that. Could she?

At dawn, she had to admit that maybe the key to the whole thing lay in the fact that, during Nash's stay in San Francisco, he'd played hooky from being Nash Prather. Maybe the key was that she'd shared something with Vincent Pratatorri. Where, then, did that leave her? Exactly nowhere, she concluded as the first rays of the sun burned across the morning sky, for

Vincent Pratatorri had once more assumed the persona of Nash Prather.

And just how likely was it, she thought as she crawled from the rumpled bed and put coffee on to perk, that Nash Prather would ever again come into her life? She figured the odds lay somewhere between "Don't count on it, sister" and "Yeah, sure, dream on, baby."

She heard nothing from him on Monday... or Tuesday. She told herself that it didn't matter, that it was nothing more than she expected, yet she found herself rushing home on Wednesday, hoping beyond hope that maybe a letter awaited her. None did, however. Her mailbox was as empty as her heart. Thursday, she played it cool despite the restlessness building inside her. Not only didn't she rush home, but she didn't even check the mailbox. Instead, she busied herself with painting... or tried to. When it became obvious that her mind wasn't on what she was doing, she threw up her hands and looked in the mailbox. Nothing. There was nothing there—just as she knew there would be. Having it confirmed, though, sent her to the depths of despair. How could he just walk out of her life without a backward glance after what they'd shared? Easily. Obviously, he could walk out easily.

On Friday, she chanced to run into Gary, who innocently mentioned having spoken to Nash. She waited for Gary to pass on a message to her. She would have settled for Nash instructing his friend to tell her anything: Hello; Hope you're well; See you soon; Go to hell! Anything! At this point she would have settled for anything. She got nothing, however. Her spirits plummeting, she told herself that she had to pull herself together. She had to forget Nash Prather, because it was patently obvious that he'd forgotten her.

If she'd had any say in the matter, Claire thought the next day, she would have chosen a diversion other than AmyAnn's regression, but nonetheless she was relieved to have anything to take her mind off Nash. Just as Claire had feared would happen following the play, AmyAnn slipped back into her solitary, silent world. Oh, not entirely back, but far enough back to cause Claire some concern. Once AmyAnn could no longer hide behind the character of Lindy Boyd, fear and insecurity, anger and bitterness once more claimed her. Claire had to nip the regression in the bud. She did so by playing in a totally unfair manner.

"You're angry with me," Claire said as she and AmyAnn sat across from each other in a small restaurant en route from Fremont to San Francisco. They had stopped for pie and coffee...or in AmyAnn's case, for pie and milk.

These were the first words that had been exchanged since they'd left the riveting performance of *My Fair Lady* nearly forty-five minutes before. The play had been staged at the California School for the Deaf by members of the prestigious National Theater of the Deaf. Claire had taken AmyAnn with no forewarning, simply because she remembered the young woman's initial and adversarial reaction to the deaf theater.

"Yes," AmyAnn signed, "I'm angry." The word *angry* was hurled from her fingers in sharp, curt gestures.

"Would you have agreed to go with me if I'd told you where we were going?"

"No," AmyAnn said flatly.

"Then I didn't have a choice, did I?"

AmyAnn said nothing. She simply let her silence speak for her.

Despite her sullen attitude, Claire knew that the young woman had enjoyed herself. There had been too many times when AmyAnn had been lost within the play, totally absorbed by the characters signing dialogue and song. Though she would never have admitted it, she had even enjoyed seeing a couple of the deaf kids who'd come to see *Two Queens and the King of Burwick*. With them she wasn't different...except that she didn't sign as well as they.

"I had trouble following the play," AmyAnn volunteered, surprising Claire with the unsolicited comment. Claire knew that she referred to the sign language used throughout. She felt AmyAnn's frustration. The young woman might resent sign language, but nonetheless she was smart enough to see that she was excluded without it. Though still far from perfect, her skills in signing and lipreading were increasing by quantum leaps.

"That's understandable," Claire said, though she could tell that AmyAnn hadn't read this last word. "Understandable," she repeated. This time, AmyAnn nodded. "You can't become proficient overnight. It takes time."

Again, AmyAnn said nothing, but Claire could see, could sense, her impatience.

Another silence passed as each finished her wedge of pie. A light rain began to fall, dotting the window of the restaurant. Reacting to the rain as always, Smudge whined.

AmyAnn, too, watched the rain. In her mind she heard the gentle pitter-patter. But only in her mind.

Pensively, she said, "Sometimes I wish I were like you. Sometimes I wish I'd never been able to hear."

The statement was provocative, leaving Claire to ask, "Why?"

"Then I wouldn't know what I was missing."

It was a question debated often among deaf people: was or wasn't it better to have ever heard? Its answer lay in the heart of who was asking the question.

"There may be some truth to that," Claire conceded, "but, personally, I think you have the advantage." Before AmyAnn could respond, Claire said, "At least you have the memory of what falling rain sounds like. At least you remember what your mother's voice sounds like. You know the sound of the wind, the sound of a dog barking, the sound of a baby crying. These are things that I can only imagine."

Intrigued, AmyAnn asked, "How do you imagine sounds?"

Claire grinned. "I imagine them visually—as colors."

AmyAnn grinned, the act once more emphasizing her youth. It was a youth that too often got lost in her adult-size problems. "Yeah? Then what color is rain?"

"Depends." Claire said, sipping the last of her coffee.

"On what?"

"On how hard it's falling. This rain is baby blue. If it were falling hard, it would be an azure blue. A storm is indigo. It also depends on other factors," she added, spurred on by AmyAnn's obvious interest. "A winter rain is ice blue, but a spring rain is turquoise—a blend of blue and green, or water and wind." *The color of Nash's eyes.* The thought came from nowhere, leaving Claire startled that it had crept up on her so silently... and that it left so much damage in its wake. She willfully ignored the pain in her heart and focused on what AmyAnn was saying.

"Wind is green?"

"Uh-huh," Claire said as the hurt dulled slightly.

"Why?"

"I guess because I think of it moving over the earth, blowing the grass, swaying the leaves of the trees." Claire shrugged. "I'm not sure exactly how I decided on the colors.... Most of the decisions were made when I was a child."

"Were you scared?"

The question came quickly, unexpectedly, straight from AmyAnn's tormented soul. Claire had the strong urge to pull the child-woman into her arms and tell her that everything would eventually be better. At some point, life would stop being bleak and would again be beautiful. Instead, she answered simply, "No, I wasn't afraid. But then I didn't know to be. Being deaf seemed normal to me. In many ways, it still does."

Another silence descended. The rain changed tempo, slipping from baby blue to azure. Claire watched as AmyAnn stared at the changing scene. The young woman seemed lost somewhere between a tomorrow she couldn't envision and a yesterday she couldn't return to. It left her square in the middle of a today she didn't know how to cope with.

"Are you afraid?" Claire asked, daring the intimate question, praying that AmyAnn would trust her enough to answer it truthfully.

AmyAnn's doe-brown eyes hazed with pain. Her mouth moved to form, "Sometimes." It sat on her lips with all the hesitancy of a newly freed prisoner, which, in truth, it was. AmyAnn had just released the admission from the place deep within her where she had kept it captive. While it was chained and bound, she didn't have to confront it. Now she did. Claire could see the ensuing struggle.

Claire smiled gently. "Sometimes just saying you're afraid helps."

For a brief second, AmyAnn didn't respond, but then she surprised Claire with a tiny smile of her own. "And then again, sometimes it doesn't."

Claire's smile widened, then began to fade slowly. There was one other question she wanted to ask. "Is fear what's keeping you from going out with Lance?" Claire knew that the young man had asked AmyAnn out a couple of times since the play had ended. She knew, too, that AmyAnn continued to reject him.

AmyAnn shrugged. "I guess." Before Claire could speak, AmyAnn said, "I know, I know, he isn't Curt."

"No, he isn't. And it isn't fair to Lance to make him pay for Curt's mistakes."

"I know, but..." AmyAnn stopped, sighed and threaded her fingers through her honey-blond curls.

"But what?"

"You're always so sure of yourself," AmyAnn said, and Claire could tell that her young friend envied her self-assurance. Claire just wished she had the confidence AmyAnn thought she did. For the most part, she guessed she *was* sure of herself—everyone seemed to think she was—but sometimes of late, when it came to Nash... The truth was that she wasn't too sure of anything where Nash was concerned. She wasn't sure what she was feeling. She wasn't sure just how deeply she'd gotten involved. The only thing she was sure of was that it had been a big mistake, as in colossally foolish, to have allowed herself to get involved with Nash on any level.

"Sometimes when I look in the mirror, I look so plain, like some part of me is missing."

Claire forced her attention back to what AmyAnn was saying. "Being deaf," she signed gently, "has nothing to do with one's attractiveness. You're still as pretty as you ever were."

"I don't feel pretty."

"But you are...and I'll bet money that Lance thinks so, too."

"Maybe he only feels sorry for me."

"Do you feel sorry for me?"

"No, but—"

"Then why should he feel sorry for you?"

AmyAnn shrugged.

"Look," Claire said, "deaf people have no more or no fewer guarantees in life than hearing people. The truth is that you and Lance may not make it as a couple any more than you and Curt did, but it won't have anything to do with your inability to hear."

Because what she'd said had been so long, because she wanted AmyAnn to understand what she was saying, she repeated this last. Or then, maybe she repeated it because she herself needed to be reminded of it again. Maybe she needed to affirm that Nash's not getting in touch as he'd promised had nothing to do with her being deaf. That she needed the reassurance troubled her a little. She could never remember needing that kind of reassurance before.

AmyAnn's comment was "You don't understand."

"Try me."

Fidgeting with the remains of the piecrust with her fork, AmyAnn hesitated. "It's just..."

"It's just what?"

"Even though Curt's older than me, he..." She shrugged again. "I don't know. Sometimes he could act like such a kid, but Lance...I mean, he's eighteen—almost nineteen. He's...he's a man."

Claire hid her grin. "You're a young woman. So what's the problem?"

"He makes me feel...confused. He makes me feel— I don't know—all quivery inside."

Amid everything else, Claire realized that AmyAnn was experiencing a sexual awakening. That was always an unsettling time in a young adult's life. AmyAnn's awakening was compounded by the fight she was waging to adjust to her disability. Claire laid her hand across AmyAnn's. "Believe me, everything you're feeling is normal. And no one's ever died from growing up."

AmyAnn gave a half smile.

Claire used the good-mood moment to say, "Promise me you'll go out with Lance just once."

AmyAnn hedged.

"Okay," Claire amended, "promise me you'll think about going out with him."

AmyAnn still hedged.

"Being deaf is one thing—being a coward is another," Claire said, repeating what she'd said once before.

"All right, all right!" AmyAnn agreed. "I'll think about it."

"Good," Claire said, pushing back her chair and picking up the check. "Now I can take you home."

AmyAnn laughed.

Later that night, unable to sleep, Claire realized that young womanhood didn't have the market on confu-

sion . . . not when it came to the opposite sex. Climbing the stairs to her darkened studio, her gown flapping
at her ankles, she sat on the floor and gazed up at the
stars peeking through the remnants of the gauzy
clouds. Trusting Smudge coiled into a ball by her side.

She missed Nash, Claire admitted. The foolhardiness of it taken into consideration, she still missed him.
She'd give anything she owned to see him again. She'd
give anything she owned to talk to him once more.
She'd give anything she owned for one taste, one sip of
his sexy mouth.

THE FOLLOWING WEEK, with still no word from
Nash—had she really expected this week to be different?—Claire threw herself into her work. She still had
several pieces to complete before her Dallas showing,
which was scheduled for the weekend. Plans included
an overnight appearance in Dallas for her to meet and
greet the public. Despite the excitement of having her
own show, she wished that the event could have been
better timed. Or, more to the point, she wished that
she'd never met Nash Prather. No, that wasn't true. No
matter how badly she hurt, she couldn't bring herself
to wish they hadn't met.

In a perversity that she made no attempt to explain,
she stopped by a video store on Thursday afternoon
and rented several of Nash's movies. She then came
home and played them. Though she couldn't follow all
the dialogue, it made little difference, for all she really
did was watch Nash. Every gesture was heartbreak-
ingly familiar—every tilt of his head, every quirk of his
lip, every lithe sway of his hips as he walked. When he
pulled the actresses into his arms and kissed them, it

was Claire who felt the pressure of his lips, the embrace of his arms.

She also felt a sadness…and a restlessness that drove her upstairs to her studio. For all of her life, painting had been therapy, a way of expressing that which she could express in no other way. Tonight was no exception. As she began to paint, she lost herself to the bold strokes and bright colors. She also lost all account of time. Somewhere near morning, completely exhausted, she tumbled into bed and fell into a deep, though troubled, sleep.

In a prearranged meeting the next day, an early spring Friday, Peg Pannell said, "You look awful."

Claire, who'd had no more than a couple of hours sleep, directed her bleary eyes toward her friend and replied, "Gee, thanks."

Despite the long night—and the very long week— she'd fulfilled her university obligations, partially packed for the flight later that evening and shipped her last paintings, the paint barely dry, to Dallas by overnight express for the Saturday showing. She'd then made a mad dash to keep her regularly scheduled Big Sister-Little Sister appointment. Even so, she'd been late. She'd been relieved to discover that Peg had gone ahead and met with AmyAnn. The three of them had then had their usual session together, and now, AmyAnn having been dismissed, Claire was meeting privately with the caseworker…that was, if she could stay awake, or more importantly, if she could keep her mind focused.

"You're working too hard," Peg said.

Claire stood, walked to the window of Peg's Mason Street office and stared out at the lavender-tinted sky. Smudge raised her head, as if trying to decide whether to follow her mistress, then settled back down. Nope, the canine seemed to say, she'd just stay put. It had been a busy day and she was dog tired.

"Once the show is over, I'll have time to rest," Claire said. *And maybe even have time to forget one tall, tanned, incredibly handsome man who walked into and out of my life with all the speed of a whirlwind and with all the brilliance of starlight.*

When Claire turned and started back for her chair, Peg said, "I hope the show's a huge success."

Claire smiled. "Thanks."

"So," Peg asked, getting down to business, "how do you think AmyAnn is doing?"

The next few minutes were spent discussing the young woman.

"All in all," Claire concluded, "I think she's right about where she should be. She lost a little ground following the play, but it was nothing I wasn't expecting. Her signing and lipreading skills are improving tremendously."

"Did she tell you about her friends?" Peg consulted her notes. "Candace and Leah?"

"No," Claire said, clearly intrigued. She hadn't seen AmyAnn, except for just minutes before, since the previous weekend when they'd gone to Fremont. A cold had kept AmyAnn in bed for a couple of days, and she had postponed their usual weekly outing.

"Apparently they decided they wanted to learn to sign and are attending the sign language classes with AmyAnn. In fact, the school is giving them a credit for a foreign language."

"Fantastic!" Claire signed. The first and only time she'd met AmyAnn's two friends, Claire had sensed their awkwardness with AmyAnn's deafness, but she'd equally sensed their caring. Plus, Claire knew that it had been they who'd told AmyAnn about Curt's betrayal. That was not only an act of courage but also an act of friendship. Claire hoped their friendship would give AmyAnn the courage she needed in at least one area. "Has AmyAnn said anything about allowing an interpreter in the classroom?"

Peg sighed. "I tried to ask her that today but was cut off with the statement that she didn't need one."

Claire, too, sighed. "If I could just get her back into some sort of normal social life, I think she would begin to concentrate on how alike other people she is rather than on how different she is. Also, I need to find some way to make her mother believe this."

"AmyAnn said her mother is seeing your friend Gary."

"Yeah, I think so. Were you able to get a handle on how AmyAnn feels about their dating?"

"She seems pleased. I think she likes Gary. And, I agree with you. I think AmyAnn feels guilty about the financial burden her illness placed her mother under. At this point, anything that makes her mother happy makes AmyAnn happy."

Claire nodded in agreement, though her mind had begun to wander. There was still so much to do. She still had to finish packing, and her plane left for Dallas at 9:38. That was less than four hours away. That—

"AmyAnn says that you've been holding out on me."

It wasn't so much what Peg said that ensnared Claire's attention as the sudden impish look that sprang to the caseworker's face. The serious discussion was definitely over.

"Holding out on you? What to you mean?"

Peg stood—all four feet ten inches of her—and
rounded the desk. "AmyAnn says you're dating Nash
Prather."

At the mention of the name that had never been far
from Claire's mind these two weeks, dark ribbons of
sensation knotted in her stomach. Her face grew warm
with feeling. "That's . . . that's ridiculous."

"AmyAnn says the two of you were seeing each
other while he was here," Peg persisted.

"Well, of course we saw each other. We were involved in the same play."

"And that's all?" Before Claire could answer, Peg
rushed forward with, "For heaven's sake, don't deny
me the vicarious thrill of a lifetime!"

"Sorry to disappoint you, but Nash Prather and I
were . . . just friends."

Claire wasn't sure that the word truly applied.
Hadn't the breathless kisses made them something
more? No matter, it wasn't the clarification of their
relationship that was at issue, but rather the temporal
status of it, and that she'd eloquently expressed in the
past tense of the verb. She and Nash *had been* friends,
the implication being that whatever had existed between them was over.

Over, as in never again.

Over, as in Nash had forgotten her.

Over, as in she wished she could forget him, too.

DALLAS WAS LOVELY, the art gallery was impressive,
and the people—both those sponsoring her exhibition
and the public in attendance—were gracious and hos-
pitably warm. Claire would have willingly forfeited the
commission on any one of her paintings to be back in
San Francisco. Failing that, she'd simply settle for

someplace where she could be alone, someplace where she didn't have to wear a false smile.

She'd flown into Dallas late the evening before and had spent another sleepless night. She'd simply been overtired and too nervous—what if no one showed up for her show?—to sleep. Come morning, she'd been given a royal tour of the city, wined and dined, then brought to the gallery, where, much to Claire's surprise and delight, patrons were already awaiting her arrival. She'd sold many pieces of art, all of which she'd personally signed, all of which the purchasers agreed to leave hanging for the duration of the exhibition, which ended the next day, although Claire would fly back to San Francisco later that night.

Careful not to let the woman talking to her notice, Claire checked the watch at her wrist—seven-thirty—as she shifted from one foot to another. She probably shouldn't have worn such high heels. Her feet were killing her, and she had an hour and a half to go. Even Smudge, ever faithfully beside her, appeared tired.

" . . . so unique . . . so spirited . . . so . . ."

Despite the fact that she longed to be elsewhere, Claire was pleased with the reception her work was given. This show was the culmination of many years of hard work. From the very beginning, her style had been different, a new way of looking at spatiality. In what one critic had labeled a spatial genesis, image flowed into image—tress grew from the sky while clouds floated near the ground. Claire had often thought that sign language had been the basis for her unusual spatial concepts. After all, sign language was spoken in space. From the beginning of her life, there had been no sound, just an acute visual awareness, just an acute awareness of images.

Yes, she was achieving the success she'd longed for and worked for. Why then did that success feel emptier than she'd expected? Why would it have seemed fuller, richer if there'd been someone to share it with?

Someone like Nash? Claire chased the unbidden thought away.

"Thank you," she said in answer to the woman's profuse praise.

No sooner had the woman stepped away than a man approached.

"Ms. Rushing, I can't tell you how much I admire your work," he said.

"Thank you."

"...bold color...the piece on the end..."

As the man continued, Claire noticed that Smudge rose from her haunches and, her tail wagging in greeting, moved off. Claire supposed the dog spotted her agent, who'd insisted on flying in from New York for the occasion. She forced her attention back to the man speaking and smiled.

Seconds passed.

Her feet were killing her!

Only an hour and a quarter to go.

Only...

Out of the corner of her eye, Claire saw Smudge. She was with a man. The man was squatting, petting the animal. The animal was lapping up the loving. Two thoughts crossed Claire's mind. One, the man was not her agent. Two, though the man's head was lowered, there was something familiar about the set of his shoulders.

Claire's heart stopped.

At the same time, she told herself that she was only imagining that familiarity. And then the man stood, glanced around the room and singled out Claire. He started toward her.

Claire's heart went wild.

One might mistake a lot of things in life—shiny fool's gold for the real thing, rhinestones for diamonds—but there was no mistaking those bluer than blue eyes. They could belong only to one man.

Nash Prather.

CHAPTER TEN

FOR CLAIRE, the world was reduced to a pure, con-centrated visuality—the rhythmic sway of lean hips, the copper-colored bronze of sun-perfect skin, the color white, for Nash wore white pleated slacks and a white shirt that lay open at the throat. At his waist, a slender tobacco-colored belt was threaded through the loops, while the same color loafers encased his feet. He wore no socks. The overall impression he gave, or so Claire thought, was one of casual sensuality. She also thought that her heart was going to pound out of her chest, or perhaps she was just going to faint.

Sweet heaven, don't let this be a dream! she pleaded, astonished, and afraid, that she could miss someone so much. When had this man become so important to her? And how odd that she had to see him again to re-alize the full impact his absence had had on her. She'd known all along that she'd missed him, but she now wondered how she would have survived had she not seen him again.

For Nash, the world had become similarly visual—a black pair of men's trousers sculpting shapely femi-nine hips, a white satin blouse rising high at the neck in a prim Victorian collar, hair piled in a haphazard fashion. The impression she gave was one of consum-mate femininity and a downright sexiness that blasted all coherent thought from Nash's mind.

Sweet heaven, how I've missed her! he thought. All at once he realized how starved he'd been for the sight of her. He hoped to God he wasn't about to do something embarrassing like pull her into his arms and kiss her in front of all these people. To guarantee that he didn't, he ran his hands into his pants pockets.

"Hi," Nash said.

"Hi," Claire breathed.

The world seemed to spin far, far away, leaving only the two of them to stand alone on the shores of their own private universe. Suddenly, Claire recovered her senses enough to realize how rude she was being to the man who'd been so generously praising her work.

"I'm sorry," she said, turning to the gentleman, "this is—"

"Vincent Pratatorri," Nash interrupted, removing his hand from his pocket and politely extending it.

The man introduced himself. "Say, did anyone ever tell you that you look like—"

"All the time," Nash interrupted with an easy, innocent grin.

A few more pleasantries were exchanged before the man, still praising Claire's talent, moved away. His departure left Claire and Nash alone.

Nash's gaze roamed over Claire's face. *God, she's beautiful! More beautiful than I'd even remembered!* He felt his fingers fidgeting in his pockets, itching for the feel of her. He forcefully stilled them.

Claire's gaze feasted on Nash, though a part of her remembered vividly how painful the silence of the past two weeks had been. Why hadn't he gotten in touch? Or was showing up two weeks later his idea of keeping in touch? Whatever the answers, she was aware of wanting him to touch her. She was aware of wanting to touch him. She cupped one hand over the other and held tight.

"I know," he said softly. "You thought I'd handed you some glib, practiced line."

Startled that he'd read her mind so clearly, Claire blurted out exactly what she felt. "What was I supposed to think?"

He nodded—sarcastically. "Right. After all, I *am* Naughty Nash Prather. Love 'em and leave 'em and score faster than a basketball team on speed."

"I didn't say that."

"But you thought it," Nash said, knowing that with his reputation she had every right to believe as she had. Still it hurt. Deeply. He sighed. When he spoke, a sadness had eased into his voice—and his eyes. "Is it so outrageous to think that there was a good reason I didn't contact you? Is it so outrageous to think that the time we spent together was special to me?"

"Was it special?" Claire asked, and was appalled at her brazenness—and at how much his answer meant to her.

"Yes!" he said, and she could see the force with which the word was delivered. Nash then surprised himself by being as bold as she. "Did it matter that I didn't get in touch?"

A part of her wanted to deny, even to herself, how very much she had been hurt that he hadn't communicated with her in any way. Another part of her, however, couldn't lie, not when he was waiting so earnestly for her answer.

"Yes," she whispered, "it mattered."

Nash had held his breath, needing to hear the truth but fearing what he might hear. He had no idea why it was so important to know that this woman had missed him. He knew only that it was. Now, as her answer glided on the silence, he allowed the words to bind him in their softness, in their sweetness. In all of his life, he couldn't remember a more exquisite bondage. It was the kind of bondage one had no desire to escape.

"I, uh... I made arrangements for a rose to be delivered to you each day," Nash said, "but the florist screwed everything up. Everyone thought someone else was taking care of the order. When the florist realized what had happened, the owner called to apologize. I called Gary. I wanted him to go explain to you what had happened, but he said you were out of town. So I came to tell you what happened myself." Before she could say anything, he added, thinking of all the meaningless words he'd said to women and of all the meaningless words women had said to him, "I didn't hand you a glib line, Claire. I swear it."

Claire's heart, like a hollow vessel, filled with emotions she couldn't explain, with emotions she didn't try to explain. Instead, needing him to tell her once more that he hadn't forgotten her, she asked, "You sent roses?"

"Yes... but the florist screwed everything—" Nash's gaze lowered to Claire's mouth "—up."

Claire, too, seemed unable to withdraw her gaze from Nash's lips. It was obvious to both of them what each was thinking. Claire grew hot. Nash grew hotter than hot.

"How much longer do you have to stay here?" Nash asked hoarsely.

Claire glanced at her watch, uncertain what she'd find. Had minutes gone by? Or had hours? "Another hour," she answered.

Consulting his own watch, Nash asked, "Until nine o'clock?"

Claire nodded.

"I'll, uh . . . I'll wait for you."

Claire nodded again.

"I'll just look around," he said, vaguely gesturing behind him.

This time Claire didn't even bother to nod. Her consent was taken for granted.

Suddenly, Nash groaned. Claire could feel the frustrated sound scraping against her senses. "Do you have any idea how much I want to kiss you?"

Knowing full well how much he did, because she wanted to kiss him just as much, she answered, "Yes."

It was the way she said the single word, as though she had breath for it and it alone, that threatened to destroy Nash's restraint. It caused all sorts of savage thoughts to rumble through his mind, all sorts of savage needs to storm through his body. "I suppose it would be frowned upon if I threw you across my shoulder and carried you out of here?"

Claire smiled. "Like a caveman?"

"Exactly, though to be honest, I suspect the caveman might be considered more civilized at this point."

Claire's smile faded in the wake of scalding-hot feelings that purled across her heated skin. The idea of being carted off over Nash's shoulder had great appeal. She wondered what kind of lover he would be. The word *naughty* leapt to mind. Interestingly, the idea of him being a naughty lover also appealed to her.

Claire was grateful for the series of interruptions that ensued. As time began to run out, everyone wanted one last word with her. Her agent, a man who could have passed for the late Andy Warhol's brother and who'd had faith in her talent when everyone else called her work too avant-garde, happily informed her that a sizable number of the paintings had already been sold. Claire was elated. Strangely, she wanted to share that elation with the man slowly making his way from painting to painting. Despite the fact it was nighttime, the man had put on sunglasses.

"Pardon me?" Claire asked when she realized her agent had asked her a question.

"Do you want a ride back to the hotel?"

Claire's gaze raised once more to Nash's back, then returned to her agent. "No, thanks."

"What time is your flight?"

"Eleven." Claire was keenly aware that she had little time to spend with Nash. In two hours, according to prearranged plans, she'd be on her way home.

"Then this is goodbye until next time," her agent said, giving her a quick, affectionate squeeze. "We'll talk. Oh, and by the way, the show was wonderful. *You're* wonderful."

Claire smiled at this man who was so much more than just her agent. "Thanks for everything," she said.

By the time all the loose ends had been tied up, Nash had disappeared. Claire wasn't exactly certain when he'd left. She knew only that, as the organizer of the event was thanking her for coming and making arrangements to transport her back to the hotel, she'd glanced up to find that Nash was nowhere to be seen.

"Transportation won't be necessary," Claire said, "I have...a friend waiting for me." At least she hoped she did.

Minutes later, she and Smudge stepped onto the front porch of the gallery. Above, a flirtatious breeze blew the stars around, while below, daffodils choked

the air with their fragrance, insects flitted around in a
nocturnal dance, and the lacy leaves of a nearby tree
swayed to the slow rhythm of the southern night music. Claire noticed three cars still parked in the parking lot. From where she stood, all appeared empty. She
was mistaken, however, for one of the doors opened
and a man stepped out. The man was Nash. At the
sight of him, Claire's heat skipped a beat. Smudge's tail
began to thwack against the concrete.

Nash watched Claire walk toward him, thinking that
she looked very much as she had the first time he'd seen
her. They had been in a parking lot then, too. Only that
time he'd just struck her with his car. It was he who
now felt as though he'd been struck—by her very presence. And he wasn't at all certain that he was going to
recover. In fact, he was pretty close to certain that he
didn't give a damn if he did or not...as long as she kept
looking at him the way she presently was...as long as
she kept moving toward him.

In heartbeats, she stood before him with her sultry
eyes, her pouty lips, her hair that begged a man to tear
it down in the throes of unrestrained passion. Suddenly, he had no idea how he'd survived the past two
weeks; in fact, he had no idea how he'd survived the
evening. All at once, he knew he was not going to survive a minute longer if he didn't... On a throaty moan,
Nash pulled her into his arms. His lips smothered hers.

Claire willingly went into his arms, just as she eagerly met his kiss with one of her own. There was no
holding back. This was what she'd wanted every night
of the past two weeks; this was what she'd wanted when
she'd seen him walking toward her in the gallery; this
was what she wanted so badly this very second that she
couldn't get her fill of him fast enough. She wondered

if she was being too brazen, too forward, then didn't care one iota if she was being either or both or a thousand other bold things. All she wanted was a deeper taste of this man.

Nash responded to her naked hunger as he'd never responded before. That she wanted him as badly as he wanted her did things to him—painful things, beautiful things, things he never wanted to end.

"Oh, baby...." he mumbled as he thrust his fingers through the fragile knotting of her hair. He mumbled something else—even he wasn't quite sure what—as his mouth slanted more aggressively over hers. And then, he groaned...and slid his mouth from hers to the sweet, straight column of her neck. There he left tiny kisses as he worked his way to the base of her throat. "I missed you," he whispered, but realized that she couldn't hear him. Angling her head with his thumbs, he raised her face to his so she could see the lips that had just kissed her. "I missed you," he said.

"I missed you," she breathed. "I thought I'd never see you again—"

He silenced her with another kiss simply because he didn't want to hear the words spoken aloud. They were too painful.

This kiss was slow and long and involved the gentle play of tongues, and then the not so gentle, sensual play of tongues as emotions heated once more. Bit by bit, touch by touch, their bodies melted into each other—he feeling all her softness, she feeling all his hard strength. She knew he was aroused; she felt the evidence of it pressed against her lower body. Uncertain why, she liked the fact that he made no attempt to hide his need. He simply let it rest naturally between them. And it did seem natural—sweet and natural and not the slightest bit complicated. It seemed like the very thing that should be happening between them—that and the glorious burning she felt deep inside her own body.

On a ragged gush of air, Nash jerked his mouth from hers. For a long time the two of them simply stared at each other, each silently telling the other that, yes, each was feeling the same thing. The same physical thing. The same emotional thing.

Finally, taking in her disheveled hair, her kiss-wet lips, and suddenly aware that they were standing out in the open where anyone could see them, Nash said, "Get in the car."

Claire did as bade and slipped into the driver's side of the rented vehicle, sliding over to the passenger seat. Smudge had already crawled in and sat impatiently waiting. Nash slid in beside Claire and closed the door. The car was shrouded in darkness.

"Come to dinner with me," Nash said.

Claire could see his lips move but couldn't make out what he was saying. "I can't read your lips."

Nash fumbled to find the interior lights. With a flick of his wrist, the car was flooded with illumination. Both he and Claire squinted against the brilliance. Realizing what she must look like, Claire raised her hand to her hair in an attempt to straighten it.

Nash's hand halted hers. "No," he said huskily. "I like it that way. It looks like we just crawled out of bed."

We.

It was the pronoun—very plural in its content—that gutted her stomach. That and the unbidden, forbidden images that sprang quickly to mind. Images of rumpled sheets. Images of bare bodies. Images of this man looming provocatively above her. Claire slowly lowered her hand from her hair. She could not lower her gaze from his, however. No more than he could lower his from hers.

At long last, he remembered to say, "Have dinner with me."

"I can't."

"Why?"

"I'm flying back to San Francisco tonight. My plane leaves at eleven."

"Fly back with me." At her confused look, he explained, "I chartered a plane."

As what he said sank in, Claire shook her head in self-reproach and smiled. "I keep forgetting who you are."

"Good. Just keep it up," he said with dead seriousness as he quickly kissed her, switched off the light and started the car.

With a totally masculine arrogance, not unappealing to Claire, he took charge of the evening.

THE RESTAURANT, which had been recommended by Nash's pilot, who had a sketchy knowledge of the area, was small but posh. Nash had called ahead for reservations from the hotel while Claire had checked out. He had obviously explained who he was and his wish for anonymity, for the manager himself met them at the door, addressed Nash by name and escorted the three of them—Nash, Claire and Smudge—to a private table. Only after he was seated in the candlelit shadows did Nash seem to relax.

They ordered a delicious French cuisine served on elegant china—fish in a rich butter sauce for Claire, tender veal for Nash. Even Smudge ate her dinner, a can of which Claire had taken from her purse and given to the waiter, off a gold-edged plate. And the wine was superb, the best Claire had ever drunk. Even the bubbles seemed more effervescent than usual as they echoed the spirit of the evening. Claire and Nash talked about anything and everything as though they'd known each other forever. Mostly they talked about completely ordinary things, which made it easy for Claire to forget the intimidating, professional Nash Prather. When they were together as they now were, they were just a man and a woman.

For all of their earlier kisses, for all of the way Nash's body had so snugly, so suggestively, fit her body, he made no further attempt to touch her, except with his eyes. They had caressed her as she, out of necessity, rearranged her hair before going into the restaurant. His gaze had said that she could pile the hair back up, but he would only muss it up again later. Surprising herself once more with her boldness, her gaze had said she'd hold him to that tantalizing threat.

It was while they were drinking after-dinner liqueurs that Nash said, "You're really very talented."

It was the first that had been said about the exhibition. Though Claire hadn't realized it until now, she'd been eager to hear his appraisal of her work. Somehow it was important what he thought.

"Do you really think so?"

"Yes. I think your work is like you—bold and confident."

"I think you're very talented," she said, "and I think your work is like you—evocative and sensitive."

"Are you talking about Nash Prather's work or Vincent Pratatorri's?"

"I know you think the two men are distinctly separate, that one doesn't exist at all, but I'm not so sure. Isn't it possible that both are just facets of the same complex man?"

"You mean that one is only the mirror image of the other?"

"Something like that."

Nash, leaning negligently back in his chair, shrugged. "Interesting theory, though I'd hardly call Nash Prather's work evocative and sensitive."

Claire sensed the scorn in his remark. "I would. You have the ability to make the viewer care about your character. You bring a real honesty to the screen."

"You can tell that from viewing one film?" Nash asked, his voice filled with incredulity.

Claire looked sheepish. "I, uh...I rented some others."

Nash's eyebrow rose.

"A couple," Claire clarified.

"I thought you weren't much of a movie watcher."

"Well, occasionally..." she said, trailing off.

"So you rented two of my movies?"

"Well, actually," she began, "it was more like... several."

"Several?"

"Several."

"Exactly how many is several?"

"I don't know—three...four...five."

"Which is it?"

"Okay, okay, five! I was curious. Besides..." She trailed off again.

"Besides what?"

"I was curious," she repeated, dropping her gaze from him to her wineglass.

But Nash would have no part of her sudden reticence. He tipped her chin up with the crook of his forefinger. "You were going to say something else. What?"

"No, I—"

"Claire?"

There was no way she could ignore the passionate plea in his eyes. There was no way she could ignore the plea in eyes that stripped her so emotionally naked. Besides, something in her needed to make the admission.

"Seeing you on film was better than not seeing you at all," she whispered.

Nash's heartbeat shattered against the wall of his chest. He was glad he didn't have to make his voice heard when he whispered, "Then you were luckier than I. I had nothing but memories. And they were damned poor substitutes."

As though he had no will of his own, he lowered his hand onto the table and covered hers. Neither could believe how hungry each was for the mere feel of the other. Claire lowered her gaze to his hand. It looked large and strong and was decidedly sexy with its smattering of dark hair. Nash felt the silken smoothness of her skin and wished he could go on feeling it forever. Turning her hand over, Claire meshed their palms. They had just entwined their fingers when the manager of the restaurant stepped to the table. He stooped and spoke quietly to Nash.

Claire was unable to read the manager's lips, though she quickly picked up Nash's reply. It was a swearword. She caught his, "Is there a back way out of here?"

"Yes, sir," the man replied, nodding toward the nearby kitchen door.

Nash stood, quickly extracted his wallet and left far more than the cost of the meal on the table. He motioned to Claire. "Let's go." At her inquiring look, he added, "The press."

Automatically, Claire glanced toward the front of the restaurant. A man stood there talking to a waiter. The waiter was shaking his head.

"How—" she began, but Nash cut her off.

"Who knows? They always find a way." Without further delay, Nash hustled Claire and Smudge out through the kitchen. At the back door of the restaurant, he turned to the manager, "What's your name?"

"Robert Brazer."

"Robert Brazer, you're in the will," he said, shaking the man's hand.

And then Claire was running, being dragged along by Nash toward the car. Smudge thought it great fun and barked. Just as Nash was unlocking the car door, the reporter rushed from the restaurant, aimed his camera and began to take one shot right after the other. Nash swore and shoved Claire and Smudge into the car. Revving the engine to life, he slammed his foot against the accelerator and sped from the parking lot. The last Claire saw was the reporter at the passenger window, his camera aimed at her.

Claire, her hand at her fluttering heart, leaned back against the seat and sighed. She felt ... To be honest, she wasn't sure how she felt. No, she did know how she felt. She felt violated. Beyond that, though, she felt something even more unsettling. It was again one of those moments when she realized that Nash was no ordinary man…and that no amount of wishing would make him otherwise.

"I'M SORRY."

They were the first words Nash had spoken to her since boarding the plane and instructing the pilot to set a course for San Francisco. Now, as the small craft sailed through the black, star-dappled night, Claire looked at the man who'd just returned from the cockpit and settled beside her. Smudge, belted in, lay snoozing in the seat behind.

"For what?"

"For what happened back at the restaurant." Nash sensed that the episode had upset Claire. He was accustomed to dealing with overzealous reporters, but she wasn't. And he felt this need to protect her.

"It wasn't your fault."

"I know, but if you hadn't been with me, it wouldn't have happened."

Claire was well aware of this. It was something she'd reminded herself of a dozen times while they'd silently driven to the airport. No matter how she cut it, the truth was that she was out with Nash Prather—and that had an unreal ring to it.

"True," she said, "but still, that hardly makes it your fault. Look, let's just forget about it, okay?"

For reasons Claire didn't want to delve into, she just wanted to put the incident behind her. Maybe it had something to do with preferring her insular world of painting. Maybe it had something to do with preferring her silent world. Maybe it had something to do with not wanting to be reminded that the man sitting beside her was a star. Maybe it simply had something to do with not wanting to share him with the world—at least for the duration of the flight to San Francisco.

Nash let the subject drop.

Once again conversation between the two of them came easily, comfortably. They spoke of Gary and AmyAnn and a thousand other things. One hour passed, then another. They drank champagne, then talked some more. Somewhere around two in the morning, Nash told her that he'd spent much of the past two weeks going over scripts, trying to decide which one to accept as his next movie.

"You don't sound too thrilled about any of them," Claire said.

"How can you tell?"

Claire smiled. "After two glasses of champagne, preceded by wine and a liqueur, I get clairvoyant."

Nash grinned. The action, Claire thought, was far more potent than any alcoholic spirits she'd consumed. His grin faded little by little until he said, "The scripts are typical of what I get sent. Lots of A and A."

Claire's look said she didn't follow him.

"Action and a—rear end," he amended quickly.

Claire vividly remembered the shot of his bare backside in *Sonora Sunset*. The scene, to a greater or lesser extent, though always tastefully done, had been duplicated in each of the other films she's viewed. She knew why the studios wanted him tied to such scripts. No man had more sex appeal on the screen. No man had a better backside. Claire brought the glass of champagne to her suddenly dry mouth.

"So what are you going to do?" she asked.

"Not what I want to, I'm sure."

"Which is what?"

"I want to direct a film version of *Two Queens and the King of Burwick.*"

"So why don't you?"

"Because no one's going to back Naughty Nash Prather."

"Why?"

"Because we're talking tons of money, which studios don't hand out capriciously. Hell, I'm not even sure Nash Prather is stupid enough to put his own money into the project."

"Then you know what I think?" Claire asked.

He looked at her as though he truly did want her opinion.

"I think the studios, and Nash Prather, are idiots."

He should have suspected such raw, unmined confidence. Laughing, he reached for her glass, set his and hers aside and said, "And I think this definitely proves you've had too much to drink."

The hand that brushed hers was warm—intoxicatingly warm. The touch sent tremors through both of them.

"I do believe in you," Claire said, wanting him to know the depth of her faith.

Needing to touch more of her, he trailed the back of his hand along the ivory softness of her cheek, his fingertips encountering her curls. He had the overwhelming urge to do what he'd wanted to do ever since she'd rearranged her hair—and that was to take it down. Completely. Slowly. With boldness, he sought through the silken tresses to find one pin, then another, which was followed by yet another.

Claire's breath became shallower with each pin that slipped from its mooring. The feel of his foraging fingers, the feel of her hair, swath by swath, tumbling to her shoulders, the devouring way he was looking at her was sexier than any act she could ever recall. She was certain that every bone in her body was melting. And the truth was that they couldn't melt fast enough. A moan vibrated in her throat as he buried both hands in the thickness of her now wantonly styled hair.

Nash heard the sensual sound, and it destroyed the last vestiges of his willpower. Groaning, he lowered his head to hers. He took her mouth unhurriedly but with a thoroughness that left not an inch unexplored. His tongue did delightful things, sexy things, naughty things—and encouraged hers to do the same. Somewhere along the way, Claire realized that not only was Nash naughty, but also that he made her feel naughty. He made her want things that she'd never wanted from a man before... and he made her want them with a power that was awesome, even frightening.

Claire's only consolation was that she could feel that Nash wanted everything she did. She sensed his restraint, for which she wasn't entirely grateful. A part of her—the heated body part—wanted him as her lover, while another part—the logically thinking part—was prudently cautious. She had no way of knowing where this relationship was headed, though she did know with a fierce certainty that she couldn't bear to be just another feminine statistic in Nash's life.

Kisses and breathless sighs later, the plane landed in San Francisco. Telling the pilot that he'd be back shortly, Nash walked Claire to her van.

"Come to Malibu next weekend," Nash said.

"I can't. My family's having a get-together."

"Then how about the next weekend?" At the resistance he sensed, he added, "I'll send a plane for you."

Claire shrugged. "I don't know."

"Why don't you know?"

She shrugged again, not really certain why she was hesitating.

"Do you like being with me?" he asked.

"Yes," she answered, unable to deny the truth.

"Do I like being with you? The answer is yes. So why shouldn't you come visit me? Smudge'll love the beach."

Still, Claire hedged. "I don't know, Nash."

"Give me one good reason."

She gave him the reason that was foremost in her mind. "I'm not sure I fit into your world."

"I live on the same planet you do."

"Not really... and you know it."

"Okay, so let's say I do live in another world. How do you know whether you fit in or not if you don't try it?" Fearing an out-and-out rejection if he pushed, Nash said, "Will you at least think about it?"

Claire nodded, signaling that she would at least do that.

Leaning forward, he brushed her lips with his, then settled lightly to kiss her with all the sweetness of silver moonlight spilling across the concrete sea of the parking lot.

When she felt weaker than a newborn babe, he withdrew his mouth from hers and whispered, "I'll be in touch."

Claire believed him... simply because her heart demanded it.

CHAPTER ELEVEN

ONE DOZEN RED ROSES arrived on Monday, another dozen on Tuesday and a third on Wednesday. Each bouquet bore a note with the simple message, "I miss you." As beautiful as the roses were with their fragrant, rich, velvet petals, Claire cherished the notes far more, for, simple though the sentiment was, it eloquently expressed what she herself was feeling. She missed Nash—in so elemental a way that she realized she'd never really understood the meaning of the word before. She also realized that missing someone hurt. Terribly. Yet every time she thought about Nash's invitation to visit him in Malibu, her feet grew cold.

Early on Thursday morning, as Claire was getting ready to make a mad dash to the university for her eight o'clock class, her mother called. Using a special telephone that enabled both women to type their conversation, they chatted back and forth.

"Sorry for calling so early," Esther Rushing typed, "but I wanted to catch you before you left for class. I wanted to remind you about Saturday night."

Several times a year, the Rushing clan took time from their fast-paced lives to enjoy each other's company.

"I haven't forgotten. I'm looking forward to it."

"Don't forget you're to bring coleslaw."

"I've got a note tacked on the refrigerator."

"Good... Oh, listen, I meant to ask you before. Do you want to bring your Little Sister?"

With all that Claire had had going on in her life, inviting AmyAnn hadn't crossed her mind, but she liked the idea immensely. Since Claire's nieces and AmyAnn were roughly the same age, it would be a good chance for AmyAnn to interact socially.

"Yeah, I think I would like to invite her," Claire typed, another idea occurring to her. This one had everything to do with Esther Rushing and the way she treated her deaf daughter no differently from any of her other children. During Claire's maturing years, her mother had always emphasized the positive, had always stressed Claire's similarities to everyone else rather than focusing on the dissimilarities. In short, much of Claire's confidence had come as a direct result of her mother's attitude toward her disability. "Would you mind if I also invited AmyAnn's mother?" Claire now typed.

"The more the merrier," came her mother's reply.

As the day wore on, Claire took her mother's words at face value. When she accidentally ran into Gary, she invited him, too, then thought of including Lance. Her nieces usually invited their current beaux, so Claire reasoned that she was really doing AmyAnn a favor. She just hoped AmyAnn agreed.

That afternoon, another dozen roses arrived. It was as Claire was reading the message—another "I miss you"—that inviting Nash first occurred to her. No, he wouldn't want to come to their simple little get-together. After all, he was accustomed to far grander forms of socializing. Yet, hadn't she sensed that he missed not having a family of his own? Hadn't he said that he'd like to meet her family someday? The question was, had he really been serious? She'd remembered thinking so at the time. Still...

That night, Claire tossed and turned, turned and tossed. With each restless movement, she vacillated between yes, invite him and no, don't. Mostly, though, she just thought of his kisses and the way they reduced her to putty...and the way his arms made her feel safe and secure and sexier than silk and satin. She had accused him of living in a different world, yet, when he held her, their worlds merged, bound together with soft sighs and softer caresses. By the dawn's pale light, she was reminded once more of just how badly it hurt—physically, emotionally—to miss someone. How could it have been only days since she'd seen him when it seemed like forever? And how could she not do something to at least try to ease her pain?

WHEN GARY OPENED his door, he was more than a little surprised at the sight of his early morning caller. "Hi," he said.

"Hi," Claire returned, hoping she wasn't about to do something monumentally stupid. "I want you to do something for me."

Motioning for her to step into his apartment, he replied, "Sure. What?"

"I want you to call Nash. I want you to ask him to fly up for the get-together tomorrow night." She hoped she was speaking calmly, matter-of-factly and not giving away the rapid thump-thump of her heart.

"Sure," Gary said, walking toward the phone, removing the receiver from cradle and dialing a number. He grinned. "I hope we can wake him up. He sleeps like the dead."

The comment prompted Claire to look at her watch. It was only a little after seven-thirty. Panic trickled through her. She hadn't realized how early the hour was, yet, when one was up much of the night, seven-thirty seemed like the middle of the day. "Maybe we should call later," she said. "I wouldn't want—"

"It's ringing," Gary interrupted.

Claire's panic did more than trickle through her; it made one rampaging gush. As distracted as she was, she still had the presence of mind to wonder how Nash slept. In pajamas? In pajama bottoms? In nothing? This last thought made her weak-kneed.

When second slipped into second, ring into ring, Claire said, "Maybe we should call back. Maybe—"

"It's about time you answered," she saw Gary say into the receiver.

Claire's heart slammed into fast gear. With that crystal clarity that always comes when it's too late to alter the course of events, she realized that she was doing a very foolish thing.

A few hundred miles away, a sleepy voice growled, "What time is it?" Not waiting for Gary's answer, Nash looked at the clock and groaned, "Good gosh, Gary, it's the frigging middle of the night!"

"Not for some of us," Gary said.

Well, it is for those of us who were up half the night, Nash thought, his mind replaying the miserable hours before sleep had stealthily crept up on him. The memory of Claire's kisses, of the sweet way she felt in his arms, had haunted, no, taunted him until the wee hours. And not just last night. It had been going on all week, and he knew that he was about three shades away from being a real grouch. Furthermore, he couldn't have cared less.

"I have someone here with me," Gary said. "In fact, she asked me to call you."

Nash, who'd pushed to an elbow and was sweeping back his sleep-tousled hair, froze.

Claire wanted to die on the spot. What in heck had she been thinking about to come over here and get Gary to call and wake Nash up?

"Claire?" Nash asked, daring to hope.

"No one but," Gary confirmed.

"Claire's there?" Nash asked, suddenly wide-awake, suddenly as far from grouchy as one could get.

"Isn't that what I just said?" Gary teased.

"Tell her hi."

"He says hi."

"Hi," Claire responded breathlessly.

"Did she get the roses?"

"Roses?" Gary teased. "I'm impressed. I didn't know you had that kind of class, Prather."

"Just ask her," Nash persisted, answering the friendly ribbing with, "And just what the heck would you know about class?"

"Did you get the roses?" Gary asked Claire.

She's suspected the question that was coming ever since she'd interpreted the word *roses*. She actually fought a blush. "Yes."

Gary grinned and said into the receiver, "She's blushing."

Claire only blushed more.

"Remind me to pay you back for this," Nash said good-naturedly.

Gary laughed. "Say, the little lady here wants to know if you can fly up tomorrow for a gathering at her family's house." Before his friend could answer, Gary said, "Sounds like fun. We're all going."

"Who's all?"

Gary told him, then asked, "So what do I tell her?"

"Tell her I'll make her a deal."

Claire knew from Gary's expression that Nash's reply hadn't been what he'd been expecting. When Gary repeated Nash's comment, she, too, was surprised. "What kind of deal?" she asked warily.

Gary conveyed her question.

"Tell her that I'll come there this weekend if she'll come here next weekend."

Gary repeated Nash's conditions. Somehow it was what she knew he'd said. "Tell him that this sounds a lot like bribery to me," she said, feeling like a tightrope walker suspended in midwire—elated, but afraid.

"Tell her it is bribery," Nash replied, then screwed up his courage to add, "Tell her those are the terms. Take them or leave them." Intuitively, he knew he had to push her or he'd never get her to Malibu. On the other hand, he hoped he wasn't pushing too hard.

When Gary repeated Nash's remark, he shrugged apologetically and said, "Looks like he's playing hardball."

So many things crossed Claire's mind. Part of her wished he wasn't putting her on the spot like this, while another part was almost glad that he was. A third part, obviously the one hurting from his absence, said for her to do whatever she had to do to see him again, while her logical side tried to minimize his request. What was a visit to Malibu, for heaven's sake? It was hardly the commitment of a lifetime. While this attitude predominated, Claire said, as though it were no big deal, "Sure, tell him I'll come."

Nash's long-held breath seeped out like air from a balloon.

Claire, though complacency personified on the outside, wondered what she'd just let herself in for. Her only saving grace was that, whatever she was in for was a week away. And in the interim, she was going to see Nash. At the moment, her heart said nothing mattered beyond that.

IF FAMILY WERE MONEY, Claire was the richest person he knew, Nash thought Saturday night. It was a conclusion he arrived at within minutes of entering the Rushing home, which was a redwood split-level, comfortable without being ostentatious. The last would have been totally inappropriate for this family, for they were the most natural people he'd ever met: John and Esther Rushing, he a doctor of medicine, she with a doctorate in English; their oldest child, Daniel, a test pilot; Ellie, married with two daughters, had followed in her father's footsteps; Mark, a criminal lawyer, with a wife and daughter.

Because of an unexpected university commitment, Claire had asked Gary to meet Nash at the airport, which he willingly agreed to do. Since Nash had arrived in San Francisco only a short while before, Gary had driven straight to the Rushings. Both Sharon and AmyAnn were with him. Lance was scheduled to arrive on his own.

"And has Mom pointed out to you yet that the greatest burden she has to bear is that her oldest child and her youngest refuse to marry and give her additional grandchildren?" These were the first words Claire said to Nash after he had met everyone. As she spoke, she looped her arm possessively through the crook of his elbow. Both felt tremors of a warm excitement skip through them. Both felt the week's emptiness being replaced with a heavy, glowing fullness.

"I had not mentioned it," Esther Rushing said, and signed, "But now that you have..." She trailed off, leaving unmarried Daniel to fill in with a moan. Everyone laughed. On the heels of that, Gary, Sharon and AmyAnn were each introduced.

"Please make yourselves at home," Esther announced to all.

"Do either of you guys know anything about putting up a volleyball net?" Mark asked Gary and Nash.

"For heaven's sake, Mark," his sister Ellie said, "they just got here. Claire and Nash haven't even had a chance to say hello to each other."

"Look, they can neck later," Mark said. "Right now we've got something important to do, like get this net into place."

Ellie and Mark's wife, a pretty, petite brunette, groaned, while Claire turned pink from tip to toe. She did not, however, back down. "You'll have to excuse my brother. He's demented."

Nash grinned and squeezed Claire's arm before disengaging it from his. "I'll be back," he mouthed.

Claire could feel the sensual power that lay behind the promise. She could feel her toes curling in anticipation. She had waited impatiently for his arrival, drawing back the edge of the draperies a dozen times to check for a car pulling into the driveway. When he'd finally walked into the house, when their eyes had finally met, Claire knew unequivocally that he'd been just as impatient as she.

Now, unable to avoid another delay—Claire was going to kill her brother!—she watched as the three men, followed by an exuberant Smudge, made their way outside and toward the unfurled net. They were joined by John, Daniel and Ellie's husband Joseph while Esther took Sharon to the bar and poured her a glass of white wine. AmyAnn and Claire were left alone.

Claire smiled and sighed. "I'm glad you came. You look great."

"Thanks," AmyAnn sighed, "so do you. You look like Holly Golightly."

It took Claire a second to realize that AmyAnn was referring to Audrey Hepburn's character in *Breakfast at Tiffany's*. Glancing down at the ankle-length, turquoise-colored leggings over which hung an oversize white T-shirt cinched at hip level with a turquoise-and-silver belt, she signed, "Is that good or bad?"

"On you, that's good."

Claire, a grin at her lips, considered the response. "Thanks. I think. Oh, by the way, Lance called and said he'd be another thirty minutes or so. He had to run an errand for his mother."

It was AmyAnn's turn to grin. "You really think you're clever, don't you?"

"You mean inviting Lance?"

"That's exactly what I mean," AmyAnn said, adding, "And don't think I don't know what you're doing."

"Of course you know what I'm doing. I'm matchmaking." At the objection she knew was coming, Claire said, "Just give him a fair chance, and if it doesn't work out, then it doesn't work out. Plain and simple and end of subject. Now, come on and I'll introduce you to my nieces." As Claire spoke, she grabbed AmyAnn's hand and started off in the direction of the den, from which music came, though neither woman knew it. She stopped at AmyAnn's tug.

"Wait," the young woman said.

Though Claire wouldn't have called the look on her friend's face one of panic, she would certainly have called it one of concern. It was there every time she encountered a stranger. It said clearly that AmyAnn knew that once again she'd have to face the fact that she was different.

"They're just like you," Claire signed.

"No, they're not, and you know it," AmyAnn signed back.

"No two people are just alike, and yet, we're all the same. Some things they can do, but you can't. Some things you can do, but they can't. They couldn't begin to do what you do on stage."

"That's not the same. That's—"

The conversation came to an abrupt halt when a teenage girl bounded from the den and practically ran into Claire.

"Oops, sorry," the girl said.

"AmyAnn," Claire said, "this is Karen. Karen, this is AmyAnn."

"Hi," Karen signed, a bright smile on her young face. "We've been waiting for you." This, too, was signed—perfectly.

AmyAnn glanced quickly at Claire. Her look betrayed her surprise at seeing the young woman use sign language. Her look betrayed one other thing, as well—relief.

"Come on and meet my cousins," Karen said, leading the way. "Did Aunt Claire tell you that Lance called?"

The last Claire saw was AmyAnn's signed, "Yes."

Lance arrived on schedule, the volleyball net went up finally, and immediately the youngsters—Lance and the three dates of Claire's nieces—challenged the oldsters—John, Daniel, Mark, Joseph, Gary and Nash— to a game. Once the gauntlet was thrown down, there was no way it could be ignored. Claire could see that Nash's enthusiasm rivaled that of his other team members. Nash did glance her way, however, with a Humphrey Bogart look that seemed to say, Gee, kid, I'd like to be with you, but I've got this manly stuff to get out of the way first.

Claire gave her warrior a thumbs-up and sent him off to do battle. The other women lined up to cheer, as well. Smudge, entering into the spirit of the game, barked and chased after the ball. Claire's mom, Claire's nieces, AmyAnn and Claire herself all signed back and forth to each other. At one point, Claire looked over to find Sharon standing to the side, observing not the game but the silent communication among the other women, communication that her daughter was a part of but from which she herself was excluded. For a moment their eyes met—meaningfully met—but then the game ended abruptly, noisily, and Esther Rushing announced that dinner was ready. The winning team—the youngsters, who'd managed to squeak out a victory—were allowed first choice from the buffet table that had been set upon the screened-in back porch.

Watching him walk toward her, Claire noted the faint beading of moisture that had popped across Nash's forehead. A curly lock of hair had fallen forward, while the back of his shirt had worked its way from his jeans. He looked devastatingly mascu-

line...which made Claire feel fundamentally feminine.

"We almost had 'em," he said, speaking of his volleyball opponents. As he spoke, he ran his hand along
the back of Claire's neck in a way that was both natural and possessive.

She felt the warmth of his touch.

He felt wayward strands of hair plunging from her
topknot alluringly tickle the back of his hand.

"They just got lucky," Claire said smugly.

"Yeah, lucky," Mark said.

"We were this close to victory," Daniel said, indicating the scant space between his thumb and forefinger.

"Speak for yourself. I was a coronary away," Gary
said, huffing and puffing. Sharon stepped to his side
with a cool drink.

"I've got to start exercising along with my pa-
tients," John said, falling into the nearest chair. "How
many people did they have on that team, anyway—
twenty?"

Everyone laughed.

"Claire," her mother called, and as naturally as the
night was closing in, Mark touched his sister's arm,
indicating that their mother was speaking to her. Automatically, Esther signed, "Will you get the bread
from the oven?"

"Sure," she replied, looking up at Nash. "Want to
help me get bread from the oven?"

Because they hadn't had a single minute to themselves since Nash's arrival, Nash would have gladly
helped her get bread from the Sahara Desert if it had
meant being alone for even the briefest time. His look

said as much. Claire's stomach turned over, sending a thousand excited butterflies into flight.

His hand tightening at her neck, he said, "Let's go."

The yeasty smell of fresh-baked bread struck both Claire's and Nash's nostrils. What registered even more than the tantalizing fragrance, however, was the fact that the kitchen was empty except for the two of them. Without a word, with mutual consent, Claire tumbled into his waiting arms.

Those arms were strong, steady, steel-like. Conversely, his lips were soft, and though he kissed her with one purpose—to consume her with his mouth—he did so with a sobered restraint. Claire sensed the restraint and wondered what it would take to destroy it . . . and just how wild this man would be when all the emotional stops had been pulled out.

His lips slipping from hers, he whispered, "Hi."

Claire smiled. "Hi."

"I thought I'd never get you alone."

"I thought you'd never get here."

"I thought this week would never end."

"Me, too," she whispered, then started to say something else, but her lips proved altogether too tempting to Nash. On a low, throaty moan, he again claimed her mouth. Leaning back against the cabinet, he drew her to him, aligning her all along the length of him—all along the very masculine length of him.

Claire sighed and slid her arms around his lean waist. At the spot where his shirt had slipped from his jeans, her hand encountered skin—bare skin, warm skin, skin faintly damp from perspiration. Unaware what she was doing, her other hand sought the same treasure.

Nash moaned, deepened the kiss, then pulled his mouth from hers as though just remembering where they were. He grinned. "Your dad's not going to barge in here with a shotgun, is he?"

Cocking her head to one side, her dark eyes glittering, she teased, "It depends on whether your intentions are honorable or dishonorable."

Nash's gaze lowered to her lips, lips that were still wet from his kisses. "Totally dishonorable," he drawled, his grin disappearing.

"Good," Claire whispered, angling her head, rising on tiptoe and pressing her mouth against his. Their lips had just met when the kitchen door opened. Nash jerked his mouth from Claire's, half expecting to see her father with a shotgun. If the good doctor had an idea of the thoughts burning in his mind, Nash *knew* it would be shotgun time. Instead of John Rushing, however, Claire's sister stuck her head in the door.

"Excuse me," Ellie said, "but I think the bread's burning."

No one came right out and mentioned the fact that the bread was a little black around the edges—Claire might have preferred it if someone had. Instead, her brothers teased until she didn't know whether to laugh or to cry or to consider fratricide. She was dying inside at what Nash might be thinking or feeling—so much so that she found it hard to meet his eyes.

What he was thinking was that, despite the ribbing he was taking, he'd never enjoyed an evening more. What he felt, though he didn't put it into words, was that he'd love to be a member of such a caring family. It was plain to see how Claire had adjusted so well to her disability. Her family cared for her, believed in her. She simply mirrored the attitudes of those around her. He hadn't been so lucky. He'd had no family to validate his self-worth. In Claire's arms, however, for the first time in his life, he felt good about himself. It was a feeling that he didn't want to lose.

Following dinner, Gary announced that he and Sharon had to leave. Lance immediately offered to drive AmyAnn home later, if that was okay with Mrs. Williams. Sharon deferred to her daughter, who glanced quickly from Lance to Claire and back to Lance. His look pleaded.

AmyAnn finally nodded.

Gary then turned to Nash. "Do you need a ride back to the airport?"

Claire jerked her head in Nash's direction. His gaze meshed with hers. "I'm flying back tonight," he said in explanation.

Nothing had been said about his plans, but she'd just assumed that he'd spend the night in San Francisco. Where exactly he would spend the night, she hadn't clarified in her mind, though at the back of it was perhaps the possibility of her house. She hadn't clearly thought that out and wasn't sure it was even what she wanted. She did know, though, that she didn't want to be separated from him so quickly.

"I'll drive you to the airport," she said.

"You sure?"

"Yeah. No problem."

Nash turned to Gary. "Thanks for the offer. And thanks for picking me up."

Goodbyes followed with Claire ultimately walking her friends to the door. Sharon, from the casual crook of Gary's arm, hesitated, then asked, "How do you sign *thank you*?" Claire showed her, and Sharon imitated the gesture.

"Thank me for what?" Claire asked, sensing that there was more to Sharon's sentiment than a simple thank-you for a nice evening.

"For showing me what I've been doing to AmyAnn." A look of anguish crossed Sharon's pretty face. "Why didn't you tell me?"

"Because we're all deaf to what we don't want to hear."

Sharon sighed, as though divesting herself of a great weight. "I wanted so desperately to believe that one morning I'd wake up and find that all of this was only a bad dream, but every morning is the same. Every morning AmyAnn can't hear, and every morning that makes me angry all over again."

Claire noticed that Gary, though silent, had tightened his hold. "Don't force AmyAnn to carry the burden of your anger," Claire said.

"That's what I've been doing, isn't it?"

"Yes. Much of what she'll feel is what she thinks you feel. However you see her—deaf and incapable or deaf and capable—is how she'll see herself."

"Until tonight, I thought that AmyAnn and I could never again share the same world. The truth is that AmyAnn's not coming back to my hearing world, but with sign language I can enter her silent world, the way your family has entered yours."

Claire smiled. "AmyAnn's very lucky to have such a smart mother."

Sharon Williams's eyes glistened with unshed tears of gratitude. "She's very lucky to have such a good friend."

AN HOUR LATER, Nash pulled Claire's van onto the apron of the airport, where private planes, looking like ghostly phantoms in the dark, were parked. The drive had been quiet except for idle chitchat. It was as though each were saving his strength for the separation that was soon coming. Even Smudge, belted into the back seat, seemed unusually silent.

Nash cut the engine and angled his body toward Claire. She turned toward him. Neither spoke. Each simply looked at the other in the pale yellow glow of a nearby light. Claire saw picture-perfect features, hair that curled slightly, eyes that were as deep and fathomless as the sea. Nash saw pretty, though not perfect, features, hair that beckoned him with its touchableness, eyes as dark as the desire he felt for her.

"I'm glad you came," Claire said.

"I'm glad you invited me," he said, adding, "You've got a great family."

She nodded in agreement. "They liked you, too. I hope you didn't mind my brothers' teasing."

Nash grinned. "I minded only if you did."

"I'm used to anything they do or say."

"Actually, I liked it. It was nice to be treated like a normal person. Most of the time people treat me like..." He trailed off.

"Like a star?"

"I guess. They treat me like the fantasy they think I am, rather than who, what, I really am. It, uh, it gets tiring."

Claire said nothing. She simply looked at him again, thinking that, more and more, the reverse was growing true for her. More and more, at least when she was with him, she had trouble remembering that he was a star. It was something she had to keep reminding herself of, for mostly she just thought of him as a man. A handsome, desirable man.

"Which one is your plane?" she asked, tamping down the tingly feeling that arose from this last thought.

"I think the one on the end."

Claire nodded. She wasn't sure why. In fact, she wasn't sure why she'd asked the question. No, that wasn't true. She was trying to say something without saying anything. She was trying to steer clear of begging him not to go back so soon.

As though he'd read her mind, he said, "I have a meeting with my agent early in the morning, so I thought it best if I went back tonight. One of the film companies is doubling its offer if I'll do their script."

"I'm sorry to hear that."

Nash's look said her comment had surprised him.

"It's just going to make it harder for you to do what you really want to do, which is make your play into a movie," she explained.

"Yeah," he said in a monotone.

Another silence stretched between them. This one Nash broke.

"Claire, I thought about staying over. I thought about staying a few hours more, but we both know what's going to happen if I stay. And I don't want that. I mean, I do want it," he amended quickly. "I want to make love to you more than I've ever wanted anything. Sometimes I..." He reached out to lay his palm along the side of her cheek, but, as if not trusting himself to stop there, he withdrew his hand without touching her. "Sometimes I can't breath for wanting it so badly, but—" he swallowed "—you deserve more. There are times now, since I've met you, that I even think *I* deserve more." He suddenly looked flustered.

"Is this making any sense, or am I making a complete fool of myself?"

"Yes," Claire said. "I mean, no, you're not making a fool of yourself."

"It's just that I've screwed everything up so badly with women in the past. This time I've got to get it right."

Something in his expression as he spoke moved Claire as little ever had. That he wanted to get it right with her brought a happiness that fizzed like champagne in her blood.

"Give me time," he said, then gave a half laugh. "I know that's supposed to be your line."

Claire smiled softly. "I need time, too. Whatever's happening between us has never happened to me before."

Her words, as honest and natural as all of her, moved Nash until he felt his throat constrict with emotion.

"Come here," he whispered, running his hand along the back of her neck and pulling her to him.

He kissed her gently, then hard and deep. She could feel his restraint straining its leash. She could feel it going, going, going... She knew the precise moment he forced himself back from the sensual abyss and gentled the kiss once more. Slowly, he raised his mouth from hers.

"See you next week," he said at the same time as he opened the car door behind him. The car was instantly flooded with light, but the light disappeared as quickly as it had come when he closed the door. And then he was gone, walking toward the plane...and leaving her alone. Behind her, though she didn't hear it, Smudge whined, as though she, too, were sad to see this man going.

Claire watched as he waved once and disappeared inside the plane.

She could never remember feeling lonelier.

CHAPTER TWELVE

As THE CHARTERED PLANE prepared to land in Los Angeles the following Friday, Claire experienced the same uneasy feeling she'd felt a dozen times during the week. The day before, AmyAnn had accused her of being afraid to spend some time with Nash on his own turf. Claire had vehemently denied the accusation. What was there to be afraid of? Now, however, she had to admit that she was feeling afraid—oh, not out-and-out fear, but tiny, disturbing pangs of the dark emotion. She knew the source of the fear. Deep in her heart, deep in her gut, she felt that it had something to do with not being able to make her world and Nash's blend. Or, more to the point, with realizing once and for all that she didn't belong in his world. It was the reason she'd hesitated to accept Nash's invitation from the beginning.

Sensing Claire's mood, Smudge pawed at her arm as though reassuring her that everything would be all right. Claire patted the dog's head and smiled.

"What would I do without you?" she whispered.

Smudge made a little noise that said, "I like you, too."

Within a few minutes, the plane had landed and rolled to a stop. The pilot lowered the ladderlike steps.

"Be careful," he cautioned Claire as she began to descend the sharply angled stairway. Smudge, her tail wagging, her head high, followed behind, as though she were embarking on a wonderful new adventure. As Claire looked around, even she felt an anticipatory excitement. No matter what else she might be feeling, it had been a week since she'd seen Nash. A miserably long week.

The sun had almost disappeared, leaving the sky painted in pastel streaks of lavender, peach and pink. Night, sweet and sultry, hung in the air like the seductive promise of a lover. Brushing back a wisp of hair that fluttered in the sudden breeze, Claire stopped and looked for Nash. She immediately spotted him—a tall, slender figure moving toward the plane. He grinned and raised his hand in greeting.

Claire automatically raised her hand, but the wave never materialized. Neither did the smile that had started to spring to her lips. Instead, a simple yet profound realization struck her: she was in love with this man. When had this miraculous thing happened? Had it been the moment she'd stepped into the path of his car and realized that an incredibly good-looking male was frantic with worry that he'd injured her? Had it been one of the brooding times he'd shared his soul with her? Had it been last weekend when he'd told her that he wanted her as his lover but that he needed time? Or had it been just this second with the dying rays of the sun splashing around him?

Whenever, it didn't matter. Nothing mattered except that she now knew it to be a heart-truth. Interestingly, the realization both accelerated and helped to alleviate the fear that had been eating at her. All of a sudden it was even more imperative that their worlds mesh, yet, on the other hand, did anything matter except that she loved him? Surely she could make their worlds compatible if she had to.

As though coming to after being knocked unconscious, Claire noted that Smudge had somehow passed her on the narrow stairway and was presently being stroked on the head by Nash, who seemed as glad to see the dog as she was to see him. Straightening, Nash's gaze met Claire's. With a relaxed, easy stride, he completed the distance between them.

"Hi," he said, brushing her lips with his.

"Hi," she whispered, the sound spilling onto the softness of his mouth.

Because Claire still stood on the steps, for once she and Nash were the same height, a fact that was emphasized when she opened her eyes to find them level with his. Even though the hour was growing late, she could see the incredible beauty of his eyes. The sight, coupled with her recent revelation, took her breath away.

"You okay?" he asked, aware of the sudden strange look on her face.

"Yes," she said breathlessly.

"You sure? The flight was okay, wasn't it?"

She smiled. "The flight was fine. I'm fine." *Except I've gone and fallen in love with you, and I haven't the foggiest idea whether that was a smart or foolish thing to do.*

"C'mon, then. Let's go."

In minutes, Nash had spoken with the pilot, retrieved Claire's suitcase and opened the car door for Claire and Smudge. Smudge jumped into the back seat, but only after her usual confrontation with the front tire of the BMW. A flick of Nash's wrist and the car roared to life, quickly carrying them from the airport premises onto the traffic-thick freeway.

With the windows down, Claire luxuriated in the rush of the wind through her hair…and in the rush of feelings that purled through her body. She'd never been in love before. She'd thought she had been with Bill, but she'd realized all too soon that what she'd been in love with was being in love. She'd never really felt this heart-to-heart, soul-to-soul feeling with anyone. She'd never felt this losing of herself, this finding of someone else. She'd never felt this giddy euphoria.

Unable to keep her eyes from the object of this euphoric feeling, Claire glanced over at Nash. He glanced over at her, smiled and reached for her hand. Silently, he brought it to his mouth and kissed her folded knuckles. His breath was warm and moist as it fanned across her skin. Instead of releasing her hand afterward, he laid it, still wrapped in his, in his lap.

A thousand sensations bombarded Claire: the coarseness of denim, the hardness of honed muscle, the sexiness of the ultimate masculinity that lay so very near. Though she tried, she could not be blasé about the intimacy. Neither could she pull her hand away. It was an intimacy that she craved—that and more. Much, much more.

Claire suddenly felt Nash's penetrating gaze. When she glanced up from their entwined hands, when she looked into his eyes, she knew without a doubt that he'd read her mind just as she could read his. He wasn't blasé about the intimacy, either. He, too, craved more. Their mutual need sent something hot silently sizzling between them. He tightened his hand, pressing hers more firmly into his inner thigh. Claire thanked the breeze that helped to cool the heat dancing within her.

"I can't believe you're really here," Nash said later. Of necessity, his hand had abandoned hers, after another brief kiss, in order to shift gears.

"I can't believe it, either."

"You won't regret coming. I promise."

As was becoming habit, she believed him. But then, she was in love with him. She would have believed him if he'd told her that north was south, east was west. She would have believed him if he'd told her wrong was right, right was wrong. She would have even believed him if he'd told her he loved her, but that he hadn't said, and only time would tell if he ever would.

Nash's house turned out to be exactly what she was expecting. Tucked at the back of a canyon, hidden behind a heavy, electrically operated gate, the white one-story house sprawled like a drunken sailor on shore leave from the very sea that lapped at the nearby beach. The grounds were a curious blend of Eastern and Western culture: massive planters of early blooming red and purple tulips, evergreen junipers gnarled by ocean-blown winds and a Japanese stone garden, where each raked swirl of crushed pebbles bore a ceremonial significance.

Inside, the house was magnificent, everything that money could buy. Claire moved with awe from room to room. In one the carpet was antique Persian, while in another there was an authentic Chippendale sideboard. In still another, there was a fireplace mantel imported from Austria. Above it hung a seascape by Dominic Serres. Another seascape by Thomas Luny hung nearby. Several brightly colored pieces of Japanese raku ceramics were scattered around the house. Not a thing—not a picture, a magazine, a single flower—was out of place.

Slowly, Claire's feeling of awe gave way to some other feeling that she couldn't put a name to at first. As she passed by perfection after perfection, however, she realized that what she was feeling was sadness. While the house was unquestionably beautiful, it was also barren. Nowhere was there any evidence of life, nowhere did she *feel* the presence of Nash. How interesting, how sad, that a man in search of his identity could find not a clue to himself in his own home. It was as if he didn't exist.

"And this is the library," Nash said, opening the door to yet another room.

Claire, preceded by an eager Smudge, stepped inside. The soft tones of polished oak welcomed her, as did the Victorian atmosphere. English club chairs clustered near an inviting leather sofa. Hundreds of books—hundreds of other worlds for Nash to escape to—lined built-in shelves, while several books lay scattered around, as though he'd been reading them and simply discarded them at will. A typewriter, more ancient than Coleridge's mariner, perched on a desk. A half dozen wads of crumpled paper had been tossed toward the wastepaper basket but hadn't made it. A couple hadn't even come close. A thigh-high pile of what Claire surmised were scripts was stacked haphazardly on the floor. There was also a foil candy wrapper on the desk, along with a forgotten mug, still partially filled with coffee, and newspapers aplenty. In short, despite its elegance, the room was disarranged and disorganized. Wonderfully disarranged and disorganized.

"I love it," Claire said with a smile.

"It's my favorite room. I dare the housekeeper to touch a thing." Looking sheepish, he trashed the balls of paper and the candy wrapper. He grinned. "Maybe I should let her in a little more often."

Claire shook her head. "No, don't. I like it this way."

Her seriousness in the face of his kidding surprised Nash. Hiking his hands to his hips, he replied, "Okay, if it's that important to you, I'll leave it looking like a pigsty."

Grinning, Claire said, "Good," then began to browse through the room. She found an old, weathered and thoroughly read copy of *Wuthering Heights*, a current photo of Nash and Gary and an old black-and-white photo of a woman. She was young, dark-haired and weary eyed. Claire turned to Nash for an identification.

"That's my mother," he said.

Claire knew that he'd spoken quietly. She could see it in the gentleness of his eyes. "She was very pretty," Claire said.

"I don't remember much about her, except that she was kind."

Claire watched as he stepped back into a world that he'd long ago run from, a world in which his mother had died and in which his father had abused him. It was a world he'd escaped from with only his dreams intact. He faulted himself for having never attained those dreams, yet it had taken…the word *grit* came to Claire—yes, it has taken grit for someone so young to have escaped with anything. But he still bore the scars of his solitary journey… and maybe he always would. It crossed Claire's mind that maybe Nash was afraid to love, even himself. Maybe he'd had such tragic luck with love, first in losing his mother, then in the ill treatment at the hands of his father, that he found it safer not to indulge in the tender emotion. Maybe that was why he'd lost himself in the arms of countless women. Maybe that was how he protected himself from ever being hurt again.

Love me, she pleaded silently. *I won't hurt you.*

"Come here," Nash said softly.

Claire lowered her gaze from his eyes to his lips. She knew he'd spoken but was unsure what he'd said. She'd been too caught up in her own loving thoughts. "I didn't unders—"

"Come here."

A warm, syrupy feeling flowed through Claire. She replaced the photo and walked toward Nash. With each step, the feeling inside her grew warmer. When she stood directly before him, she angled her head upward.

Slowly, Nash reached out and, as though she were the most precious thing on earth, stroked her cheek with the back of his hand.

"Have I told you how glad I am you're here?" he said.

"Tell me again."

"I'm glad you're here. I don't like you far away. I don't even like you across the room." As he spoke, he drew a strand of hair back from her face with his crooked finger. Those satin-soft tresses seemed to ensnare his full attention. "Have I ever told you that I like your hair falling down?"

She remembered, as clearly as though it had been said yesterday, his telling her that he liked her hair tumbling from its loosely held knot because it looked as though the two of them had just crawled out of bed.

"I...I think you might have mentioned that," she said so huskily that Nash knew she remembered the incident vividly. He remembered it, too, just as he remembered the feel of his fingers gliding through the silkiness of her hair. It was a feeling he'd promised himself he'd know again. Not this moment, but soon. Very soon.

"It makes you look real," he said.

He said the word in such a complimentary way that Claire could have easily believed that looking real was the only thing a woman should ever strive to look. Not beautiful, not gorgeous, just real. She also believed that the pulse at her wrist had begun to flutter. She equally believed that she was dying a slow death for him to kiss her. Really kiss her. Not just the fleeting grazing of her mouth in greeting.

"Did I ever tell you that sometimes I can read your mind?" he whispered, his gaze lowering to her lips.

"No," she said, her voice ragged with desire, "you never told...me." This last fractured into small syllables of sound—a pleading sound, a needing sound.

Moaning at the supplication he saw on her face, Nash lowered his mouth to hers. Greedily, hungrily, he kissed her. His nimble tongue possessed her even as he drew her to him, molding her body to his in a provocative man-woman way. Again she felt his desire; again it felt the most normal thing in the world. Her body responded with an equally normal reaction. It grew flushed and filled with need. Deepening the kiss until both were weak from wanting, he pulled his mouth from hers and simply hugged her tightly, as though he couldn't believe she were really there.

In that second she wondered how she could ever have considered not accepting his invitation to visit, when, in his house, in his arms, was where she was so obviously meant to be.

A SALT-SCENTED SEA BREEZE, like a lazy, languid traveler, meandered onto the patio, fluttering the flames of the candles that rested on the table set for two. Beside a waist-high, brilliantly colored Oriental jar and beneath tinkling wind chimes, the table stood on a pure white concrete terrace. Below, on a second terrace, underwater lights beamed through the clear turquoise water of a rectangular swimming pool. Beyond the backyard, at the base of a series of steps, lay the sugar-sand beach and the untamed sea.

As lazy and languid as the breeze, Claire watched as Smudge pawed at the water in the swimming pool. A couple of bugs flitted by, momentarily diverting the dog's attention, but then the animal went back to playing with the water—unhurried taps and slow slaps. Claire felt mellow. Mellower than she could ever remember feeling. At the same time, she felt replete. The spicy shrimp that Nash had broiled on the barbecue had been delicious, as was the sparkling champagne swirling in her glass. The fabric of Nash's T-shirt, which she'd had to borrow because she'd left behind the blouse she'd intended to wear with her jeans, caused warm sensations to ripple over her. It was stupid, it was schoolgirlish, but she knew the source of these sensations was the fact that the shirt belonged to Nash. It was easy for her to imagine the same shirt on him at some point in the past.

"What are you thinking?" Nash asked.

Leaning back in his chair, his long legs sprawled beneath the table, where they tantalizingly brushed against Claire's, he, too, wore jeans and a T-shirt that matched the one Claire wore. The T-shirt, the one he'd loaned her, was also on his mind. He was wondering if she wore anything beneath it. He didn't think so, and that was playing all kinds of havoc with his hormones.

Claire's crimson blush, which resulted from having been asked what she was thinking, was lost in the candlelight. "I was thinking how content I feel," she said, fibbing only slightly.

"Me, too," he replied, thinking that he *did* feel content. That was not always the case, particularly in this house. Sometimes he just felt lost in the vastness. That was why he spent so much time on the beach. Even though the sea was infinitely more vast, it offered a companionship that the house didn't. He didn't delude himself. The companionship he felt now was due entirely to the woman who sat across from him.

"The shrimp were wonderful," she said.

"You didn't mind not going out?" The truth was that he knew he was being selfish. He simply hadn't wanted to share her with anyone...not their first night together, anyway.

"No. In fact, I'd rather stay in." The thought of being with Nash all weekend, in such close proximity, brought another warm sensation that rippled across her. She wondered where everything would lead. She wondered where she *wanted* everything to lead.

Nash frowned. "Do you mind going out for a couple of hours tomorrow night? I've got something to do that I just don't know how to get out of."

The warm sensation curling inside Claire cooled. Even though she'd told herself that she'd make their worlds compatible if she had to, the fear she'd felt earlier resurfaced. She obviously preferred to make their worlds compatible at some point in the future—in the far future.

"No, of course not," she lied.

Nash heard the falsehood in her voice. He leaned forward and took her hand in his—naturally, as though he'd done so a thousand times before. "I don't want to go, either. I want to stay here with you, just the two of us, but—" he sighed "—this big-shot producer who wants me to do the movie for him—"

"The one who's offered you twice the money?" Claire interrupted.

"Yeah. Anyway, he's throwing a party tomorrow night and called to invite me. My agent insists I go. He wants me to at least make an appearance. I'm sorry. If you really don't want to go, though, we'll tell both my agent and the producer to kiss off."

She didn't want to go, that she could feel clean to the marrow of her bones, yet she smiled and said, "And be the one responsible for depriving the women of the world another Nash Prather movie? No way, mister. People have been lynched for less."

"I'm not interested in whether the women of the world are deprived of another one of my movies," Nash said, suddenly very serious. "I'm interested only in what one woman wants—you."

What she wanted was his mouth on hers, his arms tightly around her, his hard body... She forced her uncensored thoughts to trail away, just as she forced the nagging fear into a corner of her heart. "Then, we'll go. Business is business."

His look asked if she was sure.

She squeezed his hand. "We'll go...although all I brought was one dress, and it's pretty simple."

"It'll be fine. It'll—"

As though he'd suddenly heard something, Nash glanced toward the stairway descending to the beach. Smudge was barking, hoping to entice Nash and

Claire. The dog had flirted with the stairs ever since finding them but couldn't work up the courage to walk the beach alone.

Nash grinned, said something to the dog that Claire didn't understand, then turned to Claire. "C'mon," he said, dragging her up, "let's play."

The sandy grit of the beach ground between Claire's toes, while the white-topped waves, like watery fingers, grabbed at her ankles. Moonlight, as though tipped from a heavenly bucket, spilled across the sea, while electrical lights, buried high in trees, faintly bathed the beach. There had been few times in Claire's life when she would have called a moment perfect, but she would have called this one exactly that. With the wind in her hair, with Smudge frolicking in the sea, with the man she loved walking beside her, her hand in his, the moment was perfect. Absolutely perfect. In appreciation of that perfection, in acknowledgment of the fact that maybe she was being too quick to worry that she wouldn't fit into his world, Claire raised her face toward the stars and let the magic of the night wash over her.

Nash tugged at her hand, and when she looked over at him, he asked what he'd asked once before. "What are you thinking?"

This time, a smile at her lips, she answered honestly. "How perfect this moment is. I love the wind, the sea, the stars.... I love..." She hesitated when she realized she'd almost told him that she loved him. "I love being here with you."

Nash stopped, pulled her into his arms and kissed her as the sea lapped around them, wetting the upturned cuffs of their jeans. Though underscored with passion, the kiss was sweet and tender, an act of total communion. It echoed the sentiment she'd just expressed, saying that he, too, loved being with her. When he drew his mouth from hers, he fingered the lips he'd just kissed, kissed them again, then once more took her hand in his and began to walk the beach.

"I love the sea," he said after a while, as though sharing a secret he'd never shared with anyone else. "Sometimes I just come out here and listen to it."

"What does the sea sound like?" Claire asked as she swiped the breeze-whipped hair from her face. Seldom did she ask such questions anymore. As a child, when she'd realized that there were sounds in the world, she'd asked the question hundreds upon hundreds of times. As an adult, however, she'd come to the conclusion that it didn't matter much what sounds there were in life. She wouldn't be hearing them, anyway. Now, she wanted to know everything about this man—including what he heard when he listened to the sea.

Nash wrestled with the question, realizing that he couldn't think of a way to answer it without involving other sound values, for which Claire had no point of reference. For the first time, he realized how truly isolated she was—how much of life she'd missed. He felt a prickling of anger that she'd had to endure such silence, though he quickly hid his feelings. The last thing this woman would ever want was pity.

"The sea sounds like a friend," he answered.

His abstract description intrigued Claire. "A friend?"

"Yes. Like a friend, it's always there for me. It always listens to me. It never criticizes me. It always assures me that everything will be all right."

Claire smiled. "Did anyone ever tell you that your reasoning is profoundly and philosophically deep?"

Nash grinned. "Is that the same as being told you're crazy?"

"Close."

"Yeah. I hear that all the time." Before she could add anything more, he asked, "How do you think the sea sounds?"

"Like the color silver." At Nash's frown, Claire explained about her attributing colors to sounds.

"Why silver?"

"For water. It's clear, and as a child, I decided the color value of clear was silver."

Nash grinned again. "Did anyone ever tell you that your reasoning is profoundly and philosophically deep?"

"Is that the same thing as being told you're crazy?"

"Close."

"Yeah. I hear that all the time."

They were both grinning now, both thinking that being crazy wasn't a bad thing to be if they were being it together.

Suddenly, Nash's smile disappeared. "Tell me what your world of silence sounds like."

Claire considered the question. How did she answer something so simple, yet so complex? "Except for occasional gurgling sounds, my world is just that—silent. But," she hastened to add, "that's not a bad thing. You have to understand that I've never been used to anything else. That doesn't mean, though, that I don't regret not being able to hear. I know—or at least can imagine—what I've been denied, but I'm reconciled to being deaf. In many respects, not hearing was more confusing as a child. I wasn't certain then what things in life did and didn't have sounds.''

"Like what sound a tree makes?"

"Exactly. Only there are a lot of subtleties to learn. For example, a tree is silent unless the wind is swaying through the branches...or unless it falls to the ground...or unless lightning splits it open.''

"Interesting distinctions," Nash said.

"Yes, and for the most part they're distinctions that hearing children make without conscious effort. On the other hand, nonhearing children, if they've never heard at all, can make all sorts of erroneous judgments.''

"Like what?"

Claire grinned. "For a long time I thought that stars made a sound...and that they made different sounds depending on what time of night it was.''

Intrigued by Claire's comment, Nash asked, "What did you think they sounded like?''

"I thought they made little popping sounds when they appeared, and that they...hummed, I guess is the right word, only the hum grew louder as the night grew darker. But then, Mother explained to me that they were silent...like my world. After that, I imagined them singing a silent star song that only I could hear.''

Somewhere during their discourse, they had stopped walking. Nash now stood stock-still. He just stared at Claire with an expression that was unreadable. "Make me hear the song, too," he whispered.

Nash's face by moonlight could easily have been listed as one of the wonders of the modern world— at least Claire thought so. So compelling were his flawless features that she was helpless not to bring her fingertips to his cheek. Its slight stubble felt scratchy...manly...sexy.

"How do I make you hear my song?" she whispered back. "How do I make you hear what's in my heart?" She was aware that, by this last, she meant not only the star song but also the love she felt for him.

Wordlessly, his gaze fully on hers, he pressed his hand to her heart, as though he would be able to hear what he could feel. What he felt was the unmistakable answer to a question he'd earlier posed. No, she wasn't wearing anything beneath the T-shirt. He could never remember any single thing having such a profound impact on him. Though he felt only the top swell of her breast, his senses quickened as though she were standing bare before him. He felt his breath splinter, his heartbeat fracture into half beats. Closing his eyes, he fought to hang on to his sanity.

"You feel good," he whispered. "So good."

Claire was having her own breathing problems, her own heartbeat problems. She had one other problem, as well—standing still, for every instinct in her urged her to step up onto her toes, which would undeniably place the whole of her breast in his hand. She sighed— a serrated sough at her lips—and once more tilted her face toward the starlit sky. She fought to hang on to her sanity.

Nash couldn't resist the temptation. Placing his lips at the hollow of her throat, he kissed her...over...and over...traveling slowly up her neck to the tip of her chin. And then, angling her head downward with his, he claimed her mouth—gently, but boldly. His impatient tongue probed, then penetrated her mouth with its sweet presence. At the same time, his hand slowly edged downward to claim her breast. He filled his palm with the incomparable softness of Claire.

She gasped, he sighed, and for seconds their parted mouths merely touched rather than kissed. Their breath merged and mated.

"You feel so good," he repeated, though he had no idea if she understood him. For that matter, he wasn't entirely certain that he'd said anything coherent. All he could really be sure of was the treasure he held in his hand, a treasure that felt full, warm, divine.

Claire had no idea what he'd said, but then it didn't matter what he'd said. What mattered was the weight of his hand at her breast. Through the barrier of the thin T-shirt, Claire felt him cup her breast, felt him caress in a kneading motion, felt his thumb brush against the nipple. Everything he did felt right...so right...so unbelievably right!

"Nash," she pleaded.

Her voice, always slightly dissonant, sounded husky, broken. He wasn't certain she knew exactly what she was asking for, but he knew precisely. She wanted him to make love to her. He knew because it was what he wanted, too—more than anything! A part of him told him to take her right there on the beach, with the waves crashing around them, with their heartbeats crashing louder than the waves. Another part held him back, reminding him that, for once in his life he wanted more from a woman than a quick physical fix. He wanted the spiritual bonding that had always eluded him before. The eager, needy part told him that he could have that spiritual bonding now, that what he and Claire would share wouldn't merely be a quick physical fix, but the other part of him, a punitive part, told him that he didn't deserve her. Not just yet. He still had dues to pay for too many reckless actions.

Forcing his hand from her breast, he hauled her to him and crushed her mouth with his. This kiss was hungry. This kiss was wild. This kiss allowed Claire a glimpse of Nash's restrained passion. It was awesome, a fact evinced by the way his mouth devoured hers, by the way her neck felt like snapping, by the way her mouth stung as though honeybees sipped at her lips. Abruptly, though, he halted. Wrenching his mouth from hers, he looked over at Smudge.

Startled by the kiss's sudden cessation, Claire followed the direction of Nash's gaze. Smudge was looking up into the adjacent tree-covered hillside and barking. Both she and Nash looked beyond Smudge.

"What is it?" Claire whispered.

"I don't know. What is it, girl?" Nash said to the dog.

Smudge, her tail wagging, turned and ran toward Nash. On her way, she barked at an encroaching wave. Nash stooped, petted the dog and looked once more into the copse of trees. He saw nothing more than he had before, and Smudge now seemed far more interested in the sea than the hillside.

"What did Smudge hear?" Claire asked.

"Probably an animal. We have raccoons that come out at night."

The answer satisfied Claire...even if it didn't totally appease Nash.

"C'mon," he said to both Claire and Smudge, "let's go to the house."

His arm around Claire's waist, they started back toward the steps. Silently, they crossed the beach; silently, they scaled the stairway. As they stepped onto the concrete terrace, Nash gave one more look in the direction of the hillside. Still, he saw, heard, nothing. Cursing a profession that had made him paranoid, he entered the house and closed the door.

The incident was forgotten.

CHAPTER THIRTEEN

THE PARTY WAS LOUD.

Claire didn't have to be able to hear to make this assessment. She could tell from the way people were laughing, gesticulating and talking incessantly. The walls, the floor, vibrated with music. As she watched the dancing couples, she could feel the rhythmic beat— sharp, pulsating decibels—tramp through her like tremors of a mild earthquake.

Everyone was having a great time. Everyone except her. And possibly Smudge, who sat beside her with a bewildered look on her face. She kept her ears folded back. Claire could only assume it was to shut out the noise.

Looking up and over the crowd, Claire found Nash in exactly the same spot he'd been standing minutes before. He was talking, or rather listening, to the producer who was hosting the party. Nash had started in her direction a half dozen times in the past twenty minutes but had always gotten sidetracked by someone. Usually it was a woman. This time, however, it had been the man who wanted to produce his next movie. Nash looked over at Claire and said with his eyes that he'd be there in a minute—hopefully. Claire forced a smile . . . and wondered what in the world she

was doing here. She belonged at this party the way a
fish belonged on dry land.

"Excuse me," Claire said, stepping aside as a
woman who'd obviously had a little too much to drink
bumped into her.

The woman looked at Claire as though it were she
who'd been at fault. Claire looked at the woman, seeing only a beautiful brunette who unquestionably
shopped on elegant and expensive Rodeo Drive. For
that matter, it appeared that every woman in the room
bought her clothes at the same exclusive shops. That is,
Claire thought once again, every woman except her.
She had known that her dress, a one-piece sweater-
dress in the color purple, was simple. Hadn't she told
Nash that very thing? She hadn't realized, however,
just how sophomoric she would look compared to the
other guests.

And her clothes were only the start of the disparate
comparison. She'd never seen such beautiful women.
She'd never seen such beautiful figures. She'd never
seen so much flawless perfection! Glancing around in
hopes of spotting one ordinary person, Claire noted the
tall, brown-haired, sensational-looking Amazon on the
dance floor. So much for ordinariness, Claire thought,
recognizing the woman as the star of a television com-
edy series. Beyond her stood a woman, a stunning
redhead, who Claire thought was a movie star. To that
woman's right was another who was about to fall out
of the front of her low-cut dress. This woman had
draped herself all over Nash the second he'd arrived at
the party. Claire had wanted to smack her.

She'd also wanted to run. Where, she wasn't sure,
except that she knew it was somewhere where houses,

beachside property and people weren't perfect. As
though seeking shelter in a storm, she raised her gaze
once more to Nash, whose white slacks and sweater
showed up his sun-god tan to perfection. For the first
time since knowing him, Claire wished he had a physical flaw. Just one. Just one tiny flaw that would ele-
vate him to the status of ordinary. Just one tiny flaw
that would make him also a fish on dry land. But there
was no such flaw. However much she might wish it
weren't so, he belonged right here. However much she
might wish it weren't so, he belonged among these
beautiful, flawless people. It was a fact she might run
from, but one she couldn't long hide from.

ONLY HALF LISTENING to what the producer was saying, Nash raised a champagne glass to his lips and stole
another glance at Claire. As he had earlier in the evening when he'd first glimpsed her in the purple dress,
he thought how beautiful she was. How beautiful in a
wholesome kind of way. She had told him that the dress
was simple. While that might be true if the dress was
hanging in a closet, on Claire, however, there was
nothing simple about the way the fabric molded to the
curves of her breasts or the swells of her hips. There
was nothing simple about what the sight of her in it did
to him. More to the point, maybe there *was* something
simple about his reaction. Maybe there was something
primitively simple.

He nodded at what the producer said, though his
mind fled back to the restless night he'd spent. A good-
night kiss hadn't put out the fire burning inside him. In
fact, it had only made the flame hotter. A dozen times
he'd started to go to her, to open the door of her bed-

room and crawl into her bed. But he hadn't, even though he'd heard her moving around her room as restlessly as he was moving around his. This was one time that he wanted to give more than his body to a woman. And he wanted more than hers in return. This was one time—the *only* time in his life he could ever remember—that he was thinking about tomorrow as much as he was thinking about today.

He noticed a woman high on too many glasses of wine run into Claire, saw Claire speak and step out of the way. He had the sudden urge to save her from the madness going on around them.

"Well, that sounds fine, Harold. Let me have a little more time—"

"We don't have time," the producer said. "We need to move on this right now. I want to start shooting..."

The producer launched into the shooting schedule he was proposing. Nash settled back impatiently, glancing over at Claire and wishing to hell that they were home...curled on the couch...with his mouth doing the wildest things to hers!

WITH EACH PASSING second, Claire felt more and more alienated from what was going on around her. A quiet panic, like a seaport fog, crept slowly over her. She couldn't explain why, though she knew that it was completely out of character, totally foreign to her confident nature. She looked around, aware on some level of seeking an exit from the room, planning an escape route should she need one.

For a moment she thought that Nash's conversation with the producer was coming to an end—Nash

looked over at her—but then the producer started
again. Claire sighed and unconsciously stepped closer
to Smudge. She smiled at a woman, a beautiful blonde
who looked vaguely familiar, as the woman edged up
to the nearest canapé tray. The blonde spoke to her,
but, because she wasn't facing Claire, Claire couldn't
make out what she said. The woman said something
else, then turned to Claire for a reply.

"I'm sorry," Claire said, speaking softly. "I didn't
understand you."

The woman—who wasn't simply beautiful; she was
a downright knockout—smiled. "I don't know how
anybody's hearing anybody in all this noise," the
knockout said.

At any other time, Claire would have simply announced that she was deaf. Now, however, she let the
music, the noise, take all the blame. It troubled her that
she did.

"It is noisy," she said, wondering why she had been
so evasive and why she was speaking so quietly. The
only conclusion she could come to was that she didn't
want to appear any more different than she already felt.
In a room full of perfection, she didn't want to wear a
placard announcing how imperfect she was.

"I said I love your dog," the blonde said, leaning
down to pat Smudge on the head. "I have a black Lab.
They're great company, aren't they?"

"Yes," Claire responded, hoping that she hadn't
misunderstood. Again, Claire was struck by the overwhelming feeling that she'd seen this woman before.
But where?

The blonde said something else, which Claire didn't catch a word of, then, as though spotting someone she knew, smiled prettily and said, "Excuse me."

Claire nodded and watched as the woman crossed the room. A sinking feeling in the pit of Claire's stomach told her where the beauty was headed even before she reached her destination. The sinking feeling was right. As Claire watched, the woman slid her arm around Nash's waist, as though she was accustomed to doing so. Nash glanced up, grinned hugely and crooked his arm around her. The woman kissed him soundly— on the mouth. Claire felt her stomach, sinking feeling and all, turn over. She also realized who the woman was. She was the blonde soap opera star who the tabloid had said Nash was squiring around town. What the tabloid hadn't said was that the two of them—Nash with his dark looks, the blonde with her fair—made a perfect—how she was growing to hate that word!— couple.

Had the two of them been intimate? The question ripped through Claire's heart, followed by an even more devastating question. Were the two of them still intimate? There had been no mention of Nash's dating status. There had been no announcement of how he felt about her. The truth was that she'd just assumed a couple of things: one, that he wasn't seeing anyone else; two, that he cared about her. Suddenly, those assumptions seemed based on shifting sand. Suddenly, Claire just wanted to escape, both the party and her naiveté.

A nearby door led to a patio. Claire, Smudge at her heels, slipped unobtrusively through it and onto the redwood patio. Because it was already occupied by several couples, each engaged in various lovers' games, Claire moved on, seeking privacy in the darkening shadows. She just wanted to be alone. To think. To feel. To forget, and conversely to remember, the sight of Nash's lips pressed against the blonde's.

Following Smudge down a pathway, Claire came to a gate. Beyond it, at the end of tiered steps, lay a swimming pool and a cabana. Lanterns faintly lighted the area, while in the distance the sea, churned by a brusque wind, crashed to shore. Though the moon was full and proud, clouds drifted past it with a threatening message of rain. It had sprinkled off and on all day, leaving Claire and Nash to stay indoors much of the time—indoors and in each other's arms.

Had his arms been only a fool's paradise? Was it a paradise that she shared with other women? Was it a paradise that the blonde knew as well as she? The questions hurt. What hurt even more was that Claire didn't have any answers. On a deep sigh, she closed her eyes and willed the pain and uncertainty away. Neither heeded her command, so she was left to share the night, and her heart, with their burdensome weight.

She had no idea how long she'd stood there when she suddenly became aware of a presence. She knew without turning around whom she'd find, though turn around she did, as if she were powerless not to confirm the presence's identity. It was Nash—exactly as she knew it would be. He stood several feet away, just staring at her with an expression that said he was trying to piece a puzzle together. The wind whipped at his hair and flapped the white slacks around his legs, making him look a little wild, a little savage and a lot desirable.

"What's the matter?" he asked softly—with lips that had just kissed another woman.

Claire turned away and back to the sea. She was uncertain whether she was trying to escape his question or his appealing appearance. Maybe she was merely trying to escape the lips that, no matter whom they'd just kissed, still made her heart patter with longing.

Undaunted, Nash stepped to her side, touched her arm and, when she angled her face toward his, repeated, "What's the matter?"

"Nothing's the mat—"

"What is it, Claire?"

She felt her answer coming, and even though she condemned it as childish and petty, she couldn't stop herself. "I was standing here wondering if I should have a face-lift or breast implants or if I should just bleach my hair blond."

Her response caught Nash totally off guard.

Stupid, stupid! she chastised herself, looking back out to sea. Why had she said that? *Because you aren't perfect,* came the reply. And that was the whole crux of the matter, wasn't it?

Sighing, Claire brushed the wind-teased hair back from her eyes. "Just forget—"

Nash clasped his fingers around her arm and hauled her back to face him. The action, which wasn't exactly rough, but then again wasn't exactly gentle, silenced Claire. Along with the hard look comprising Nash's expression.

"Don't you dare do any of those things," he said, as though he had something personally at stake. "Don't touch your face. Don't touch your breasts. Don't touch your hair. You got that?"

His commanding attitude caused Claire to tilt her chin upward. "I thought you preferred blond hair."

Slowly, Nash released his hand, though his gaze continued to hold hers. He didn't play coy. "If you want to know who she is, just ask."

"I know who she is."

Nash gave a "do you now" look.

"The tabloid said that you and she were dating."

Nash's look hardened one more. "I thought I told you not to believe everything you read."

"Then you're not seeing her?"

"Define seeing."

Claire's temper flared. "Dammit, Nash, you know what I'm asking!"

Her temper, her statement, ignited his temper. "Yes, I know what you're asking. I also know what you're implying. You're implying that when I'm not with you, I'm with her...or someone else—maybe even half of Hollywood. Do you honestly think that what I've been handing you is a line?"

Claire didn't answer. Was that what she believed?

At her silence, Nash raked his fingers through his hair. "Thanks for the vote of confidence." Something in his reply spoke more of hurt than of anger.

Claire reached out her hand, then drew it back. "I'm...I'm sorry," she said to Nash's profile. "It's just...it's just that every woman there wanted a piece of you...including the blonde in the tabloid. And I felt...I felt so left out."

Nash turned his head toward her. "Do you believe I've been handing you a line? In your heart, is that what you believe?"

Claire shook her head. "No," she answered honestly. "I don't believe that."

"Do you believe I hold you, then go to another woman?"

"No." *But you've never told me that you love me.*

"Do you believe I kiss you, then go to another woman?"

"No." *But you've never told me that you love me.*

"Do you believe I spill my guts to you, then go spill them to somone else?"

"N-o." This time her voice cracked. *Tell me you love me!*

"Then, don't ever...ever..." He didn't finish what she was never to do again, for he grabbed her, pulled her to him and buried her deep in his arms. Claire held him as tightly as he held her. Nash thought how wonderful she felt; Claire thought how strong against the wind they were when they stood together. It didn't matter if he didn't say he loved her—not when he held her like this.

Finally, he leaned back, his eyes finding hers. "Women are an occupational hazard. It's tiresome, it's boring, but that's the way it is. I told you once before that my reputation is deserved. I've played too fast and too loose. I wish I could change that, Claire. I wish I could strike every woman that came into my life before I met you, but I can't." Here his voice broke. Claire felt it in the shudder of his breath. "Tell me how and I will."

Claire said nothing. There was nothing to say. What he was asking was impossible, and they both knew it.

"If it's any consolation," he said, offering all that he could, "I haven't been with a woman in a long while—way over a year. I just got tired of...feeling nothing. I got tired of using and of being used."

"You don't have to tell me this," Claire said. And he didn't. Suddenly his past, other women, weren't important. The only thing that was important was now—the wind...the sea...his arms.

"No," he countered, "I want you to know. I don't want you to have to ever ask this again."

"I won't—"

He ignored her. "Marilyn—she's the one in the tabloid—and I are friends. Nothing more. Years ago, I worked for about three months on the soap opera she does. That was where I met the deaf person who I later wrote about in my play. This deaf woman was one of the soap's characters for a while, too. Anyway, Marilyn and I became friends. It's that simple. Occasionally, we've gone out together—to cry on each other's shoulder." He brushed back a wisp of hair that had tumbled onto Claire's forehead. When he spoke, Claire knew that his voice had lowered to a husky whisper. "We've never been lovers. She doesn't love me. I don't love her. How could I when I'm in love with someone else?" Nash's blue eyes darkened to the color of the sea that writhed with the force of the wind. "How could I love her when I love you?"

Claire was uncertain whether he'd actually said the words or if she'd just willed herself to think them.

As though reading her mind, Nash took her hand in his, drew her wrist to his mouth and kissed the tender underside. "I...love...you," he whispered against her skin.

She could read the words by the flutter of his breath, by the motion of his lips. She could *feel* what he was saying. A sweet pain began in her heart.

He kissed her hand again, then pulled it aside and said, "I know I have no right to ask it, I know I don't deserve it, but love me back. Just a little. Please."

This last word, like a humbled prayer, fell from his lips and at her feet. Claire suspected that he'd never asked another human being to love him . . . and that it wasn't easy for him to do so now. She suddenly realized how very privileged she was. She realized, too, that she couldn't see him for the tears in her eyes. Were there tears in his eyes, as well?

"I do love you," she whispered, adding, "more than I can ever say."

Time stood still, hung in a lover's suspended animation. Rain, a gentle sprinkle, began to fall. Neither Claire nor Nash noticed. And then, suddenly, they were both laughing, crying. Suddenly, Nash was drawing her up and into his arms and swinging her in a circle. Suddenly, he was letting her slip the length of him, her body sliding along every curve and jut of his. Suddenly, they were dead serious as his mouth met hers.

Claire thought that he'd kissed her every way that a woman could be kissed, but he found one other way. This time he kissed her as though worshiping at an altar—a slow, sacred, spiritual kiss that opened up her heart until the love spilled over into her very soul. She felt cherished, adored. If she could remember but one moment of her life, this would be the moment, for in it was warmth enough to last a lifetime.

Bracketing her face with his hands, he withdrew his mouth, whispering once more as he stared deeply into her brown eyes, "I love you."

"I love you," she echoed, touching his cheek with her fingertips. It was only when she felt his wet skin that she realized it was raining. Even as the realization dawned, sprinkles gave way to fat, fast-falling raindrops. "It's raining," she said.

Nash glanced up, as if her announcement came as a complete shock. Sure enough, it was raining—if raindrops upon his lashes verified anything. Draping his arm around her waist, he said, "C'mon. Let's go home."

HOME.

By the time they reached it, they were soaked, though neither cared in the least. They had raced the storm back inside, said their brief goodbyes to their host, then made a mad dash for Nash's car. It was en route to the BMW that the heavens had opened up, wetting all that foolishly stood beneath. Grinning and giggling, Nash and Claire had given in to the inevitable—they simply let the rain drench them. In fact, Nash had pushed Claire against the side of the car and kissed her—long and hard and wetly. Smudge, her ears dripping water, had simply stared at the couple as though the two of them had completely lost their minds.

Now, an hour later, a fire roared in the hearth of Nash's bedroom. Nash and Claire, both freshly showered, sat on the floor before the blaze. He wore jeans and an unbuttoned shirt, while she wore his massive terry robe. She had found it lying across the foot of her bed when she'd emerged from the shower. Its feel upon her skin was warmer than the shower or the fire or the coffee that steamed in a mug beside her.

"Getting warm?" Nash asked as Claire stroked a brush through her hair. Minutes before, he had towel dried his hair and had then attmepted to dry off Smudge, who looked like an enormous drowned rat. Smudge had licked her thanks and had wandered off to a quiet corner to catch a few winks.

Claire felt cozier than she could ever remember feeling. Just the fact that she sat in Nash's bedroom was enough to conjure up cozy feelings—to say nothing of the sensual feelings that sitting only feet from his bed caused. Actually, she wasn't sure where to lay the blame—the bed or the sight of his chest. Both pretty well sent her senses reeling.

"Yes," she answered, unaware that her voice sounded like that of a throaty siren.

Nash, though, was totally aware. He was also aware that no woman had ever looked more desirable to him. Without makeup, her hair wet and straight, her body scented with cleanliness and soap, Claire made his pulse race as no other woman ever had. A thought occurred to him: he'd never allowed a woman into his bedroom, he always met them on their ground or on neutral ground, but never on his. Claire, however, belonged here in a way he couldn't explain but was perfectly willing to accept.

"Here, let me," he said in a voice husky with feeling, taking the brush from her hand.

Moving to her side, he began to thread the bristles through her damp hair. She tried to ignore the satiny feel of his hands in her hair; she tried to ignore the fact that her elbow occasionally grazed his hair-dusted chest; she tried to ignore the hard thighs straining against denim. She tried...but failed. So she just gave in and allowed herself to enjoy the wonder of his love. On a deep sigh, she lolled her head to the side.

At the seductive picture she presented, Nash moaned and wrapped her hair around his fist. He pulled her mouth to his, whispering something about not being able to get enough of her. Obviously feeling the same as he, she opened her mouth to his, inviting him to take more and more and still more of her. In seconds, she lay on her back on the carpet, Nash leaning over her. He kissed her deeply, sexily, his tongue doing things that were carnally wicked and exquisitely wonderful.

"You *are* naughty," she whispered as his wet mouth slid from hers.

He grinned—a very naughty grin. "Am I?"

"Yes," she whispered.

"And does that bother you?"

"Oh, yes," she said, making it obvious that it bothered her in the very best way.

He started to grin again, but the grin faded. "How do you sign *kiss?*"

Claire placed her fingertips at her mouth and then on her cheek. As though performing a religious ritual, Nash placed his fingertips on her lips and cheek.

She smiled. "No, you're supposed to touch your own lips and cheek."

"I like it better my way," he said, repeating the gesture with his own interpretation.

"Actually, your way has merit," she said, her voice going breathless as he lowered his head once more over hers. Her hands splayed against his bare chest, her fingers weaving themselves in the thick matting of rich brown hair. This time it was she who drew her mouth from his in order to trail kisses down his throat and onto his chest. He groaned at the sweet contact of her mouth on his skin. Claire felt the rumbling sound and recognized it for what it was. It made her want to kiss every inch of his body, which she eagerly began to do.

Abruptly, Nash rolled onto his back, bringing her with him until she rose above him, her face flushed, her hair falling around her. Her lips were parted, as were the lapels of her robe. Nash's gaze lowered to the swells of her breasts, breasts that threatened to tumble from the cloth confines. Slowly, he reached out, tracing the delicate line of cleavage with one trembling finger.

Biting her lip, Claire closed her eyes. She felt Nash's finger disappear inside her robe, then felt the finger glide over the upper curve of her breast. It teased and tantalized before all of his hand eased to cup her breast—sweetly, silently, shamelessly. She opened her eyes.

She found him watching her as his hand knew her intimately—feeling, touching, caressing. For all the women he'd known, he was touching her as if he were touching a woman for the first time. Claire saw this and relished in it. When he pulled his hand away and belted the robe more tightly around her, she tried not to appear disappointed.

"Sleep with me tonight," he whispered.

She understood his wording. He meant exactly what he said—sleep with him. Not make love with him, but sleep with him.

"Yes," she whispered, knowing that she would give him as much or as little as he needed.

Later, in bed, his body spooning hers, Claire felt relief that he'd demanded nothing more. Oh, a part of her wanted more, but at the same time she couldn't get it out of her head that he'd been with some of the most beautiful women in the world. She wasn't quite ready to compete with them. As sleep finally overcame her, her last thought was in the form of a question. Would she ever be ready to compete?

THE FOLLOWING MORNING, Claire awoke to an empty bed. Not even Smudge was at her side. She had just made the discovery when the tempting smells of frying bacon and perking coffee wafted around her nose. She smiled, stretched and thought what a strange but satisfying night she'd spent. Would anyone believe that Naughty Nash Prather had taken her to bed and not taken her as his lover? The smile at her lips ebbed away. Maybe that wasn't altogether true. In a metaphysical sense, they had become lovers. Through talking and touching, through the sharing of heart and soul, they had become bound together in a way that the mere physical act of making love couldn't have accomplished. The truth was that she knew him better than she knew any other man—including the man she'd gone with for years.

How was that posibble?

She didn't know; she simply knew that it was.

Slipping from bed, Claire confronted herself in the bedroom mirror. She moaned, and reaching for a hairbrush, she piled her hair up as best she could, tightened the belt of Nash's robe, which she'd slept in, and padded her bare feet down the hallway and into the kitchen. She stopped in the doorway at the sight that greeted her. Wearing only jeans—jeans not even buttoned at the waist—Nash was breaking eggs into a bowl. Smudge lay at his feet.

When Nash heard her, he glanced up and smiled. "How do you like your eggs?"

Crossing to him, she slid her arms around his waist. "With a kiss," she said, pressing her mouth to his.

She felt him groan, a rough purr deep in his chest. Blindly searching for a rag, he wiped his hands and enfolded his arms around her, kneading her shoulders through the robe.

When she tried to end the kiss, he protested, saying, "Uh-uh, you started this." For the next few minutes, he leaning against the island in the kitchen, she intimately situated in the V of his spread legs, they dined on the taste of each other. It was far headier than the breakfast that followed.

After the meal, they dressed and walked the beach. They looked for shells, built a sand castle, which the sea inevitably leveled, and played with Smudge, who loved the Frisbee that Nash so expertly sailed through the air. The only thing that Nash and Claire didn't do was talk about the fact that it would soon be time for her to leave. Ignoring it, however, didn't make it go away. Four o'clock, the hour that Nash had hired a plane to return Claire to San Francisco, rolled round just as both he and she knew it would. The drive to the airport was silent, Nash simply tucking Claire's hand in his lap, where it was tacitly understood it was to stay even if he did abandon it to perform the mundane task of driving.

Pulling in next to the small plane, Nash cut the engine and angled toward Claire. She expected him to say any number of things: I don't want you to go; I've loved having you visit me; I love you— Any of those would have been appropriate. She was not prepared, however, for what he *did* say.

"Marry me."

Even though she was skilled at reading lips, Claire thought that surely she'd misunderstood him.

"Marry me," he repeated, removing all doubt as to what he'd said.

Why had this proposal surprised her? Wasn't it the logical progression of events when two people declared their love for each other? And wasn't it what she wanted? Didn't she want to spend the rest of her life beside Nash? The answer to each of the questions was a resounding yes. Yet . . . Yet what? The truth was that his proposal hadn't surprised her as much as it had panicked her . . . in much the same way that his asking her to visit him had panicked her. She felt herself hesitating once more.

Nash saw that hesitation. His expression said he'd even been expecting it. "I know it's sudden, Claire. I know we haven't known each other that long, but I also know we love each other. Surely that counts for something."

"Of course it counts for something. It's just—"

"I know," he interrupted, gently laying his finger across her lips. "You're scared. It's a big step. I'm not taking it lightly, either." He grinned in one corner of his mouth. "In fact, I suspect I'm about as scared as you. I've never asked anybody to marry me before." His grin faded. "I know I may not be the best you can do, but—"

"Don't say that!" she said, now placing her fingers at his mouth to silence him.

He pulled her hand away and continued. "I don't come to you lily-white," he said, anguish in his beautiful eyes, "but I swear to you that I love you...more than I ever thought it possible to love anything or anybody."

"Nash, I—"

"Just think about it. Take all the time you need, because I'm talking about our being together for the rest of our lives." He kissed her wrist. "Will you think about it?"

Would she think about it?

In actuality, she thought about little else during the ensuing week. Nash and his proposal were on her mind from the moment she awoke until the moment she fell asleep. Even while sleeping, she didn't always get a respite. More often than not, she dreamed of Nash, always awaking with a deep longing to see him. Throughout, she agonized over what her answer should be. Just about the time she thought she'd made up her mind to cast all reservations aside, she'd remember how out of place she'd felt, how flawed she'd felt, at the party Saturday night. The truth was that she wouldn't be marrying just any ordinary man. She'd be marrying Nash Prather...and his golden, glittery world.

She was still vacillating that Friday afternoon when she stopped by the supermarket on her way home from the university. Her arms speckled with paint, she just needed a few items, and then she'd race home to Nash's letter, which she knew would be awaiting her. The items piled in her grocery cart, Claire had just stepped up to the quick-check lane when the weekly *People in the*

News tabloid caught her eye. It actually did more than catch her eye. It clipped her at the back of her knees. Once more, Nash's perfect face graced the cover. Along with another face. That of Claire herself, though hers was half-hidden in the embrace that she and Nash were engaged in. Malibu Beach. Someone had taken their picture the Friday night they'd been on the beach. As stunned as she was, she clung to a thread of logic. The photographer couldn't know who she was. Could he? She answered her own question when she raised her gaze to the bold type running across the top of the magazine.

Naughty Nash Romancing Deaf Woman.

CHAPTER FOURTEEN

ANGER, AS HOT as a flash fire, blazed over Claire. It was quickly doused by a wave of mortification as she remembered what she and Nash had been doing on the beach Friday night. My Lord, had whoever taken the photograph seen them kissing? Had he observed them as Nash caressed her body? The mere thought mortified her anew. This was followed by another burst of fury that someone would callously encroach on something that had been private and intimate.

As powerful as her anger and mortification were, they were threatened by a third feeling. This one she couldn't easily classify. It had been inspired by the word *deaf,* which stared back at her from the tabloid. It was as though the word had reached out and tripped Claire, slamming her face down in the truth, forcing her to see herself—really see herself—for the first time. Or more importantly, forcing her to see herself as others saw her. Nash wasn't romancing an artist of growing renown; he wasn't romancing someone who taught at a university to students who clamored to take her course; he wasn't romancing a woman who was a decent human being, a person kind to kids and pets. He was romancing a *deaf* woman, a one-dimensional, singularly faceted being. Something about reducing her to this lowest common denominator galled her, an-

gered her and, though she still had no name for the
emotion, made her feel as if she stood naked before a
highly critical world.

Was this the way everyone saw her?

There was no time to consider the question, for the
checker smiled and began to unload the shopping cart.
As Claire rummaged through her purse for her check-
book, she grabbed her sunglasses and slid them on in
case the checker, the bag boy, the woman who'd pulled
in behind her connected her with the tabloid picture.
Once more, Claire felt as though she'd been shoved
naked onto a stage. Once more, she felt a fire-hot anger.

Her mood didn't improve. In fact, it grew markedly
worse. When the doorbell unexpectedly rang at a
quarter to nine, Claire wasn't certain whether to be
grateful for or further annoyed at the interruption.
When she opened the door, both gratitude and annoy-
ance gave way to surprise.

Nash stood on the threshold, a copy of the tabloid
in his hand. His expression was unreadable. Conversely, Claire's was as clear as rainwater. It said that
she'd already seen the magazine.

"You've seen it," Nash said unnecessarily.

"This afternoon. At the supermarket."

"I'm sorry. I wanted to be the one to tell you."

Claire fleetingly wondered if she would have felt
differently if the news had come from Nash. No, she
doubted she would have. She also fleetingly realized
that he looked his usual gorgeous self. On the other
hand, she could never remember feeling so dowdy...so
plain...so...one-dimensional.

"I'm sorry," Nash repeated. It was taken for granted that he meant the incident in general, her learning about it as she had in particular.

"It wasn't your fault," Claire responded, wondering for the first time just how distorted her voice sounded to Nash. For that matter, how did he see her? As the deaf woman the world saw?

"May I come in?" Nash asked, slashing through Claire's gray introspection.

She stepped back in invitation and started for the kitchen.

Nash caught her arm. "Hey, wait. What kind of greeting is this?"

"I thought I'd make some cof—"

Nash's mouth silenced her, telling her, and pretty effectively, that coffee came in a very poor second to what he had in mind.

As always, the kiss destroyed Claire, sending her into orbit around the earth, yet curiously, she once more felt emotionally naked. And this time for a reason other than Nash's sensual expertise. This time she didn't want to land back on this planet, simply because she knew that it could be a brutal place. This stark realization stoked the fires of her anger.

Nash sensed her mood, her withdrawal, and drew his mouth away. His eyes roamed over the pinched lines of her forehead, the tightness around her mouth, the anger-brightness in her sable-dark eyes.

"You're really upset, aren't you?" He'd expected a negative reaction—his own had been negative—but he hadn't expected this degree of...*hostility* was the word.

Something that had been only tenuously held together up to this point snapped. "You're damned right

I am!'' Claire said, threading back hair that no doubt looked a fright. And, furthermore, she didn't care how frightful it looked! ''I don't know how you can be so calm,'' she charged.

''What makes you think I am?''

''You look calm to me.''

''You wouldn't have thought so several hours ago when I was chewing ass.'' At her interested look, he added, ''I've been on the phone all afternoon chewing out whoever got in my way—secretaries, reporters at the tabloid, the editor in chief himself. I even took a bite out of my lawyer.''

''And?''

''The secretaries told me I'd have to talk to the reporters. The reporters told me I'd have to talk to the editor in chief. He assured me that none of his fine, law-abiding reporters would trespass on private property, although it was his job to run a magazine, which necessitated that he buy photos from free-lance photographers, and, well, he couldn't be reponsible for how they got their photos.''

''And do you believe him? Do you believe it was a free-lance photographer?''

Nash shrugged. ''Who knows? The Dallas photo was obviously bought from a free-lancer.''

This announcement grasped Claire by the throat. ''What Dallas photo?''

''You didn't read the article?''

When Claire shook her head, Nash opened the magazine to reveal a fuzzy photo taken weeks before as they were leaving—fleeing—the Dallas restaurant.

Claire groaned. ''Isn't there anything we can do?''

"I talked to my lawyer and apparently we don't have
leg to stand on . . . which I knew we wouldn't have."

"Why?"

"People in the public eye are fair game."

"But somebody trespassed on your property."

"Who do I charge?"

"Can't you sue the magazine for libel?"

"How? They didn't lie. I *am* romancing you."

"And, of course, I *am* deaf," Claire said sarcasti-
ally.

The uncharacteristic vehemence in her tone startled
lash. Claire was oblivious to this. She was too intent
n raking her fingers back through her hair and rail-
g. "I don't believe this. People invade your privacy
nd there's nothing you can do about it. They observe
timate acts—"

"Claire, you're getting worked up—"

" . . . and there's nothing you can do!"

"Claire—"

"How can you take it lying down?"

"It's part and parcel of my life."

"Well, it's not part and parcel of mine."

"You'll learn to adjust."

"No . . . no, I don't think I will. Furthermore, I don't
hink I want to try."

The short, crisp delivery, the harsh words caught
oth Nash and Claire by surprise. Especially Claire.
Clearly, she hadn't known she was going to say what
he had.

"What does that mean?" Nash asked.

She sighed. "Just forget—"

"No, you don't say something like that and then just
ay forget it." Nash had the look of a man who'd ar-

rived to do battle on one front, only to discover that th
enemy had shifted to another—and that the enem
might not be the enemy he'd imagined. "I have a feel
ing that something's going on here beyond the fact tha
a reporter snapped a photo."

Claire had the same feeling, though, to be honest
she wasn't sure what that something was. She fell bacl
on her old stand-by complaint. "Nash, we're from
different worlds."

Nash swore—and none too gently. "No two peopl
are from the same world. Besides, I'm not sure that'
what's at issue here. I'm not sure it's ever really bee
the issue." Nash had no idea where he was headed witl
his accusation. He knew only that he was flying by th
seat of his pants, pure instinct his only instrumen
panel. Considering Claire's usual confidence, he
harping on their differing worlds didn't make sense. I
wasn't fitting into character. It never had. Somethin
more had to be at stake.

"What is the issue, then?" she asked, eager to hav
someone explain to her what she was having a devil o
a time understanding herself.

"You tell me."

Heaving a weary breath, she admitted, "I don'
know...not really. It's just..."

When Claire hesitated, Nash prompted. "Jus
what?"

Another wave of anger washed over Claire. "Dam
mit, why couldn't they have called me something besides deaf? Anything! Purple, two headed, a horribl
human being. Anything!"

Nash frowned while Smudge glanced up sharply
from where she lay before the sofa.

"That bothers you?" Nash asked.

"Yes!"

Genuinely perplexed, he said, "Why?"

"Because I'm more than deaf!"

"Of course you are."

"Don't patronize me!"

"I'm only agreeing with you."

"Well, don't!" Claire shouted, knowing that none of what she was saying made any sense. In fact, it was utter and complete nonsense. Suddenly, as though all the wind had died out of her sails, she sighed and said, "I'm so tired of competing with perfection."

"What perfection?"

"The perfection in your world. Your house is flawless, your friends are flawless, you're flawless."

"My house is lifeless, my friends, for the most part, are really nothing more than acquaintances, and I'm not even close to flawless."

"Have you checked your mirror lately?"

Nash looked as though he'd been slapped across his handsome face. "Yeah ... and for the first time in my life, since meeting you, I see someone staring back. But that someone is far from flawless."

His words filled Claire with a deep warmth ... and a deep sadness. "What I see is flawless." Her voice lowered. "And you need someone just as flawless ... someone who reporters can label something besides deaf."

What she'd said hurt him. She could tell by the dullnss that jumped into his usually vibrant blue eyes.

"Let me get this straight," he said. "You're turning down my proposal—and that is what you're doing, isn't it, Claire?"

She said nothing. Was that what she was doing? To be honest, it sounded like exactly what she was doing.

"You're turning me down because I'm flawless?" He half laughed, though there wasn't an ounce of mirth in the hollow sound. "That's one for the books." He laughed again. This time it was obvious that his hurt had turned to anger. Maybe it was this anger that, like a fire, cleansed the cluttered forest of his mind, making it possible for a thought to surface that perhaps had been hiding in the background all along. The anger also made him reckless enough to say what caution may have prevented before.

"Tell me something, Claire. Have you ever had a relationship with a man who wasn't deaf?"

Like an abrupt, hard-hit ball, the question plowed into Claire's stomach. "What does that have to do—"

"Have you?"

"Of course I've dated—"

"A relationship. Not a casual date."

"I, uh...haven't had that many relationships," she said, thinking of only one—Bill. Bill, whom she hadn't loved, but had felt secure with. Secure? What an interesting word. What a significant word?

"How many?"

Claire hedged.

"Three?"

Nothing. Claire said nothing.

"Two?"

Nothing.

"Bill?"

"I don't see—"

"Only Bill?"

"—what this has to do with anything."

"Is Bill the only man you've ever had a relationship with?"

"Yes!"

Nash's expression said that everything suddenly seemed clear. He shook his head. "You know, I've been walking around feeling like a fraud, but the truth is, you're a fraud, too, lady."

"What do you mean?"

"That your confidence is a sham...at least in one area of your life."

"That's absurd."

"Is it? Then why has your only meaningful relationship with a man been with a deaf man?" He answered his own question. "I'll tell you. Somehow you have it in your mind that a deaf man is the only safe man."

Because he was stepping all over her emotional toes, Claire's anger bubbled again. "You're making a lot of reckless assumptions."

"I don't think so. I think I'm finally getting to the crux of the matter. Maybe you are afraid of the comparisons between our worlds, but the truth is you'd be afraid of any man's world if it was a hearing world."

"I think you have a fertile imagination," Claire said, her anger rapidly rising by heated degrees.

"And I think you're copping out," Nash retaliated.

"Which is something you're an expert at, right?"

He frowned. "And just what do you mean by that?"

"You want to make your own movie, but you're going to cop out and do another one that you really don't want any part of...simply because it's the safe thing to do." She hadn't meant to say what she had; it had just tumbled out in an eye-for-an-eye, tooth-for-a-tooth fashion.

Nash looked as if he'd been struck.

Claire would have given anything—anything!—to have been able to recall her words.

"I'm sor—"

"No, you're right," he said, his voice thick with emotion. "I do know all about copping out. God only knows, I've done it long enough. And, God only knows, I've had my fill of it." Here his thick voice lowered. "I've waited a lifetime for you, Claire, and if you're not prepared to make the same commitment to me that I am to you, then you can just forget the whole thing."

Now it was Claire who looked as if she'd been struck.

Nash saw her pain but could not find it in himself to regret what he'd said. He regretted only that circumstances had forced him to say it.

"You know where to find me if you want to commit to this relationship, but I want a full commitment. Anything short of that is a cop-out I won't tolerate—not anymore. I'm tired of hearing about our different worlds. The real issue is that you're afraid to let me into your world. If you don't trust me any more than that, Claire..." He stopped, as though having trouble mustering what he had to say. "If you can't believe in my love for you, regardless of what you are or what you aren't, if you can't trust me enough to let me hear your star song, then forget about us."

Forget about us.

The words lingered in the stale stillness long after Nash had walked calmly to the door and left. He

adn't kissed her, he hadn't looked back, but he hadn't
iven her an easy way out. Furthermore, he'd left her
vith far too much to think about . . . and with the fear
1at everything he'd said had been the truth.

A WEEK LATER, on a breezy Saturday afternoon, Claire
nd AmyAnn went shopping. Following that, they
topped by an ice-cream parlor for sodas. Claire wasn't
ungry, but then she hadn't been all week. Neither had
he slept. In fact, she'd done little except replay her
onversation with Nash. The net result was that she
vas bone tired, soul weary and no nearer any under-
tanding of what she was feeling than she had been
vhen Nash had walked out the week before. She did
now, though, that the strain of trying to act normal
ll week was about to get to her. She felt as though she
vere ready to unravel into a hundred ragged threads.

"Mother's taking sign language," AmyAnn said,
igning unselfconsciously. She then launched into the
lifficulties her mother was having and the humorous
nistakes she'd made. Despite her preoccupation, Claire
ealized AmyAnn's pleasure at her mother's commit-
nent.

Commitment.

The word was never far from Claire's mind. She
vanted to commit to Nash for the rest of their lives, but
he couldn't. Not until she knew exactly who—or
vhat—she was. This identity crisis was new to her,
.omething she'd never in her wildest dreams thought
he'd have to face. It had slowly dawned on her that
naybe she'd waited all these years to come to terms
vith her disability. The tabloid had forced her to real-

ize that, no matter what she did with her life, there would always be those who saw her only as deaf.

"Candace, Leah and I speak in sign language," AmyAnn said, "in class, in the cafeteria, every where." The teenager giggled. "It drives everyone crazy, so everyone asks what we're saying, so then we have to teach them. Mrs. MacMurtry—she's our English teacher—said that pretty soon we'll have the whole school..."

Claire smiled, but her mind was elsewhere—on Nash's accusation. *You're a fraud*. Yes, she was a fraud. She'd spouted equality for disabled people. She tried to make her Little Sister believe that she was the equal of any and all, and yet, when push came to shove, Claire was forced to realize that she very much felt her own inadequacy. At least in one area of her life, at least in her relationships with men. A man who shared her quiet world offered her security, safety, a comfortable sameness. Not only didn't Nash share her silent world, but the world he belonged to glittered as brightly as neon.

"...beginning Monday..."

The words snatched at Claire's consciousness. She had no idea what AmyAnn was referring to. "I'm sorry. What did you say?"

AmyAnn looked at her Big Sister as though confirming something that she'd suspected; namely, that she had only a fraction of Claire's attention. "I said," she repeated, bending to give Smudge the last of her soda, "that beginning Monday there will be an interpreter in the classroom with me."

Claire knew what a concession this was for AmyAnn and admired her courage. It was a courage she wished she could find in her own life. "I'm glad. I know what a difficult decision it was."

As she often could, AmyAnn suddenly looked far older than her sixteen years. "It's hard to be different."

"Yes . . . yes, it is," Claire said, understanding only too well. For silent seconds, the tabloid headline flashed once more in Claire's memory: Naughty Nash Romancing Deaf Woman. Yes, she knew exactly what it felt like to be different.

"I saw the magazine," AmyAnn signed.

Claire wasn't surprised. Several people had mentioned seeing it. She'd even had a reporter from a local newspaper request an interview. Claire had turned him down—nicely, she thought, considering that she'd have loved to tell him to go take a flying leap off a high bridge.

"It upset you, didn't it?" AmyAnn asked.

"Yes. I found I didn't much like being thought of only as deaf."

"Me, either," AmyAnn said. "No matter what else I am, being deaf is all people seem to see. But you know what I think?"

"What?"

"I don't think it matters how others see us. I think it's only important how we see ourselves. Okay," she amended, "I think it's nice when those we care about see us in a positive way."

Claire smiled. "Are you sure you're only sixteen?"

A smiling AmyAnn flipped back her golden Little Orphan Annie curls. "Well, I'm almost seventeen."

"That must account for the wisdom."

AmyAnn's smile faded. "Gary said that you and Nash broke up."

Shrugging, Claire admitted, "I don't quite know what we've done."

"He cares for you," AmyAnn said.

"Yes, but how does he see me?"

"Why don't you ask him?" AmyAnn said simply.

"What if I haven't got the courage?"

"Being deaf is one thing—being a coward is another."

Claire smiled. "Now, where have I heard that before?"

AmyAnn didn't return the smile. In fact, AmyAnn was dead serious when she replied, "From the woman who taught me how to be wise."

HOURS LATER, on that same Saturday, Nash stood on the beach of his Malibu home. A solitary figure silhouetted against the pink-and-gray iridescent twilight, he stared out at the endless, rolling sea. Overhead, swooping low in a lazy white V, a lone sea gull cawed in commiseration with Nash's miserable mood.

Had he been too hard on Claire?

The question had plagued him night and day since he'd walked out of her life a week before. One moment he thought no, that he had a right to expect the same commitment from her that he was willing to make. The next moment he thought yes, that surely he could be generous of spirit and realize that Claire was entitled to lapses of confidence like everyone else. Surely he could imagine how demoralizing it must have been to see her whole life, her whole being, reduced to a single element—a single deaf element. God only

new that he'd suffered from the same limiting dis-
rimination. No matter how hard he tried to appear
therwise, the world saw him only as a pretty face and
tight pair of jeans.

Tucking his hands into the back pockets of just such
pair of jeans, Nash sighed. And couldn't he under-
tand playing it safe with relationships? Claire had
onfined hers to someone who'd shared her world. He,
n the other hand, had avoided anything meaningful
y scattering himself so thin that there was nothing to
ive to any one person. Claire had found safety in a
ingularity, he in a plurality.

And yet, it hurt him as he'd never been hurt before
o think that... That was just it—he didn't know what
he thought. She kept talking about competing with his
vorld of perfection. Did she honestly think that he saw
er as imperfect? The truth was that she was perfect in
 way he never would be. Did she think he'd grow tired
f her? How could he grow tired of something more
recious than his own heartbeat? Yes, she had hurt
im.

She'd also angered him. She was supposed to be the
onfident one, the one who gave substance to his
hadow. He realized now that her confidence was what
ad first attracted him to her. He wanted her to be
trong and sure and certain. But wasn't he being un-
air to expect her to always be so? As a human being,
idn't she have the right to sometimes be the weak one?
Didn't she have the right to expect to sometimes lean on
im? Wasn't love that give-and-take, that loan and
orrow? And the truth was that her love had given him
 confidence he'd never had before—a confidence that
urely he could share with her.

Furthermore, hadn't he always been a scrapper, street fighter? Wasn't fighting what Vincent Prata torri did best? And was there anything more wort fighting for than Claire? Was there anything mor worth fighting for than their future?

No.

Absolutely nothing!

And if he left right now he could be in San Fran cisco in a few hours. The thought sent adrenalin sloshing through his veins. Galvanized into action, h whirled, his bare toes digging into the moist sand. He' taken only a few steps, however, when he saw the fig ure walking toward him. He stopped. Disbelief slice through his body even as he wondered if he was hal lucinating. If he was, he was good at it, for he not onl' had conjured the perfect image of Claire, but also ha conjured the perfect image of Smudge.

At the sight of Nash, standing tall and lean in th sunset, Claire's heart went crazy-wild. The house keeper, who'd electronically released the gate from th house when Claire had identified herself, had met he at the mansion door and explained that Nash was o the beach. The walk down had been the longest jour ney Claire had ever made. What if it was too late t pick up the broken pieces of their relationship?

Please, God, don't let it be too late!

Nash stood rooted to the spot. He was dimly aware that the surf was licking at his legs. Claire carried he shoes in her hand. The same surf played around he ankles, creating the illusion that Claire, like a Botti celli masterpiece, had somehow risen from the sea. No she was more beautiful than any work of art. With hai wind-wild and black as midnight, with a face pris

nely clear of makeup except for a hint of rose at her
ps, she was . . . perfect.

She stopped before him. Stopped and said in a voice
at was more beautiful than any sound Nash had ever
eard, "What do you see when you look at me?"

Nash had the feeling that his future, their future,
epended on his answer. And there were so many re-
ponses he could honestly give. He could tell her that
hat he saw was a beauty that took his breath away. He
ould tell her that what he saw was the other half of
imself. He could tell her that what he saw was the only
appiness he'd ever known. The truth was, though,
at only one answer really mattered.

"That's simple," he said, his voice husky with feel-
g. "I see the woman I love."

Tears stung Claire's eyes, blurring her vision until
ash was but a clouded image. He had told her—and
ith a heartfelt eloquence—how he saw her. Only one
uestion remained. How did she see herself? Interest-
gly, she found that answer just as simple as Nash's.
he was the woman who loved Nash Prather.

For now and for always.

EPILOGUE

A MONTH LATER, on a starlit night, Claire and Nash awaited the ceremony that would unite them as man and wife. The patio of Nash's home, the chosen scene of the wedding, had been converted into a fairyland. White satin ribbon hung in swags, culminating in dozens of giant, frothy bows, while pale pink rosebuds demurely peeked from delicate greenery. Tiny cymbidium orchids, their petals in pastel shades of pink, lavender and magenta, floated in the nearby swimming pool. Stands of burning white candles cast a golden gleam, a romantic beacon in scared commemoration of lovers everywhere.

A gentle murmur, in the impatient notes of anticipation, tripped ever so slightly through the gathered crowd. Though only a few guests had been invited, Nash had spared no expense at flying everyone in earlier that afternoon. All of Claire's family was in attendance, along with AmyAnn, who would attend Claire, Sharon Williams, Lance Randle and Peg Pannell.

As for Nash, beyond Gary, who would be serving as best man, he'd invited only two people, his agent and Marilyn Collins, the beautiful blonde from the tabloid. Marilyn had proved herself to be not only Nash's friend, but Claire's, as well. In the past weeks, when every reporter in the world, it seemed, was trying to confirm the rumor that Nash Prather was engaged and find out who the elusive woman in his life was, it was Marilyn, with the wisdom of experience, who'd helped Claire keep her emotional balance. No one, however, had been able to help Nash keep his, and his precarious state had nothing to do with the news coverage. It had to do with impatience. Never had any man so eagerly counted the hours to his wedding.

For the third time in as many minutes, Nash checked his watch.

"Will you take it easy?" Gary said. Both men stood at the improvised altar. Each man wore a black tux with a pleated white shirt. As usual, Nash's handsomeness and Gary's plainness posed an interesting and contrasting study in appearances.

"For crying out loud, what could be taking so long?"

"Woman things that I'm sure neither you nor I would understand."

"You don't think she's climbing out a window, do you?"

"If she has any sense, she is," Gary teased, adding, "Remember, I've lived with you."

"Yeah, well, buddy, just remember I've lived with you, too. Frankly, I think you need a woman to clean up your act."

Gary's gaze wandered to Sharon Williams. She sat talking with Lance and Peg. "I'm working on it," Gary answered. "Believe me, I'm working on it. Oh, by the way, I meant to tell you. The limos will be here at precisely two o'clock."

As best man, Gary would have to make sure that all the wedding guests were gone by 2:00 a.m. Once the house was vacated, the honeymoon would begin. After much discussion, both Claire and Nash had agreed they'd rather stay cloistered at his house—walking the beach, swimming in the surf and the pool—than go elsewhere. There would be plenty of time for travel later. Right now, all they wanted was each other and some privacy. To ensure the latter, a security guard had been hired. Part of his job was to remain discreetly out of the honeymooners' way.

Nash nodded at his friend's announcement concerning the limos, then once more checked his watch. It was only a minute past the last time he'd looked. "What in the world is keeping her?"

At the same time that Nash was grumbling, Claire was arranging—or rather, rearranging for the twelfth time—the tiny pink rosebuds in her hair. Nash had asked her to wear her hair up in the loose knot that he'd come to love. He'd told her, and brazenly, that he intended to thoroughly enjoy taking it down later that night. At the thought of what else he'd promised for later that night, Claire's body tingled. They had yet to be lovers. Although Nash had made no attempt to hide his desire for her, he likewise had made it clear that he wanted them to be married when they took that final physical step. Claire understood that, for a man who'd made love too casually in the past, it was his way of telling her how special she was to him. She understood, yet she was growing impatient.

"Here, let me," AmyAnn said, taking over the job of positioning the rosebuds in the ebony strands of Claire's hair. The women's gazes met in the mirror. Both smiled. "There," AmyAnn said, signing, "You look beautiful."

Did she? Claire wondered, hoping that the white raw-silk suit, with its slim skirt and jacket with a peplum, wasn't too simple, yet simple was her style. That simplicity was reflected in the single strand of pearls that Nash had given her as a wedding gift. As lovely as the flawless pearls were, however, he'd given her a far more valuable wedding present. The night before, he'd announced his plan to make his own movie. Win, lose or draw, he was going to direct a film version of his play. Knowing that he'd already won by simply pursuing his dream, Claire had wept with happiness.

Her wedding present to him had equally moved him. She'd sensed that it had because he'd said nothing for a long while, then had silently pulled her into his arms. He'd then taken down the valuable Serres and hung Claire's painting in its place. The subject of the painting was simple, yet complex. It was of the two of them walking the beach, yet each of them had double images, symbolizing the identity problems that each had experienced. In the distance, though their hands joined, the blurred images blended. In each other, each had found himself.

They both had grit—Nash to undertake a risky project in order to realize his dream, she to honestly admit that his hearing world intimidated her. AmyAnn, too, had grit. Claire had no doubt of that. She still sensed the young woman's anger, her frustration, but mostly she just sensed that AmyAnn was getting on with her life. Although she wasn't yet dating Lance, she did see him as a friend. If their relationship was meant to be more, it would be so in time.

"Have I told you how proud I am of you?" Claire asked.

AmyAnn, wearing a pale pink dress, answered, "I don't think so. But then you didn't have to. You told me something far better. You told me that I could be proud of myself."

Her eyes glistening with tears, Claire pulled AmyAnn into her arms. In seconds both women were sniffing back tears, laughing and sniffing again.

AmyAnn was the first to sober. "What happens to us now?" She remembered vividly how shadows could whisper and knew that, for the most part, they had grown silent because of Claire and the optimism she'd brought to her life.

"What do you mean what happens to us?"

"Will you still be my Big Sister? I mean, I know you'll be moving here, and if you move here, how can you still be my Big Sister?"

For all of AmyAnn's sixteen years, for all of the maturity that had been foisted upon her the past months, she suddenly looked like a child again. Trying to be brave, trying to hide her vulnerability but not quite making it, Claire fought the urge to pull her back into her arms.

"I still have commitments in San Francisco. Nash knows this. We'll be dividing our time between here and there. Our relationship—yours and mine—won't change at all. We'll still see each other just as we always have. Besides," she added, unable to keep herself from brushing back a wisp of golden hair from AmyAnny's forehead, "don't you know that whatever happens, we'll always be friends?"

This time it was AmyAnn's eyes that first glazed with tears.

"C'mon," Claire said, dabbing at her own eyes, "help me get married before Nash changes his mind. C'mon, girl," she likewise signed to Smudge.

The dog, a collar of white satin ribbon and pink roses tied around her throat, rose, waved her tail and thrust her head high. She seemed to know that few dogs ever got to be an attendant in a wedding. She seemed to likewise know that this house was now home and Nash part of the family. Somehow or other, she'd come to terms with that fast little sports car.

"Ready?" AmyAnn asked Claire, adjusting another flower in Claire's hair, then handing her a bouquet of roses and petite orchids.

"Ready," Claire said, boldly taking the first step toward a new life.

The next few minutes, the next few hours, would forever remain in Claire's mind as a montage of sights and scents, touches and tastes. The sight of Nash as she walked toward him stripped every coherent thought from her mind. Never had he looked more splendid. Never had he looked sexier. Never had she been more certain of what she was doing. The sight of her reflected in his eyes was humbling. He made her feel pretty. He made her feel special. He made her feel loved.

Along with the sight of Nash, their guests and the kind-eyed minister, Claire noted the plush smell of roses, the shimmering glow of candles, the feel of Nash taking her hand in his. She saw a breeze feather through his hair, saw him sign—where had he learned how? she wondered—"I do" when the minister asked if he took her for his wife, felt a gold band slip onto her finger. She felt his lips on hers, whispering that he loved her, saw the pleased grin on Gary's face and the tears of joy in her mother's eyes.

And then they'd become separated, she, he, being passed among family and friends, each bestowing good wishes for their future. Sometime later, they'd cut a cake, she feeding a bite to Nash, he feeding a bite to her. Her nose somehow got tipped in frosting. Everyone laughed and Nash swiped it off with his thumb, then put his thumb to her lips. The frosting tasted sweet. Just like Nash. She felt a warmth flutter through her. Nash felt it, too, and lowered his mouth to hers. Everyone applauded.

Claire wished they were alone.

In time—minutes, hours, she wasn't sure—they were. The champagne had been drunk, the cake eaten, the bouquet thrown by the bride and caught by a jubilant AmyAnn. Claire had given a final hug to Gary— the last of their guests to leave—before Nash had walked him to the door. Smudge beside her, Claire had stayed on the patio. She felt an odd sense of unreality as the star-streaked night closed in around her.

She was married. To Nash Prather. No, she was married to Vincent Pratatorri. For all that the world saw him as a movie star, she saw him only as a man. Her man.

Nash stopped short as he stepped back onto the patio. The sight of Claire standing, staring into the night, sent a heated wave of feeling lapping over him. She was his. His wife. His woman. From now till death do them part. In some way that he could only term spiritual, she was more than this, however. She was part of him and, as such, she completed him in a way he'd never been completed before. She also eased the

oneliness of the past. He could never not remember
eeling alone, from the time he'd seen his mother bur-
ed to the time he'd walked the streets of New York.
Even with Gary as his friend, a part of him had been
alone, simply because there was a part of him that he
could not, that he dared not, share with anyone, for
ear that someone would hurt him as he'd been hurt
before. But Claire was different. She would not hurt
him. She could not hurt him. Because she was his very
heartbeat. Just as he was hers.

Claire felt the brush of his lips at the back of her
neck even as his arms slid around her waist. He pulled
her against him, into the solid strength of his body. She
leaned her head against his chest and nestled close to
him. She could feel his heartbeat, strong and sure.

"I thought they'd never leave," she said softly. "Is
that terribly ungracious of me?"

Nash's only answer was the tightening of his arms
and the whisper of his lips in her hair. They stood thus,
feeling the salty breeze flicker the stillness, feeling the
black night hugging them tight, feeling the stars twin-
kle and shine.

"Can you hear them?" Claire asked.

She could tell from the rumble of Nash's chest that
he replied, "What?"

"The stars. Can you her them singing?"

Nash listened. In the silence, he heard the buzz of
some insect, the restless roar of the sea, the wind as it
lanced by his ear. But did he hear the stars? He wanted
to. God, how he wanted to!

Taking his hand in hers, Claire pressed his palm to
her heart. Once before he'd sought the star's song in
her heartbeat. Perhaps now, with love choreographing

the beat, she could make him hear the silence of her world.

Nash felt the rhythmic pulsing of her heart, the subtle shape of her breast. Nash felt her love. Slowly turning her in his arms, his gaze seeking hers, he whispered, "The only song I hear is your heart telling me that you love me."

A smile gently tilted the corner of Claire's mouth. "Then, you do hear the stars. That's the song they're singing."

Love split wide Nash's heart, spilling a heated desire throughout his body. He was going to die that moment, on that very spot, if he didn't kiss her. Even so, he forced himself to temper his need. Wedging her face in his palms, he lowered his mouth to hers... softly... sweetly. His tongue mated with hers, coiling, curling, in a slow, sinuous, sensuous ballet. When Claire whimpered, he deepened the kiss, drawing his hands down her body—along her shoulders, her back, her hips. He pulled her into him until she could feel every inch of him. Every aroused inch.

"I love you," he whispered.

"I love you," she whispered back.

"I want you," he rasped.

"I want you.... I do... I—"

Her words were once more silenced by his kiss. This kiss, however, was deep and throaty and filled with primitive need. It was also delivered as he scooped her into his arms and started for the house.

"Five minutes," he whispered as he lowered her to the carpet in front of the master bath. "If you're not out of there in five minutes, I swear I'm coming in after you."

His threat was delicious and almost worth challenging. Almost, but not quite, since the truth was that she was as eager as he. "Five minutes," she promised.

In somewhat less, she emerged wearing a simple white satin gown that lovingly, seductively caressed every feminine curve of her body. If she'd been worried about competing with all the women that Nash had known, which a part of her was, that fear vanished the moment she saw him. He'd been in the act of undressing, his fingers fumbling with the stud at the cuff of his shirtsleeve. His tux jacket lay forgotten on a nearby chair, while his bow tie dangled from his neck. His shirt hung enticingly open. At the sight of Claire, his fingers stilled. He looked as though he'd been struck on the head by a severe and powerful blow.

Nash's mouth went absolutely dry.

As did Claire's at the sight of the bare, hair-dusted chest that lay beneath the parted shirt.

It was she who crossed to him, for, in all honesty, it appeared that Nash was unable to move. He simply stared at her, as if he could not trust himself to believe what he was seeing. When she stood before him, she took his hand in hers and, with a curious deftness considering that she trembled from head to foot, unfastened his sleeve cuff. She then reached to unfasten the other. He stopped her, however, drawing her hand, her wrist, to his mouth. He kissed the erratic pulse that throbbed against his lips. His gaze burned into hers.

"Do you have any idea how beautiful you are?" he asked, and she could tell that the words had been roughly spoken.

"I'm not beau—"

"Yes, you are," he said, kissing her hand once more and bringing it to his chest, where he abandoned it to hard muscle and crinkly hair. At the same time, he slowly began to remove the pins, the sweet-scented flowers, from her hair. With each strand that surrendered to his touch, Claire felt his heartbeat increase its tempo. She felt her own increase when he softly whispered that he loved her.

"I love you," she whispered, knowing that her voice had been nothing more than breath.

"I know," he said, burying his fingers deep in her hair and drawing her mouth up to his. He kissed her. Deeply. Provocatively. His tongue tasting, touching, tempting her.

Claire's hands restlessly sifted through the dark hair of his chest, then lower and lower until her fingers trailed through the thicket of hair on his belly. He gasped . . . and whispered some dark something that shattered her senses. Her sanity fled completely when she felt his fingers draw the thin straps of her gown from her shoulders. The gown, as though its only desire were to do Nash's bidding, slithered downward . . . over her breasts, her waist, her hips. It lay on the floor in a cloud-colored heap.

Slowly—so slowly Claire thought she would die—Nash's gaze lowered to her dark-tipped breasts, her small waist, the jut of her hips. His hands followed his gaze, his lips his hands. Claire cried out softly as his hands, his mouth touched her in warm, womanly places. With Bill she had known safety. He had been like her—same of same, kind of kind. Likewise, he'd demanded nothing more from her than she'd wanted to give. But with Nash things would be different. With

Nash things would not be safe. Soaring above the clouds was never safe. Furthermore, he would demand everything of her—not just what she wanted to give, but everything that she as a woman, a wife, had to give. And, in the sensual bargain, he'd make her like giving it.

"Nash?" she whispered, wanting, needing to begin this giving journey. She knew exactly what road she wanted their journey to take.

"Hmm?"

"Let's have a baby."

"Uh-uh," he whispered, his lips brushing across hers. "Let's have babies. Lots of babies. A houseful of babies. Starting right now."

Claire felt herself lifted into his arms, felt the softness of the bed as her body melted into it, felt his lips cover hers as he struggled to remove his clothing. She helped by drawing the shirt from his shoulders, but her effort was thwarted by the sleeve cuff that was still fastened. Her effort was equally jeopardized by the fact that Nash's hands seemed busy with other jobs... like slipping off socks and unzipping pants. When he finally turned his attention to the cuff, he swore, broke the stud and sent the shirt sailing to the floor.

At the sight of him, golden and bare, Claire closed her eyes. Immediately, though, she felt his hand at her cheek. Her eyelids fluttered open.

"Look at me," he said. "I want you to look at me when I make love to you." As he spoke, he lowered his body to hers—hard to soft, warm to warm, man to woman. "I love you," he whispered as his mouth sipped at hers. Hers sipped back. "I love you," he said as he kissed the column of her neck. She squirmed beneath him, bringing their bodies ever closer, ever more intimate. "I love you," he said, kissing one breast, then the other, before once more finding her moist mouth.

"I love you," she whispered, running her hands down his corded back and over his tightly muscled hips. And then it was happening. Slowly, gently, as naturally as the change of seasons, his body eased into hers.

Each ceased to be, existing only as an element of the other. Somewhere in her mind, her heart, Claire knew that this was the way all loving should be—the losing of oneself in someone else. The losing of oneself so completely that one no longer cared about safety or caution. Nash, too, knew that this was the one moment he'd waited his entire life for. He had searched his heart for some way to let Claire know that she was different from all the faceless women who had come before her—that with not a single one of them had he made love, but rather experienced only something fleeting and physical—but now he knew that telling her wouldn't be necessary. She knew. That he could feel in the core of his heart.

At that second when she sexually splintered in his arms, he put his mouth to hers and whispered words of love. He followed her, soaring as high in the sky as she. He called her name and heard her whisper that she loved him . . . more than the very life that pulsed in her veins.

It was then that he truly heard the song of the stars . . . a gentle, sweet symphony played in the discordant, dissonant notes of his lover's voice.

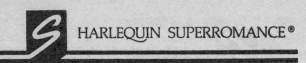

HARLEQUIN SUPERROMANCE®

Books by Sandra Canfield

BSSC

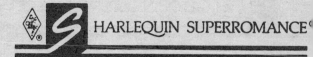

COMING NEXT MONTH

#522   JUST BETWEEN US • Debbi Bedford
When Monica Albright volunteered to be a Big Sister to
troubled teen Ann Small, she never expected to fall in
love with the child's father. But now that the inevitable
had happened, she and Richard were running the risk
of alienating Ann forever.

#523   MAKE-BELIEVE • Emma Merritt
Marcy Galvan's roots were in San Antonio. She had
her business, her family and her Little Sister,
Amy Calderon. Brant Holland's life was in New
York—his business needed him there. Though love had
brought them together, would their obligations keep
them apart?

#524   STRING OF MIRACLES • Sally Garrett
A lot of slick young legal eagles had made a play for
lawyer Nancy Prentice, but she was saving herself for a
real man: Mark Bradford. The only problem was that
Mark had always treated her like a sister. Well, no
more. Now *she* was going to take the initiative . . . !

#525   RENEGADE • Peg Sutherland
Former country-and-western star Dell McColl lived up
to his reputation as a renegade. He never backed down
from anything or anyone. Then he met never-say-die
Daylene Honeycutt. Daylene wanted two things from
Dell. She wanted *him,* and she wanted to sing in his
bar. Dell refused to give in on either count. Never again
would he be responsible for a woman's destruction on
the road to stardom.

HARLEQUIN®

Temptation®

the **Fortune Boys**

A funny, sexy miniseries from bestselling
author Elise Title!

**LOSING THEIR HEARTS MEANT
LOSING THEIR FORTUNES....**

If any of the four Fortune brothers were unfortunate enough to
wed, they'd be permanently divorced from the Fortune
millions—thanks to their father's last will and testament.

BUT CUPID HAD OTHER PLANS!
Meet Adam in #412 **ADAM & EVE** (Sept. 1992)
Meet Peter #416 **FOR THE LOVE OF PETE**
(Oct. 1992)
Meet Truman in #420 **TRUE LOVE** (Nov. 1992)
Meet Taylor in #424 **TAYLOR MADE** (Dec. 1992)

**WATCH THESE FOUR MEN TRY TO WIN
AT LOVE AND NOT FORFEIT $$$**

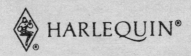

HARLEQUIN®

THE TAGGARTS OF TEXAS!

Harlequin's Ruth Jean Dale brings you
THE TAGGARTS OF TEXAS!

Those Taggart men—strong, sexy and hard to resist...

You've met Jesse James Taggart in FIREWORKS!
Harlequin Romance #3205 (July 1992)

Now meet Trey Smith—he's THE RED-BLOODED YANKEE!
Harlequin Temptation #413 (October 1992)

Then there's Daniel Boone Taggart in SHOWDOWN!
Harlequin Romance #3242 (January 1993)

And finally the Taggarts who started it all—in LEGEND!
Harlequin Historical #168 (April 1993)

Read all the Taggart romances!
Meet all the Taggart men!

Available wherever Harlequin books are sold.

HARLEQUIN®

Temptation®

Rebels & Rogues

Alex: He was hot on the trail of a career-making story . . . until he was KO'd by a knockout—Gabriella.

THE MAVERICK
by Janice Kaiser
Temptation #417, November

All men are not created equal. Some are rough around the edges. Tough-minded but tenderhearted. Incredibly sexy. The tempting fulfillment of every woman's fantasy.

When it's time to fight for what they believe in, to win that special woman, our Rebels and Rogues are heroes at heart. Twelve Rebels and Rogues, one each month in 1992, only from Harlequin Temptation.